THE DARK TRIAD

Kelly Anne Womack Machu

Copyright © 2021 by Kelly Anne Womack Machu

First edition Nov 2021
Paperback ISBN: 9798490478706

Book formatting by Fowler Ink
Cover book design by Kelly Anne Womack Machu
Editing by Whitney's Book Works

I dedicate this book to my husband, Joe. The best husband, father, partner, provider, and friend a girl could hope for. Thank you for always relinquishing the remote control to me so that I could watch any and every television show involving murder investigations, as they were my inspiration. I know this, my first published book, comes as a complete surprise to you, but that is the way I needed it to be. I did not want to disappoint you if I failed. God, you, and our three boys are my rocks and my entire world. I would not change a thing. Twenty-five years of marriage, and I love you more. Thank you!

A debut novel by Kelly Anne Womack Machu

Chapter One

Augustus

I held tightly to the Bible which I kept tucked underneath my bed, the one that Pastor Dan had given me a while back, and closed my eyes, bowing my head.

God, it is me. Augustus. Thank you for all that you have graciously blessed me with. My life, the one I am living now, is more than I, a sinner, deserves. Please, Father, forgive me of my sins. I know withholding the truth from the people that care about me, and I for them, is wrong. Please help me to find the courage I cannot seem to locate on my own, the courage to confide in those who mean so much to me. Lord, I buried my father's dead body all those years ago with hate, anger, and disgust in my heart. I love you, but I remain without remorse. Forgive me of my sins. Amen.

I really was nothing like him. He was immune to love and compassion. My father, Stefan, was dead now. A fact that continued to bring me boundless joy. He perished fifteen years ago, but up until that moment when he took his final, pathetic breath with me looking down on him, he was an emotionally void, angry bastard, who should have never walked God's Earth. No doubt the gates of Hell swallowed him with its outstretched arms of evil. Stefan was a murderer, a coward who preyed on the vulnerable, the seemingly unwanted. Oh yes, he thought he was so fucking smart because he was able to hide his habit from my mother, Mia. She knew better than to ask too many questions about anything, let alone where he was going when he disappeared late at night.

My mother was what you would refer to as damaged goods. A woman emotionally, physically, and spiritually devoid of happiness, peace, or purpose. He worked hard to make her that way. He controlled her. He destroyed her. She had endured a lifetime with a man who loved no one, nothing, and who was without a soul or morals. My mother was a tiny woman, standing at just five feet tall and so very thin, which I suspected was because of her anxiety. She was not beautiful, but she was attractive in her European way, despite the dark circles she carried beneath her eyes and the wrinkles around her mouth that had become more pronounced throughout the years. Her blonde hair that she always wore up in a neat bun atop her head had grayed only slightly. Despite the fact that she had lived in the good ole US of A for over forty years, her German accent was still prominent and difficult for others to decipher, not that my father gave her opportunities to interact with outsiders.

My parents immigrated from Germany to the United States in the 1970s, the end! Honestly, that was all of the information my father permitted me to have on the subject. My childhood attempts to obtain specifics from my mother were always unsuccessful and seemed to add to her anxiety. She adamantly refused to provide any details of her life prior to moving to America. There were no photo albums of her or my father's life in Germany, their childhoods, or even of their wedding day. No, there were no pictures at all until I was born, and even then, they were limited to a small album containing photos of me early in life, always on our front porch or in the blueberry fields, and ALWAYS with just my mother. When I was about ten or so, I asked my mother where her parents were and if I could meet them. She fought to hold back tears and her voice tremored when she replied that she and my father had no parents, no siblings, no aunts, or uncles to visit. I did not have the heart to press the issue because even as a child, I knew how fragile she really was. But I always suspected, no, I was certain that she was not telling me the truth. She demanded, begged really, that I never ask my father any questions about life before he came to the United States. She claimed he had an extremely difficult life in Germany, and the memories were much too heart-wrenching to rehash. A lie, of course. One of hundreds that I would be told throughout my childhood years. Heart-wrenching? Really? A man with no soul felt no pain or joy, or anything human for that matter. He was incapable of experiencing a genuine emotion, nor did he attempt to pretend to. He was as cold as ice every single day of his life, without exception. The fear of that man still, even as an adult, and even though he was dead, felt like a steel dagger drilled through the pit of my stomach. I spent the majority of my childhood staying out of my father's way, always conscious of how close in proximity I was to him and always ready to retreat.

I could not remember asking for much, as far as kid stuff or toys go. I had a bicycle that always had flat tires, a couple of old metal trucks, and an outdated computer that I was only allowed to use for schoolwork, when my father was not using it. My father forbade my mother and me to use the internet, and my father went to great lengths to ensure that I did not. He actually downloaded a parental lock on the access to the internet, and it would be years before I was smart enough to figure out how to undo that. I remembered often worrying that no one outside of the property we owned even knew of my existence, that my father could do whatever he wanted to me, even kill me, and who would come looking for me? I knew my mother loved me deeply and losing me would be the final devastation that drove her into permanent insanity, but the unkind reality was that she could do nothing to stop him from doing whatever he wanted to the both of us. Prisoners.

I had but few positive childhood memories, like the excitement I would feel when I would catch a glimpse of the field workers playing with their kids after working all day. The moms and dads seemed so happy to spend time together. Their affection toward each other made me smile but it also made me sad and angry. I was denied that type of love and companionship from my father. They ran, kicked soccer balls, laughed, and sang songs in Spanish together in the evenings.

My father had three Mexican families that he permitted to live on the property, as long as they worked for him during blueberry season and took care of the equipment and property in the off season. He demanded that they not send their children to local schools. My mother told me that my father insisted on home schooling only, like me, and remaining on the property unless he gave permission to leave. She said most migrant workers were sent away by farm owners when the weather changed, and the work was completed. I can only assume that he kept them on the farm and provided them with year-round housing because the last thing he wanted was a revolving door of strangers knowing too much about him. Too hard to keep prisoners if too many people were aware of our existence, and his crimes, even in the middle of nowhere.

My father permitted me to go outside only with my mother or to the blueberry fields with him, where he would let me help the workers harvest the berries. Hector, who was in charge of all of the field workers, would make a loud whistle noise and wave me over to take a break and play with them when my father left for town to bring back supplies or mail bills. Hector's son, Javier, was my age, and despite the language barrier, we got along really well. He looked like his mom, who looked more American than Spanish. I very much looked forward to spending time with him, although the stress of worrying about my father finding out was always weighing on me. I guess he was what someone with a normal childhood, who was not a prisoner, would call a friend. Hector treated me like I was a part of his family, too. He always had a positive outlook on life and a tremendous smile on his face despite working twelve-hour days under the scorching sun in the stagnant summer air. He often told me that God blessed him with the opportunity to work and take care of his family, with a sturdy roof over his head. He spoke good English, too, for never having been formally educated. He would tell me and Javier stories about Pine Barrens and how the first settlers here worked hard, mining coal, hunting for food, and building homes for their families along the water. He, despite not having much of anything valuable, was genuinely thankful for what he did have. Love, his life was filled with the love from and for his family.

He knew a lot of silly jokes, too, and I laughed a good hard belly laugh no matter how many times Hector told us the same joke. He taught me how to pray and to thank God for my blessings. On more than one occasion when I silently prayed with Hector, I prayed that my father would die, and that Hector would become my dad. As soon as we saw the dry reddish dust kicked up by my father's truck coming up the really long dirt and rock road that led to the farm, we would quickly scatter like mice. Hector would rally all the workers quickly back into the fields with a loud whistle noise, and I would run like hell to my front porch where my mom sat asleep in the rocking chair. I was quite sure she knew that I had snuck off to be with Hector and the kids, and I think she pretended to be asleep, so she did not have to tell me that I couldn't go. It was like a game for all of us, our fun secret, and we enjoyed every second, though those moments were scarce.

Sometimes in the evenings, when I had the opportunity and the nerve, I would study my father's face, at a safe distance of course, tucked behind our black and brown checkerboard sofa in the TV room. It was always darkest in that room. Actually, it was completely void of light, except for the glow of the television. The room was small with light brown walls and only one window that my father insisted be kept closed with the blinds down. Always. After my mom would put me in my pajamas, kiss me goodnight, and turn my bedroom light off, I would wait just long enough to hear the little kitchen radio she played every day stop playing. I knew that meant that she had gone upstairs to her bedroom as well. I would wait just a few minutes and then quietly make my way down the hall, past her bedroom door, and down the wooden staircase. Next, I would lay on my stomach and carefully crawl low to the floor, dragging my belly until I reached my safe spot behind the couch. There I would lay on the musty, shaggy green carpet for hours, peering my head out just enough to see his profile but always cautious not to get caught. Always hoping for a glimmer of humanity, a grin, a laugh at a television show he was watching, but behind those mean, cold, steel blue eyes lived a soleless, empty man. God, he really scared the hell out of me.

I loved reading books as a young child, and my mother did her best to home school me properly. I beamed with confidence and pride as she praised my advanced learning capabilities. She told me that I was smart beyond my years and that someday I would grow up and could be anything I wanted. She was proud of me, and her face would light up, and she would giggle when I was able to answer all of the questions on one of her quizzes correctly. That was how I would always remember my mother, in that exact moment of time when, for just a brief period, she was elated and carefree.

My father, on the other hand, would grow angry and incredibly impatient when he noticed that she was spending too much time in a day teaching me lessons about history or challenging me with math problems. He told her to stick to the basics because blueberry farming was all a son of his needed to understand. Despite my mother's fear of my father, she continued to teach me everything she could, but mostly when he was not home. She would sneak books to my room at night with a small flashlight so that I could continue reading without him knowing. Even though we had each other, we were still helpless, helpless and hopeless, together.

In one of the history books my mother gave me, I learned that during the 1970s, when thousands of families immigrated from Germany to the United States, they chose to start new lives in New York, Baltimore, and St. Louis because of the opportunities for employment and education for their children. My father, however, did not. As far as I could tell, there were really only two reasons why a man would move his young wife thousands of miles from her homeland only to assume residence in the Pine Barrens of New Jersey. Poverty or the need for seclusion, and money did not seem to be an issue for my parents. They purchased forty-six acres of sandy, acidic, good-for-nothing soil, except of course, for growing and harvesting New Jersey blueberries, and that was the only thing my father cared about when he wasn't hunting for victims in the darkness. I was nothing like my father.

Chapter Two

Stella

I picked up my vibrating phone from the nightstand, but I already knew who was texting me. It made me laugh anyway.

Well, how did it go last night???????

I knew Brie was not going to be satisfied until I gave her the details of my blind date last night. I replied with a quick, "I'll call you when I get out of the shower" text. Brie's next text was a long chain of unhappy emoji faces and naughty gestures that also made me laugh. I still had four hours until my shift started, but I decided to get up and get moving before I fell back asleep again. At thirty-four years old I should know better than to drink wine until 2:00 am, especially with work the next day, but I got caught up in the moment, and my first date since my breakup with Thomas. It'd been nearly four months since I last saw Thomas, but the reality of loss stung as if it were yesterday. I could still smell the sexiness of his cologne when I closed my eyes, a perfect mix of mahogany and bergamot with just a hint of sage. After we'd make love for hours, I would smell that intoxicating scent all over my body, and I hated to shower it away. I would wrap myself in his shirt, content to lay in bed watching him sleep, memorizing every inch of his beautiful face. I remember the softness of his perfectly sculpted lips on my neck. No doubt that it was his physical attributes that drew me to Thomas.

He was by all accounts, the perfect man. He was one of those guys who didn't have to try at all. The kind that stole your breath when eye contact lingered just a second or two longer than it should. The subtle way he ran his hand through his golden, brown hair when he was flirting with me. His deep blue eyes swallowed me, rendering me incapable of looking away, or even wanting to. Thomas had a smile that lit up a room. He was an infectious presence, the kind of guy people naturally gravitated toward. The beautiful, kind, funny, hypnotic man who was nothing less than perfect, and I fell quick and hard. Stupid-high-school-girl hard. Brie tried, without success, for a year to shake me out of the lust-struck haze, as she so often referred to my emotional state during that time.

She warned me that I was but one kiss, one lustful, lingering eye glance, one secluded lunch break pulled off the road in the heat of passion, or one text message on a phone carelessly tossed on the kitchen table from losing my job, the respect of my fellow officers, Thomas, and my self-esteem.

Well, Brie was wrong, but only about losing my career that I loved and was so proud of. Nope, I did not lose that. I was, however, forced into an immediate transfer from Philly to Podunk, NJ, also known as Pine Barrens. And that was it, my life fell apart, just like Brie warned. I made three critical errors. I had a sexual relationship with my partner. I had a sexual relationship with my *married* partner. I fell in love with my married partner. I made no excuses other than I was human and it just happened. My actions were unforgiveable, selfish, and reckless and, in the end, damaging to unwilling, innocent bystanders. I knew I would never be the same person. I would not want to be that person ever again.

Thomas and I always talked about being careful not to get caught and what would be at stake if we were. He, without a doubt, had more to lose than me. Thomas was married just a year before we were partnered together at the East Philly Police Department. Jenna. Jenna and Thomas had been together since eighth grade, through high school and even the first two years that Jenna went away to the University of Florida. Thomas had remained steadfast and faithful until that point. Sometimes absence didn't make the heart grow fonder, it made the need for intimate human contact grow stronger.

Thomas was in the Police Academy when he slipped up and cheated on Jenna. After a grueling physical day at the Academy and the excitement of a long weekend ahead, the beers started flowing fast and early, as he put it. One thing led to another, as it often did, and Thomas spent the next forty-eight hours having drunk sex with a girl he met at the at Erin's Sports Pub. It was a favorite spot for law enforcement and the business casual nine-to-five crowd. Thomas didn't go into too much detail, and to be honest, hearing him talk about hot, sloppy, drunken sex with someone else stung just enough to trigger my jealous bone. It was bad enough that I had to physically share him with his wife. I didn't want to wonder if he was reminiscing about that savage weekend with "her" when he was on top of me, inside me. One thing that I do know for certain is that being publicly mortified via social media with pictures of your long-standing boyfriend in an enthusiastic bar kiss, the get-a-room type of kiss, is a relationship bullet through the heart. That was the end of the Thomas and Jenna story, until of course, chapter two began when they ran into each other five years later at a laundromat. Ironically, they had lived in the same building for six months, before this "meant to be reunion," as Jenna often told anyone that would listen.

At that point Thomas, despite his good looks, charm, and profession was lonely. He, a police officer for almost five years, avoided bars on his days off. He said that too much personal drama unfolded at bars, and people felt the need to tell you things in a state of intoxication that they would never let pass their lips during any given sober moment. And then you had to live with that knowledge, careful never to repeat the secret that would ruin a life. He said he tried dating websites, as did I, but he said, laughing sort of, that all he finds at this age were women desperate to release their drying up eggs, newly divorced and in pain, or his least favorite, the "no names please" lunch hour screw. Running into Jenna seemed like the answer to the loneliness and so they quickly got engaged again.

As the months passed, Thomas realized that his feelings for Jenna had changed and that he was no longer excited to get home to her, to hear her voice, to make love to her. Thomas said that he truly had hoped he would find those "can't live without you" feelings again that he once had for Jenna. Although Thomas didn't want to get married right away, Jenna got pregnant while on the pill. Very curious? They had a small ceremony at City Hall and an intimate dinner for two. There was no honeymoon, no long getaway. Thomas said they both went back to work the following Monday. Jenna was a newly-employed real estate broker and really had no time off to enjoy even a quick jaunt.

Two months later, Jenna miscarried. Thomas described the void in their relationship as cavernous and beyond repair. Jenna devoted all of her time to her career, and as the billboards proved, she was setting the bar of success in the real estate market in Philly. When Jenna wasn't working, or at client meetings, or on work related phone calls, she was out with friends or spending weekends with her parents. Thomas secretly hoped that she would find someone to love her like she deserved.

I was firm in my opinion that she intentionally stopped taking birth control in order to trap and retain Thomas. That damn karma, she was an evil bitch. Just so I would not end up in hell, and the fact that it was the God's honest truth, I, in no way, was pleased with what Thomas and Jenna endured, especially the loss of a child. Regardless of my feelings for her, Jenna did not deserve to find out that Thomas and I were lovers, especially not the way she did. Like Brie always said, those damn cell phones would be the end game for cheating spouses everywhere. It should have come as no surprise that in a moment, while Thomas lay asleep on the sofa, Jenna read the very explicit text messages between Thomas and me from the night before. Jenna in turn called every cop on the squad, including our superiors, to tell them about their disgraceful fellow officers not suited to serve amongst them. The final nail in my coffin was Jenna posting the text conversions on her Facebook page. Touché! I never spoke to Thomas again, nor had I spoken to my former colleagues. There was no other option available for me, the female officer, the whore, the home wrecker. My walk of shame, head down style exit from the station that day, was the closing of a chapter in my life that I wanted to forget, move on from.

Chapter Three

Augustus

I must have been about twelve when the suspicion and curiosity finally surpassed the numbing fear my father filled me with. What did he expect? A twelve-year-old kid, with no friends, no real entertainment, void of a father figure, and left with just the companionship of an emotionally-damaged shell of a mother that he created. It wasn't enough for me anymore, not that it ever really was. This life they forced upon me wasn't fair, I didn't ask for it. I realized then that my fear was slowly giving way to hate and anger. Such a dark, unhealthy, loathing anger. I wanted him dead, but not drop-dead quick dead. No, I wanted him to suffer a painful, slow, agonizing death. He made me what I am today: a liar.

On a muggy, windless July evening, I decided that this was the night I was going to find out what he did out in the dark. I'd spent my childhood looking out my bedroom window as he made his way through the acres of lush blueberry fields with his flashlight glowing until the light disappeared into the darkness. The thought of following him into the pitch-black darkness terrified me. After all, Pine Barrens was home to nightmarish tales, none more infamous than that of the Jersey Devil. The Jersey Devil was the thirteenth child of a woman named Ms. Leeds, who, as legend said, upon news of her thirteenth pregnancy, cursed the unborn child and wished him dead. The story went on to say that Satan, hearing the mother's wishes, took advantage of the opportunity, and when the baby was born, it took the form of a hideous, evil creature with the head of a horse, large prominent horns, and the tail of a serpent that savagely murdered and decapitated all twelve siblings and both parents. Legend dictated that, even to this day, he spent his nights slithering through the darkness of the thick wooded Pine Barrens terrain, watching and hunting prey. Prey, which mostly consisted of deer, snakes, and farm animals. However, he had been known to, if opportunity afforded, abduct children as they lay asleep in tents from all of the local campgrounds that were nestled up and down the Wading River. The stolen children were never seen again, or at least that was how the legend went.

As if that weren't traumatic enough for a kid who

actually lived in the isolated, creepy barrens to know, there were other mysteries and unsolved disappearances, all of which were apparently well known by those who dwelled in the barrens. I remembered overhearing my father a many years earlier, during one of my recon missions behind the old chair in the TV room, that he had been to town earlier that day for supplies and was told by the clerk at the store that the mutilated remains of what appears to be two females were discovered by a couple who had been hiking one of the thousands of trails that led everywhere and nowhere. They were miles into the forest when they stumbled upon the gruesome discovery. My father told my mother that there were news media vans parked in town and vehicles that were marked with bold letters, FBI, CRIME SCENE UNIT, STATE POLICE, and the local cops as well. He said there were helicopters that seemed to be looking for something from above, but that he was unsure if they were law enforcement or media. I remembered thinking that it was odd how concerned about the situation my father appeared. He went on to tell my mother that he would not be going back to town until all of the outsiders were gone. *Why not*, I thought. What did it have to do with him? He only went to town for farm supplies and food, right? I'd imagined he was the most invisible resident that the barrens had produced, so why did he seem threatened by the law enforcement and news media?

My head still reeling with the terror of being taken by the Jersey Devil, or whatever other ungodly creature may be lurking outside my house, I slowly crept to my closet and pulled out the too tight, torn sneakers from the floor, slipped them on, which took a few minutes because they were probably two sizes too small now and smelled musty. I cautiously opened my door and paused just long enough to make certain that my mother was not still awake in her bedroom. No noise at all, expect for the buzzing of the insects and critters outside in the thick, breezeless, summer air. The marshlands and brackish waters beyond our property drew hordes of enormous strawberry flies and mosquitos that looked like they had been genetically modified, filled with steroids and released into the barrens. They thrived in this muggy, damp marsh-like wilderness. I gingerly stepped only on the carpeted part of each wooden step to avoid the creaking of the old staircase. I avoided grabbing the railing, as that made a horrible screeching sound due to years of pulling on it and the lack of upkeep on my father's part. Already, big drops of sweat rolled down my back, and the fear of my father standing on the other side of the front door as I opened it made me feel physically ill. I could feel the thump of every rapid heartbeat as it pounded inside my chest.

Finally, there I stood at the bottom of the staircase,

frozen and uncertain of my next move. I knew if I opened that door there was no turning back. Whatever I discovered, if anything, I would have to live with for the rest of my life. A sudden jolt of courage came soaring through every muscle in my body, adrenalin if you will. I stood straight up, took a deep breath, and reached for the doorknob.

Chapter Four

Stella

The buzz of my cell shook me from my trance, agonizing over Thomas and the derailment of the life I once loved, in a town I once loved. I picked up my phone and read the text message and could not help but smile. It was Ty, my blind date from last night.

I had a wonderful time with you last night. I really hope to see you again! Have a wonderful day!

Direct, polite, and respectful, just like I would expect from Ty. I was pleasantly surprised when he walked into the bar we decided to meet at last night. He looked exactly like the picture he posted on the dating app. Not ten years older, or fifty pounds heavier, just handsome, well dressed, and confident. This was the first time in my life that I'd been out on a date with a black man. Not because I was avoiding opportunities, I just had never met anyone like him. His face and dazzling smile had me swiping YES quicker than I'd like to admit.

I did enjoy my night out with him. I forgot how satisfying a little sexual flirtation could be. I didn't sleep with him, but God, I thought about asking him back to my crappy little apartment. Aside from the embarrassment that thought conjured up, I knew it would be a mistake and possibly the beginning of something I wasn't ready to start. He truly was a gentleman, though, which was extremely rare. Usually, bellying up to a bar until closing time with a guy somehow meant "green light" and wandering hands. No, Ty was raised by a good woman. That was evident, but even so, I needed to focus on my new position within the Wading Pines PD. I sent him a quick response with that stupid smiley face emoji and plugged my phone into the charger on my nightstand.

Thanks again for last night. I had a great time with you, too. Let's talk soon once I get myself situated with my new job.

I regretted sending that the second I did. It sounded like such a blow off, but in all honesty, I guess it was. I was in no condition, emotionally, to start a new romance, and he deserved better than waiting around for me. Continuing to text or even see him was just stringing him along. No, Ty was too good for that. He deserved better. I promised myself that no matter how lonely and pathetic I got, I would not reach out to Ty again.

As I stood looking around my little bedroom adorned with the most obnoxious paisley flowered and yellowing wallpaper, I fought off the urge to burst into tears again. Fuck, how I missed my modern-day apartment in Philly and living with Brie. Everything just really sucked right now. I was a creature of habit who despised change of any kind. It was not supposed to be like this for me. This stupid, little one-bedroom house I rented from the coffee shop owner here in Chatsworth was no doubt circa 1800, and never been updated. I certainly was not going to sink a dime of my money into renovating this shit hole. I didn't own it, and I didn't want to own it. I was hoping that this would be a temporary situation, but realistically, who was I kidding? I could never go back to Philly. I would never show my face there again. People never forget a woman who slept with a married man, regardless of how much time passed, and then somehow, over time, it also became solely her fault. I had no idea if Thomas was still at the precinct, married or divorced, but I had to let it go. It took all of my will power not to ask Brie about him. Not to inquire as to his whereabouts, not that she would know. She was outspoken and against the torrid affair from the get-go.

I had been in this house for a couple of months now, and Mr. Avery, the landlord, was super sweet and non-intrusive. Truth be told he was the most adorable old man in the world. He was at least eighty, maybe even older, but he opened his little eatery, three hundred feet from my house every day at 5:00 am, seven days a week, and worked until 3:00 pm when he would flip the antique sign on the door over to read "CLOSED," put his Sherlock Holmes hat on, lock up, and make his way up the concerningly aging flight of ten wooden steps to his little apartment over his shop. He was a definite gem, as was his very rustic, yet clean little shop. Mr. Avery must have achieved celebrity status decades ago, because everyone, from the kids who rode up on their bikes for candy to the daily dwellers, also known as the gossiping old men at table three every day, referred to him as the mayor. Mr. Avery's chuckle at hearing that from his loyal customers always made me laugh, too. So, I guess it wasn't all doom and gloom here, and honestly, the locals were incredibly warm and welcoming when I went in for coffee, which was almost every day.

Everyone now knew my name, and everyone not only said good morning in a genuine, cheery voice, but they asked me how I was doing and actually waited for my reply. A totally foreign concept to me. It took some getting used to, as the Philly morning coffee routine meant head down, no eye contact, place your order, don't sit, grab your coffee when called, pay, and get out. If you were lucky, you would get a low grunt from one of the miserable employees that slightly resembled a thank you, but it also could have been a fuck you. No friendly locals, no chatter, just human cattle herded about quickly to get to jobs they didn't want to be at. I guess maybe I was slowly becoming accustomed to that part of the culture shift. I knew that I had no choice but to put my big girl panties on, be grateful for a new opportunity, and move on. No rearview mirror life for me!

I made my way over to my closet and pulled out my uniform. The closets in this little house were about two feet wide and four feet deep, and oh yes, they were adorned in the same wallpaper. I imagine over one hundred years ago when this house was built people didn't have too much, especially not full wardrobes and fifty pairs of shoes, so closet space wasn't much of a concern. It honestly didn't matter much to me. I only hung my uniforms and threw my shoes in there anyway. I was more of a jean, t-shirt, and hoodie girl when I wasn't working. Although, Brie mentioned every time she saw me that I was way too young to dress for comfort in lieu of catching potential mating candidates. Brie had a way with words, which was why she was so good and highly respected in her marketing firm. *Note to self, do not forget to call Brie back on my way to work!* I quickly threw my t-shirt and underwear in my hamper and turned the shower on. It took a few minutes for it to go through the clunking, sputtering, and warming up routine, so I pulled my magnifying mirror out from underneath the bathroom sink.

This bathroom was so antique that it actually made a comeback in the magazines I thumbed through at night when I was bored. Big black and white squares covered the floor, and the vintage pink clawfoot bathtub could actually be worth a fortune at an auction. The sink seemed like a last-minute makeshift decision, or maybe a used piece to replace the broken original. Nevertheless, it didn't match and ruined the overall charm of the bathroom. The sink itself was modern pink, and the cabinet below was a very unflattering lightly colored wood. Nope, not a fan, but again this was not my forever home. I had to dump my pink, makeup-stained Victoria's Secret bag on the bathmat to attempt to find the tweezers, which I did after a minute or two of profanities, as if the cluttered mess inside the bag was someone else's fault.

Thank God, I pulled this mirror out. I discovered, without effort, two dark scary hairs on my chin that emerged overnight and grew to what looked to be a half an inch. How the hell did this happen? Why were they so dark? My hair was naturally blonde, very blonde as a kid. I could only imagine twenty years from now what I was going to look like. Would I have a full-grown beard to contend with every morning? I yanked them out quickly which was when I realized that the bathroom was completely silent. The shower had finished the awakening song that I had grown accustomed to, so I jumped in.

My drive to the police department was only thirty minutes, well, unless I got stuck behind a run-down farm type truck hauling blueberry or cranberry loads. That actually happened more often than one would think. I pulled out my phone and dialed Brie, but it went straight to voicemail, which meant she was in a meeting or with a client. I turned the radio up loud, put the windows down, and took very deep breaths. Lee Brice was singing "A Woman Like You," which was one of my all-time favorites. I belted out the lyrics as if I were auditioning for American Idol. "Nails on a Chalkboard" was how Thomas and Brie both described my vocal capabilities. They were not wrong. Before my mind could shift back to another self-pity session, I decided to focus my attention on my surroundings. After all, I would be patrolling this area now that my desk training duty had been completed. Pine Barrens was such an odd stretch of real estate. I guess I could best describe it as beautiful and mysterious, with a rich, yet dark history.

I did a lot of research on my new neck of the woods. Apparently, in the 1800s it was a mining town, and a successful one at that. I read that somewhere in these woods there were still remnants of the equipment they used and the houses they built and occupied. The article I read went on to say that it was virtually impossible to find this area, as it was so deep in the lush and somewhat overgrown forest, but the guy that wrote the article obviously got to it because the article was complete with many black and white photographs, adding to the creepiness of the writer's words. The author said the terrain was treacherous, and as much as they thought they were prepared, they quickly realized they were not. As if the area was protected by spirits, the skies opened up and rain pounded their heads and soaked them to the bone as they slowly approached the ruins. The author and his crew ran for cover under what looked to be the remains of a small home, only to find that they were standing in quicksand. The crew was able to pull themselves to safety. He described what happened next "as if the spirits were satisfied with their scripted warning and our subsequent reactions. The clouds parted, the rain ceased, and the sun rapidly warmed our cold and wet bodies. I took just a few pictures, disturbed nothing, and retreated, vowing never to return or reveal the exact location of the sacred rubble."

So, while lurking in the woods for archeological finds and pissing off ghosts was not my idea of a fun day, the Cranberry Festival scheduled for early October was.

Some of the town folks described it to me as the best day of the year. A sea of vendors selling food, wine, candy, clothing, jewelry, artwork, garden sculptures, oddities, and of course, everything cranberry. I was told thousands of people attended the two-day event. There was even a committee that met every week, right at Mr. Avery's little shop, throughout the year planning the event. Mr. Avery wanted me to think about joining the committee. He said I would have great input and suggestions regarding safety, as an experienced police officer. I was not sure if he really thought that or if he secretly hoped that it would be a perfect way for me to get to know people and do a little socializing. I had not unloaded my heaping shit-show past on Mr. Avery, but he was the sort of wonderful soul that just knew damaged goods when he saw them, and who felt compelled to help. The two old guys from table three, the permanent fixtures, chimed into the conversation to brag that they were able to hire the best musical acts in New Jersey every year. They also worked with local campgrounds to bus the weekend campers into the event in the hopes they would generate even more revenue for the town. Before I had time to stop myself, I agreed to be a part of the committee. Mr. Avery smiled his warm and comforting smile, and whatever reservations I had about joining the group, slipped away.

Chapter Five

Augustus

I was standing on the front porch. I did it! I faced my fears and opened the door and closed it behind me. My heart was still racing, and I was a bundle of rattled nerves, but there I was on the front porch. I reached into the pocket of my hoodie and felt the small flashlight that was still there, but I had to get through the fields and to the barns with just the light of the full moon. It was a clear night and the stars were particularly bright, so I knew I would be okay. It was as if the universe was rooting for me, encouraging me to forge ahead. Complete the mission. Figure out, once and for all, what my father was doing in the darkness, without, of course, being caught.

The stairs of the porch were old and buckled in spots, but I knew just where to step on each board to avoid the screeching response they made when they struggled to manage weight. I had been practicing for so long in preparation of this night. As I stood at the bottom of the stairs looking up at the house, it struck me for this first time that my parents put no effort into the upkeep of the old farmhouse, which I imagined must have been a real beauty decades ago. The wrap around porch was really wide and long, and I spent much of my childhood on my knees pushing an old toy dump truck up and down the length of the porch as my mother sat in her chair watching me. Yet looking back, I was sure she was a million miles away, lost in her own thoughts and sadness. So much of the white paint was either chipping or gone altogether. It made me sad. The house was sad. My mother was sad. My life was sad.

Our driveway was not paved, or even properly stoned. It was sort of a mix of weeds, dirt, and rocks that had collected over the years. The driveway empty. My father always left his beat-up old truck at the barns. Never in the driveway. My mother had once told me that he liked to walk and that was why he did not bring his truck home. Of course, I believed her, until I did not. My father parked his old truck at the barns to avoid waking us up when he turned the engine over and drove off into the darkness teetering between late night and early morning. Whatever he was doing, he apparently needed privacy doing it. I often wondered if my mother knew what he was doing. Had she ever been brave enough to follow and confront him? Did she discover something so horrible that it caused her to withdraw even further into her own head? That would actually make sense. After all, for all intents and purposes, she was a prisoner here in the sense that she had nowhere to run, no friends or family, no money, no skills. Had my father been a different man when they first met back in Germany? Was he charming and gentle? Did he take her on fancy dates and twirl her around on a dance floor late into the night? Were they once happily in love, and if that were in fact the case, what happened to change all of that?

It had not rained in days, so the dirt path I followed through the blueberry bushes made it easy to move at a quick and steady pace, even in the dark. When it did rain, the fields were thick with reddish mud that stained shoes and pants for good. Soil that was only good for growing blueberries. It would not be too much longer before it was time to harvest the blueberries again. I very much looked forward to this because it meant I could see Hector and the other kids. Lost in my own thoughts, I didn't realize how close I already was to the barn until a strange noise delivered me back to my present situation. I stood there in the field, mentally paralyzed with fear, unable to move my feet, and terrified to even breathe. Did I turn and run? Should I wait to see if I heard it again? Maybe it was just my imagination. No, no, wait I saw movement just beside the barn and a light, although dim, definitely the glow of a flashlight. I got down on my stomach, but I was still able to see the glow. I heard the clanking of metal and a thump, thump, thump. Digging! Someone was digging with a shovel in the blueberry fields. I laid on the dirt completely silent. Was it my father? Was someone stealing blueberry bushes? Is that what my father was doing at night, patrolling for thieves? The digging went on for what felt like an hour, and I was too petrified to move. Whoever it was, I was close enough to be seen should they shine the flashlight in my direction. Suddenly, the barn door opened, and I could see my father's truck. Oh God, he started it and began slowly backing out of the barn. Whatever he was doing, he was done, and I wasn't going to find out tonight what exactly it was. Why the hell was he bringing the truck home? That was not his usual routine. Shit, I was dead! My only thought was to run and to run like hell. I took off fast, running at a steady pace, but breathing hard. My heart felt like it was going to explode, but if he got to the house before I did, he would kill me, actually kill me, and no one would know. *Just keep running.*

Chapter Six

Stella

My cell rang just as I pulled into the parking lot of the Wading Pines PD. It was Brie. I still had a few minutes, so I picked up.

"Okay, okay I shall give you the cliff notes version of my date that was incredible yet a one and done meeting, but I only have a few minutes before my shift. I am meeting my new partner today."

Silence.

"Brie, are you there, sweetie? Brie?"

Her voice was low and flat, void of her usual happiness and spunk. "I really need you, Stella. I am having more of those issues I told you about at work, and I am coming down to stay with you for the weekend tomorrow after I get off. I should be there by six. Stella, I am so worried about my career. I don't know what to do or who to trust. I have no one to turn to. I hate that you live so far away, especially now. I'll see you tomorrow."

Brie did not give me the opportunity to respond or ask any questions. Instead, she hung up. I could only assume she was calling me from her office and concerned about the "thin walls." I felt a sudden surge of anger that grabbed me by the shoulders and caused every muscle in my neck to tense up. That sick old pervert of a boss she had must have done or said something to Brie that upset and embarrassed her once again. This unfortunately was not a new situation. Brie was brilliant, creative, endearing, and really great at her job. Everyone loved her, from her colleagues to her clients. Brie had a natural gift of making everyone feel center-stage important, always. She treated everyone as if they were the most important person in the room, in that moment. The building custodial staff, the restroom attendant, the file clerks, it did not matter. She genuinely cared about all of them as human beings.

I think Brie's personality is both a gift and a curse. Everyone in the office felt comfortable talking to Brie when they had a personal or professional problem. She would close her door and listen to a coworker talk, cry, or vent until they felt better, even if it meant she would lose valuable productive hours of her own. People thrived on her advice and empathy and appreciated her complete confidentiality. I referred to her as the Oprah Winfrey of the office. I made the mistake of asking Brie why she felt so compelled to spend hours listening to the receptionist talk about her husband's infidelities, thus causing Brie to stay in the office and work into the night to meet a client's deadline. Oh, I'd never make that mistake again. I got the death stare and the lecture about us all being God's children and born to help others. Brie always said that she refused to be a "title reactive" person. I understood what she meant. It was simply Brie. True, good, honest, and beautiful Brie. Unfortunately, Brie was second in command at the office. Second to Will Bayo, the pervert.

Will Bayo was in his mid-sixties and the director of the marketing firm Brie worked for. He was a closet drunk who had a bright red nose every morning as a result of his evening ritual of sitting in his garage drinking beer alone and avoiding his wife. He had a face that only a mother, if she were half blind, could love. He was, in a nutshell, a truly ugly man, inside and out. If I had to compare his looks to someone or something, I would say he was a cross between Monty Burns from the *Simpsons* and Franklin, the cartoon Turtle with an attempted comb over of what little hair he had left. Oh, Brie, me, and a bottle or two of cabernet, and we would laugh at that for hours while watching Netflix in our jammies.

Will had an ivy league education and a high dollar successful investment portfolio and let anyone who would listen know it. Brie said he never left a meeting with clients, staff, or board members without showboating and tooting his own horn, as if he were responsible for any of the company's success or brilliant ideas that Brie and her team achieved. A few months back, Brie caught one of the board members rolling his eyes at Will's showboating attempt during a late-night board meeting that had already gone much longer than anticipated. She said she was incredibly tempted to reach out to that board member for advice but was petrified Will would get wind of it and she would be blackballed in the industry. On one occasion, Will had the nerve to insist that Brie accompany him to lunch with other company leaders and insisted she drive with him to further discuss a new project, but when they arrived at the cozy little Italian restaurant, she realized it was just her and him. He lied. Total creep. Brie said she would have cried if it were not for the fact that she enjoyed watching him fumble with all of the bells and whistles in his sporty black Mercedes that he was way too old to drive. Ha, end of life crisis? However, the unfortunate reality was that he continued to make unwanted, inappropriate, sexually-charged comments to her, and he was becoming bolder in his behavior. He went so far as to tell Brie that the only thing stopping her from being the next director when he retired in a few years was him if he chose not to support her when the Board Chair asked for his opinion with respect to succession. I told Brie over and over again to record their conversations with her cell phone and nail his ass at the next board meeting. It was not her style, though. She hated confrontation even more than she hated being the center of attention. I could only imagine what that pathetic piece of shit had done to her now. I guessed I would find out this weekend. I turned my car off, locked it, grabbed my bags, and headed into the precinct through the backdoor.

I smiled and gave a quick wave to Margie, who was the PD's version of a desk Sergeant except she had no formal academy training or skills. She answered the phones and dispatched accordingly. She had to be nearing sixty, but she never missed a beat. She knew everything there was to know about the WPPD. She was for all intents and purposes, the receptionist, but I didn't think this place could function without her. She was always super peppy, and in really decent shape for her age, too. She had big, curly blonde hair and was always in full makeup. Her nails were long, and she wore screaming bright-colored nail polishes. "The brighter the better, honey," she told me when I complimented her on her weekly choice of polish. She made certain to fill me in on all the dirt and gossip over the past few months, too. Shocking how much drama there apparently was out here in Podunk, New Jersey. I was certainly not complaining, though since, despite her lack of law enforcement education, she handled my office training while she continued with her other responsibilities. I guessed if I had to admit it, she was the real one in charge here, and I think everyone liked it that way. She was an absolute riot to talk to. We usually spent the good part of our mornings drinking coffee and discussing her one-night stand hookups she scheduled on her 'over fifty' dating apps. Sadly, she had the social life that I did not, so I really looked forward to those mornings. The days were long, and I hated being stuck in an office, which was why I pursued a career in law enforcement in the first place, but all that was behind me now. Today, I get to meet my new partner. It was his first day with the WPPD, so I was not the "newbie" anymore. I liked the thought of that.

I threw my duffle bag in my locker, threw my hair up in a messy half bun, half ponytail on the top of my head. Brie referred to it as my traveling bird nest. I didn't care. I liked it this way, a sexy mess. Having poker straight hair without bounce was boring. I looked better with it lifted and a little messy. Okay, and the fact that I was super lazy may have contributed to my love of the bird nest. I closed my locker and headed to my captain's office. I wasn't given much information about my partner, only that he lived in South Jersey and was pretty new to law enforcement. Come to think of it, I didn't even know his name. I wondered why he had chosen the Wading Pines

PD. The captain's door was closed, but I could hear him laughing. I figured that he must be on the phone, so I plopped down at my desk and fired up my computer.

I was by myself in the "pit," as the other officers referred to it. Realistically it was an old, yet exceptionally large, family dining room. The PD was headquartered in an old, well-kept Victorian type mini mansion. Apparently, the previous owner, who died over twenty years ago, had lost his wife and had no other family members, so in his will, he left the home to the police department. He had been an officer, too, a lifetime ago, and was very fond of the community and law enforcement. My captain, Captain Jesse Ryan, told me that prior to these digs, headquarters was nothing more than two double wide sixty-foot trailers.

Captain Jesse was a naturally beautiful man. At forty-eight years old, he was in excellent physical condition. His short, blonde, military-style haircut, his bright green eyes, and chiseled face were striking. His laugh was infectious. He was the nicest police captain I had ever met. He never pulled rank and didn't treat his subordinates like children. He was personable, likeable, and thank God, gay because I could see myself getting into a whole bunch of trouble otherwise. He was married, and his husband Joe was equally as impressive. Being the only gay cop in a small town like this did not seem to concern him one bit, and from what I could see in my two short months here, he was well-liked and respected by everyone. He and Joe were very affectionate toward each other and comfortable. They had a great life together. Joe was a fifth-grade teacher at Wading Pines Elementary School. Marge told me that was how they met.

In Philly, the department was large and always chaotic with people rushing around and talking on phones or pounding keyboards. Captain Hanks was a screamer, and his shrill could peel the paint from a wall. I was always jumpy around him because you never knew what would set him off. I did not miss that. This was peaceful. The other two officers on duty today were already active and the radio was pretty quiet thus far.

I was just a click away from the Philly News website when I heard Captain Jesse's door open. He hadn't been on the phone. He had someone in his office. Following closely behind Captain Jesse was another man who looked to be maybe thirty years old or so. He looked nervous. He was very handsome, dark hair and blue eyes, probably about six feet tall. He was muscular but not obnoxiously so. I stood up from my desk as they made their way toward me. He blushed just a tiny bit when our eyes met. He was truly adorable.

Captain Jesse spoke up, "Hey, Stella, good to see you! Well, he's finally here. Meet your new partner. I'd love to stay, but I gotta run over to the school. Joe forgot his lunch again, and you know he's a bear when his belly is rumbling." And just like that he was out the back door.

It was a lot to process, and my new partner and I just stood silent for a moment with that deer in the headlight look. I spoke up first and told him my name and that I was pretty new here, too. He stuck his hand out to shake mine.

"Hi, my friends call me G. I'm really excited to be here and to meet you. Which desk is mine?"

He was definitely a little nervous, but that was understandable. The first day on a new job, any job, was brutal. New people and new processes were overwhelming, and if he wasn't from this town, then that had to be a lot to handle all in one day. I pointed to the desk opposite mine.

"That's yours," I said. I told him he lucked out because I was already trained via desk duty hell, so he didn't have to suffer the same consequences because we were partners and riding together. I would be filling him in and showing him the ropes as they say. Captain Jesse had said to use the first few days to get acquainted and show him around the barrens. Show him where the schools are, the hospital, where our troublemakers hang out, etc.

"Hey, G, let me know when you are ready to head out, and I'll bring you to meet the Jersey Devil."

He looked up at me and smiled. "We're already close friends," he said. I told him to meet me out back, but no rush, and he gave me the thumbs up. I headed up to see

Margie for the keys to my patrol car. She had that look on her face like she was about to burst if she didn't tell me what she wanted to say.

"What, Margie? What?"

"Oh, nothing. I was just thinking you are single. I bet he is single, and what a fine piece of law enforcement ass he is."

"No playing match maker, Margie! I mean it. I am not looking for a relationship right now, and when I am, he will not be a cop." I never gave Margie all the gory details from my Philly disaster, so I thought she was pretty shocked at my tone.

She held her hands up and mumbled in a defeated and scorned voice, "Message received, just trying to help," which of course made me feel instantly terrible for reacting that way. I grabbed her hand and told her she was a really good friend and that someday I would explain to her why I felt that way. Margie smiled. "I'll bring the wine."

Chapter Seven

Augustus

My throat burned and sweat dripped down my back as I sprinted through the blueberry field toward the house. I had to get there before he did. I noticed the glow of a light on in Hector's bungalow off to the right of me, but it was further away than my house. I had no choice but to just keep running toward home. There was no guarantee that he would not check my room before he went to bed, so waiting it out was not an option. I wasn't far from the edge of the field when I tripped over something and went down hard on my knees. I knew from the stinging that I was cut and bleeding, but that nothing was broken. I hurled myself to my feet and finally reached the front porch where I crawled on my hands and knees up the stairs, opened the front door, and quickly leapt inside. I was cautious not to slam the door behind me. I could barely catch my breath. I could see the headlights of my father's truck as he approached the house. Did he see me? Did he know?

I kicked my shoes off and noticed they were covered in blueberry mush. Shit! Would he notice that? There would be no reason for me to have been in the fields. We aren't due to harvest for a few weeks. I was out of time. It was too late to grab the shoes. I heard his truck door slam and sprinted up the stairs and closed my bedroom door behind me. I stood there against the door, in the dark, trying to catch my breath and finally realizing how painful my stinging knees were. Nothing I could do about it, though. I took my pants off and threw them behind my bed. I would worry about throwing them out without my parents knowing tomorrow. I needed to slow my breathing, and my heart rate. I climbed into bed and faced away from the door. My father had not made his way up the stairs yet. He must be in the kitchen. I was too wired and panicked to sleep, and I desperately needed water. I was able to convince myself that calming down was the only way I was going to sleep. At that moment, I heard the creaking of the stair boards as my father made his way up. I laid perfectly still, my back to the door, when I heard my doorknob turn and the door open, but no footsteps into the room. Seconds later, the door quietly clicked shut, and I could hear my father walking down the hallway to his room. Did he always look into my bedroom at night, or did he see me in the field? Did he notice my shoes? As terrified as I was of getting caught, I knew I had to get back out there to see what he was digging and why. He was up to no good, of this I was certain.

"Augustus. Augustus, wake up." I opened my eyes to see my mother standing over me, talking to me, but in a whisper. The look on her face scared me, and I quickly sat up and asked her what was wrong. She calmly replied, "Augustus, were you out in the blueberry fields last night after I went to sleep? Don't you lie to me, Augustus. I saw your shoes by the front door. You are incredibly lucky that I woke up so early today. If your father saw those shoes..." Her voice trailed off too low for me to understand what she said, but I knew what she meant. He would kill me, not punish me, kill me.

"Mom, did you clean my shoes off?" She nodded a quick yes. "Mom, yes, I was out there last night. I need to know what he is doing at night. Aren't you even curious? Why are you so afraid to ask? Why are you so afraid of him?"

This time my mother seemed annoyed when she answered. "Augustus, I cleaned your shoes before your father could see them. Where are the clothes you wore?

They must be filthy, too." I pointed over my shoulder, and she got down on her hands and knees and retrieved the pants from behind my bed. She gave them a once over and then pulled my blanket off my legs. "Oh, Augustus, you are hurt. We need to clean out those cuts. I will worry about your pants later. You go take a bath now."

"Mom, answer the question, why are you so afraid of him? What did he do to you?"

She hesitated but answered, "He didn't hurt *me*, Augustus. He, he, well, he is just a very strange and private man. He does scare me, but I, I, I... That's enough, Augustus! No more talk about this. Take a bath!"

"We can leave here. We can leave him and run away, far away, somewhere he would never find us."

She let out a long sigh and sat on the edge of my bed and took my hand in hers. In such a loving tone, she said, "Augustus, it is likely that someday I will have no choice but to explain all of this to you, but not today. I do want, no, I *need* you to know how much I love you and how sorry I am for not being stronger. You deserve better than this life you have had thus far. You should be going to school and to parties with friends, not held hostage here."

"Am I? A hostage, I mean?"

With tears forming in her eyes, she replied, "Augustus, I believe that your father is capable of very bad things.

He certainly is not the man I thought I married, and I have no doubt that he would physically punish us both if he felt as if we betrayed him, defied his orders."

She stood from my bed, but I wouldn't let go of her hand. I looked her in the eyes and said, "Mom, you deserve better, too. I love you, Mom." She bent down and kissed my forehead for a few seconds, and I felt her warm teardrop roll down my cheek.

"I love you, too, Augustus. Please do not sneak out into the darkness again. It's not safe. Your father is dangerous, evil."

I stayed in my bed for a while trying to remember every detail of what I saw last night. I thought too about what my mother had just told me and figure out my next move. I could not just stand by and do nothing anymore. I was no longer a little boy, and I needed to take care of my mother, protect her from my father. I had to find a safe way for us to leave here. I loved my mother, but I was going back out there tonight. I knew the key to ending his reign of terror and obtaining our freedom was out there, in the dark, in the blueberry field where he was digging. If I got caught, I could run to Hector's. I knew he would protect me from my father. I wished I could speak to Hector and ask for his help. Ask him if he knew what my father did out there in the dark, but it was too risky to involve him. He had a family and people that depended on him. I did not want anything to happen to them because of me. I pulled off my blanket and swung my legs slowly over the side of the bed and gently got to my feet. God, my knees were a mess of dried blood and dirt and blueberry stains. Sitting in a bathtub was going to hurt like hell, but I knew I had no choice.

I headed downstairs freshly bathed and dressed in clean clothes. As I made my way down the stairs, I could see the shoes I had worn at the bottom, near the front door. Whew, my mother did an excellent job making them look clean again. I slipped them on and was about to head out the front door to the porch when my father called my name from the kitchen. The sound of his voice, cold and angry, made the hair on my neck stand. A cool shiver ran down my spine, despite the already high humidity that seeped into the old house. I stood in the doorway of the kitchen looking at my father, who was eating eggs and toast my mother made him. Always eggs and toast, every single morning for as far back as I could remember. He did not make eye contact with me, which I preferred. He continued to read the newspaper, never looking up, and said "Augustus, I am taking Hector with me to look at a new harvesting equipment in New York later today. It is a long ride, and we may have to spend the night if it gets too late to drive home. You are not to leave this farm.

You are to stay close to your mother and help her. I told Hector's wife, Olenka, to knock on the door if she needs anything while Hector is gone. Do you understand?" He looked up at me with those mean eyes, the eyes that had terrified me my entire life. They were evil, dark, and hateful and filled me with dread and fear, oftentimes completely paralyzing me head to toe.

I quickly replied, "Yes, yes, I understand. Is it okay if I go outside now? I am just going to ride my bike, but only on our property."

He seemed annoyed but finally nodded his head. "Fine, Augustus, but stay out of the blueberry fields." I nodded and turned quickly toward the front door. Once I got to the front porch, I realized that I had been holding my breath. I exhaled and leaned onto the porch railing for a second. I think maybe I was in shock. Why did he say that? I had never ridden my bike into the fields. Had he seen me in the fields last night, and this was some sort of sick game of mental torture? I had no way of knowing, and maybe I was reading way too much into it. The bottom line was that he would be away tonight, perhaps all night. It was like a sign from God. Tonight, I'd find out the truth. I'd find out what he had been doing, what his secrets were.

I felt energized and ready as I left the house that morning. I had intent and purpose today that only I could fulfill. No one else was going to make life better for my mother and me, or even at the very least, normal. I knew that. It was up to me. I was controlling my own destiny now, and my mother's. I jumped on my beat up, old bike and headed down the driveway, feet dragging to steady myself through the crappy rocks. I decided to ride around the perimeter of the blueberry fields to see if I could find any clues or obvious signs of disturbances in the dirt. I noticed instantly just how much we really needed rain. The air was thick and muggy, and the bugs were relentless. The red brackish dirt cloud I created as I rode along our farm stuck to me like paint and stung my eyes. Fortunately for us, blueberries thrived in these conditions.

Our farm was surrounded on all sides by a fortress of tall green pine trees that seemed to go on forever. The wooded terrain behind those pines was a mix of thick green and brown overgrowth, moss, dead trees, animals and animal skeletons, and waterways that stretched in all directions, hundreds of miles long, snaking deep throughout the barrens. It was beautiful, and it was disturbing all at the same time. I did not find the sense of peace people claimed to experience after spending time in these woods. The woods made me feel trapped and hopeless, like prison gates. Last month, after I successfully disabled the parental control lock my father put on the computer and learned how to permanently delete browsing history, I did some research on this area of New Jersey. I read newspaper articles, some that dated back over fifty years ago. All were witness accounts of hikers and campers that were accidentally separated from their group and lost in the barrens. Many were rescued within days, but unfortunately, some were never recovered. One hiker described the three nights he spent lost in these woods as harrowing, stating that the shrill screams, which encompassed him in the darkness as he hunkered under a large dead tree, were unbearable and literally drove him to the brink of insanity. He told the reporter that they sounded both human and animal and were always close by, but not close enough to be seen in the blackness. By day, he followed various waterways hoping to come across people canoeing or hiking, but every waterway led to another, and another, and he was out of food, water, and the energy to continue. By the Grace of God, at the point of exhaustion and breached mental capacity, a hunter spotted him and was able to safely guide the hiker back to civilization. I had always had a healthy fear and respect of the woods, which had kept me exactly as my father wanted: imprisoned.

Chapter Eight

Stella

G came out the back door just as I pulled around in our patrol car. He threw a string bag in the back and jumped in. "Not bad, not bad," he said.

I laughed. "What were you expecting? That we used old pickup trucks and dirt bikes to patrol?"

He nodded and grinned big. "Well, uh, yeah, exactly that."

My God, his teeth were perfect. I didn't know if I'd ever seen teeth that straight and white. His lips were soft and full, the kind of lips a woman would pay thousands of dollars for. I wanted to smack myself at the thought. *Okay, Stella, stop! Haven't you learned your lesson?* It didn't help that I hadn't had sex in months, not since Thomas, but I knew I had to control myself.

"Where is our first stop?" G asked.

"I think I will begin this tour by showing you where we will spend most of our weekends on duty."

As we drove down Route 563, I pointed out some of the more interesting places, not that there were many.

"That's Piney's," I said. "It's a local sort-of bar. I haven't been there yet, but Margie loves the place. She says they have the best cheeseburgers in New Jersey, but I am not certain that Margie has ever left the county, so you will have to make up your own mind."

G laughed. "Will do, will do. How come you haven't been there? How long have you lived here?"

"Well, I have only been here a few months, and I don't know. I guess going to a bar alone in Pine Barrens at night doesn't sound like fun to me. I am not the alone at a bar type, you know. Don't get me wrong, I look forward to having a social life, but with training and not having time to make friends other than work people, it hasn't been a priority. However, my best friend is spending the weekend with me, so perhaps tomorrow night I shall grace Piney's with my presence."

"Maybe I will join you ladies, if you don't mind?"

"You are welcome to join, newbie." I didn't tell him about my date with Ty. That would simply be too much information, too soon.

I threw my left blinker on and made a sharp turn onto the long dirt road to the campground. "What is this place?" G asked.

"This is where, unfortunately, you and I will spend many weekends on duty from April fifteenth through November first. This is Waving Pines Camping Resort." G shook his head and laughed. "This Campground at full capacity is temporary home to over 2,000 obnoxious, drunk, clueless, rude, golf cart riding assholes. Assholes that you and I will have to deal with. The state police used to oversee the campgrounds, but Margie says that changed about two years ago when an officer was severely burned by a drunk with a can of gasoline, a fire pit, and a cigarette. It didn't end well for him, either. The officer's partner shot and killed him on the spot."

"Ah, so we are sort of the cleanup crew, huh?"

"Exactly, and to make matters worse, 70% of the campground's population is seasonal campers who leave their trailers here for the entire season. They are like a cult that hates the 'transient campers' that are only here for weekends in their tents, travel trailers, or one of the cabins on the lake. Needless to say, when the cult and the transients share space at the Recreation Center where the band plays on Saturday night, it always ends in a knockdown, drag out, gang style fight. Last weekend, Jack and Erin were on duty. You'll meet them at some point. They were called out here six times in forty-eight hours. Two brawls, one golf cart in the lake, one fire that got out of control, and two escorts off the property at the request of the owners, Beth and Tony."

"Wow, that is incredible. It sounds like this place can be pretty dangerous, huh? I heard there has also been gang activity in the area. Have you had to deal with that, too?"

I shook my head. "Nope, not yet. Actually, I haven't been briefed on any gang activity. There are tons of motorcycles through here every weekend, but the majority of those guys are weekend warriors and charity event riders. They are a pleasure in comparison to the campers."

I drove through the entire campground, so he could understand the layout. The little cabins on the lake had no bathrooms, no air conditioning, and no heat, but they were booked solid every weekend. The lake itself was pretty cool. The bridge that spanned across the entire lake was at full capacity with kids and adults tossing fishing line into the water. It was a catch and release lake. I showed G where the bath houses were, the line of demarcation between the seasonal side of the campground and the transient side. On our way out of the campground, Beth was standing outside the little camp store that offered food, ice cream, brochures, and other camping needs. She waved at us, and I pulled over to introduce G. Beth and Tony were great people. A few years back, they decided that the corporate life in Manhattan was sucking the life out of them, so they cashed in their stocks, quit their jobs, and bought this camping resort. It hadn't been easy. They worked day and night, and Beth said the cost of the insurance needed for the resort had tripled over the past two years due to reckless camper incidents resulting in claims that the insurance company had to pay out. She really did look exhausted, and I wondered if her and Tony regretted their decision. I made the introductions and told Beth that I hoped I didn't see her this weekend.

She replied, "Oh, please, say a prayer for us, Stella, please."

We pulled out toward the long road that would bring us back out to Route 563, but I made another sharp left out of the campground instead.

"What's back here?" G asked.

"This is yet another problem the campground has just about every weekend. It's actually the state park. The free state park where weekenders who don't want to pay for a camping spot at the campground go to throw up a tent and party, except alcoholic beverages are prohibited, not that it stops them from bringing them in. To make matters worse, there is no fence separating the state park from the campground, only a shallow waterway utilized by tubers and kayakers. The state park campers have been known to wait until dark and then make their way through the water and onto the campground property, stealing everything they can and using the pool and bath houses. Beth's security guard Hank caught a couple having sex in the pool in the middle of the night. Hank also caught a group of teens getting high in the main bath house. They ran off in all directions, so no one was caught. Hank is well into his sixties, so he can't really give chase anymore. Instead, they call us, and we take reports. As part of our patrol, Captain Jesse promised Beth and Tony that we would ride through the state park reminding the campers that alcohol is prohibited and crossing over into the campground was trespassing. Okay, lets head back to the main road and head over to the schools." After a quick drive through of the camping section of the park, I told G that our next stop was to meet Captain Jesse's husband, Joe.

"So, Officer Stella, what's your story?"

I laughed. "Which story would that be?"

"You know, the Stella story. Where are you from? Why did you transfer here?"

Shit, I had not put much thought into answering this inevitable line of questioning. Stupid, Stella, really stupid. We would be together hours on end, patrolling and answering calls, so of course, he wanted to know my story. It was the starting point of any new partnership. Damn it. "Well, it isn't a very exciting story, but I grew up in Maryland. I had a normal, healthy childhood. No trauma or drama, no residual issues resulting in necessary weekly therapy sessions with a shrink. I am an only child because, hey when you get it so right the first time, why jinx it." G smirked. "My parents are still married. My dad is a County Sheriff, and my mom takes care of their farm." I got a raised eyebrow from G. "What's with that look, Officer G?"

"Nothing, nothing, just something I would like to do one day as well."

"It's not a big farm, and mostly just lots of chickens. My mom sells eggs and cut flowers that she grows during the summer months. It is her true passion in life. She spent twenty years working for an insurance company and felt nothing but unappreciated, unfulfilled, and depressed. Chickens and flowers were the cure. We talk a couple times a week, and I visit as often as I can. Boring, right?"

G shook his head and replied, "Not at all, sounds like the American dream to me. Nice. So, that answers half of the question, but what about here? You know, at this specific police department? I can't imagine that you went into law enforcement with the overwhelming desire to be here, right?"

"Uh, I would say it is your turn first, Officer G. What is your story? We most certainly have the time, and I am driving, so spill."

Chapter Nine

Augustus

Behind me, at a slow and steady pace, I could hear my father's truck approaching. I pulled off the dirt road, stood with my bike balanced between both of my legs, and waited for him to pass me by. He slowed almost to a complete stop to remind me of the instructions he had given me earlier. Hector leaned over from the passenger seat and smiled and gave a quick wave as my father continued on his way, leaving a cloud of red dust in his tracks. I wanted to run right through the fields to the area where he was digging, but I did not trust him. If he knew I was out there watching him in the dark, he may expect me to do just that. He could have pulled over after his truck disappeared from my sight to watch me. As anxious to find out the truth as I was, I would remain cautious and wait this out a bit.

I could hear a faint voice in the distance but could not ascertain where it was coming from. I turned around to see Javier yelling and waving to me. He was on his bike, too. I bet Hector told him to spend time with me since my father would be gone. I could not have been happier. "Hola, Augustus. Can I ride with you?"

"Hey, Javier, you said that perfectly! You have been practicing your English." Javier smiled big and nodded. He followed me for what felt like miles around the dirt roads that denoted our fields.

It was incredibly muggy, and after a while, I could feel the sunburn on the tips of my ears and the back of my neck. I knew sleeping tonight would hurt like hell. I turned to Javier and told him to follow me. We rode to the biggest barn that sat in the center of the smaller structures because I knew that was where the water hose was. I jumped off my bike, letting it fall to the ground and quickly turned the nozzle. It had been laying in the shade, so the water was immediately cool and refreshing. I held the hose over my head and allowed the water to soak me. Then, I drank until my stomach hurt. I handed the hose to Javier, and he did the same. We sat in the grass near the barn for a while until I told Javier that I had to go home to check on my mother. I didn't want my mother to be worried about me.

"Okay, bye, Augustus." Javier patted me on my shoulder, thanked me, and off he went toward his little house on our property. I was super exhausted but spending those hours with Javier, riding our bikes, laughing, and talking was just awesome. I was really proud of how hard he must be working to learn the English language. He was so very blessed to have a mother and father that love him and wanted him to succeed.

By the time I reached my front yard, I was completely dehydrated again. My mother must have known because as I let me bike fall to the ground, she opened the door and handed me a big glass of lemonade and sat down beside me on the top step. I drank every bit of that lemonade. "Oh, Augustus, you are filthy."

"I know, Mom, isn't it great?"

She laughed and hugged me tight. "It makes my heart so happy that you had such a good day. I saw you and Javier riding your bikes together and having a good time. You just looked so excited and carefree. I am so deeply sorry that you don't get more days like this. I love you."

"I know, and I love you, too. Don't worry, one day, you and I will have a better life." I kissed my mother and jumped up before she could reply. "I am going to take a bath and a nap, okay? Can you wake me up when dinner is ready, please?"

"Yes, Augustus, yes I will. Get some rest. It's just us tonight."

"Augustus, Augustus, wake up, sleepy head. It's dinner time." Mom was sitting at the edge of my bed, smiling and shaking me awake.

"Okay, okay, I'm up, Mom. I'm up." My belly was howling. All that exercise today really gave me an appetite. Once Mom realized that I was wide awake and starving, she went back downstairs. Oh, the smell of whatever she was making was absolutely amazing. My mouth watered. I couldn't remember ever being this hungry or smelling anything as delicious before. I jumped out of bed and threw a t-shirt and shorts on and headed downstairs. I ran down the stairs as if the house were on fire. Mom was in the kitchen filling up a plate for me, and I plopped down into my usual seat.

"Mom, what is this? The smell is incredible. It makes my belly growl."

"Aw, thank you. Since its just you and I tonight, I made a special dish that my mother used to make when I was a little girl." That stopped me in my tracks. Did my mother just mention her mother? Mom saw the look of shock and awe on my face and simply said, "Augustus, I have made up my mind that whenever I can, I will try to tell you about my family from back home. Everyone deserves to know their family tree, but it will have to be our secret. This dish I have made you tonight is Jager schnitzel, an authentic German meal. This must be our secret dinner, Augustus. Your father wants no reminders of life before America in this house. Eat, enjoy! I have made desert for you, too. German cake that my grandmother used to make me when I was a little girl. Oh, you will love it. Our secret!"

I thought this exact moment in time, in this universe, was the happiest I had ever been. I was at ease, eating and laughing, having dinner with my mother. I needed nothing more than this, but I knew it would be short lived. He would be back, though, and tonight I needed to make my way out to where he was digging in the blueberry fields before he returned. I may never get an opportunity like this again. I must wait until Mother goes to bed. I didn't want to worry her. Tonight was the happiest I had ever seen her as well. I felt blessed, like Hector told me I should, and I bowed my head and thanked God for this time with my mother tonight. I was nothing like my father. I felt. I loved. I hated. I enjoyed. I stressed. I hoped. Nothing like him at all.

After dinner, my mother and I cleaned up the kitchen, did the dishes, and placed the uneaten food into a black garbage bag. We had a pretty big dumpster on the farm that was emptied by the local waste management company twice a month. I headed over to the dumpster, garbage bag in hand, and hurled it in. Evidence gone.

When I got back to the house, my mother was sitting on the porch with a small black book held tightly against her chest. "Augustus, come sit with me. I have something to show you."

The look on her face was one I had not seen before. Perhaps, a combination of happiness and pride. I did as she asked and sat next to her on the top step. The thickness of the summer air and the choir of insects and animals faded as my mother opened the little book.

"You ready, Augustus?"

"Oh, I am, Mom. I am." I could tell she was holding back tears, but not the sad kind. She opened the book to the first page. A black and white picture of a man and woman stunned me. "Mom, that lady looks just like you. Is it you, but how?"

She let out a loud laugh as tears started to stream from the corner of her eyes. "No, sweetie, this is my mother and father. Your grandparents, Johanna and Albert Becker. They are still living in Germany, at least I hope and pray they are. A few years back, the pain of missing them for all of these years became just too much for me to bear, and I wrote them a letter, without your father knowing, of course. It was a risky chance I had to take. The older I get, Augustus, the more I long to see my parents again." My mother seemed lost in her thoughts until I took her hand in mine.

"Mom, did they write back to you? What did they

say?"

"They wanted me to take you and leave your father and come home to Germany. They even sent money for the journey."

"So, what happened? Why didn't we go?"

"Your father happened, Augustus, your father happened. He found the letter they sent and the money in my dresser drawer. He was furious, so angry I thought he may kill me. I was terrified. He warned me that if I attempted to leave with you, he would have me arrested and that I would never see you again." Bigger tears welled up in her eyes now and streaked her cheeks. I squeezed her hand tighter.

"Don't cry, please. You did what you could. This is not your fault. One day, we will get to see your parents. We will."

She hugged me tight and cried for just a bit longer. "Okay, no more tears, let me show you a few more pictures." She turned the page, and another black and white photo of a baby immediately brought a smile to my face. The baby looked like me.

"That's you, right? It looks just like my baby picture!"

"Yes, yes, it does!" We sat for over an hour looking at the old photos and talking about my mother's childhood. She looked so normal and content in each picture. Innocent, blind to how her life would turn out, living in another country, held prisoner with her own child. The sky was now dark except for the low glow of the moon and the dots of stars, barely visible behind the overcast clouds and thickness of a summer night in the barrens. "I don't expect your father will be home before noon tomorrow. I will wake you up early and make breakfast for you and I." She kissed me on the forehead as she stood to walk back inside the house with her book in hand. "I'm going to bed. I love you more than life itself. This day has been the most precious to me since I left Germany. If I didn't have you, Augustus, I would have no reason to live."

"I love you, too, Mom, and do not worry anymore please. One day, you and I will visit my grandparents."

"I pray that is true. Good night, my beautiful boy. Make sure you get to bed soon as well."

I decided to walk for a bit. It was dark but not pitch black, and I was not afraid. I watched for the light from my mother's bedroom window to go out, which it did several minutes later. She was in bed. She will undoubtedly have the best night sleep she has had since she was a child, safe at home with her parents. I waited just five minutes more before I went back into the house and to the kitchen. I slowly opened the drawer next to the stove where I knew the flashlights were and grabbed two. I paused for a moment to be certain she was not coming back downstairs. All was still so I made my way outside and toward the blueberry fields.

Chapter Ten

Stella

G paused, a long pause, as if trying to decide what information he was going to divulge to me. Curious. I nudged him with my elbow, and he laughed.

"Okay, fair is fair. My story isn't quite the American dream, Stella. I was born and raised in Ocala, Florida. My early childhood memories are all good ones. Happy ones. My mom and dad just seemed really happy together. My mom stayed at home with me, and my dad was in the Navy, but he really didn't have to travel much. Dad was actually stationed in Florida indefinitely. Oh, and as you so eloquently put it, since my parents achieved absolute perfection with me, there was no need for further babies that may not be as fabulous as me."

"Cute, very cute. Go on, next chapter please."

"Well, that's where it all goes to hell. My mother was

killed in a car accident when I was just seven. My dad was driving, and I was in the back seat. A drunk driver drove straight into the front passenger door, killing my mother instantly."

"Oh, G. I am so sorry! Now I feel like such an ass making you talk about this."

"It's okay, really. It was a lifetime ago."

"So, what happened to you and your dad after?"

"Well, that's where it all *really* goes to hell. My Father, I guess, didn't think he could raise a child alone, so he met and married a woman within six months of my mother's death. She was odd and pushy. She had him wrapped around her finger, too. Talk about a whooped man. He still spent time with me and went to all of my baseball games, but it was never the same. By the time I turned eighteen, I was desperate to get out of that house and away from her, and trust me, it didn't break her heart, either, when I joined the Navy and left home for good. My father has since passed, but she is still alive in my childhood home. My father left everything to her, which did not surprise me at all. Your turn, Officer Stella!"

I did not know what the hell came over me or why I felt such a connection with my partner already, but before I could stop myself, I was telling G the story of Thomas, my walk of shame, and subsequent current circumstances. I was quite certain that he never expected me to open up so soon, as evidenced by the deer in the head light look, mouth hung open, expression.

"God, I am sorry. Why in the hell did I just unload all of my personal baggage on you? Listen, I have not told anyone else about why I am here, and I would really appreciate it if you would refrain as well."

He put his hand softly on my shoulder. "Stella, we are partners. I would never betray your confidence. Listen, everyone has a past, or at least something in their past, that they are not proud of. In my opinion, not that you asked, but Thomas acted like a coward not supporting you or reaching out to make certain that you are alright after you endured public humiliation. That's just not cool."

"Yeah, that thought has crossed my mind a few hundred times, but I am over him, over the embarrassment and guilt, and adamant to make a life for myself."

"Here in Pine Barrens?"

"Well, I don't know. I guess it's sort of growing on me. I don't hate it anymore. I will say that much. After we leave the school, I'll drive you by the breathtaking mansion I am renting." G shot me a look of confusion as if he weren't quite sure if I was kidding.

I turned onto Creek Road, which, like most roads in the barrens, was long and wooded and rich in water supply with bugs on steroids. About three miles down on the right, I turned into the parking lot where a large sign read "Welcome to Pine Barrens Elementary School, home of the Devils."

"Home of the Devils, huh? That's original." We both laughed. "Wow, I must say that this isn't what I expected for a school in the middle of nowhere. This is state of the art, beautiful."

"Yup, I said the same thing when Captain Jesse brought me here a few months back. Apparently, the military facility nearby sends the children of their stationed men and women here, so Uncle Sam gave the school a huge grant to rebuild the old run-down school that stood before this one. Cap says that this school is double the size of the old one. Let's park the car, and you can meet Jesse's husband."

I pulled my cell out and sent a quick text to Joe letting him know that we were outside and to come say hello. I knew Cap told him we would be stopping by for a quick hello and introduction with the newbie.

G and I leaned against the patrol car chatting while we waited for Joe. It was ridiculously hot today. The gross kind of hot that made you sweat everywhere. Sweat rolled down the back of my neck, and I was glad I put my hair up. I jumped when G sprang forward from his leaning position and slapped the side of his neck hard.

"Jesus Christ, it got me good. Fucking strawberry flies! Big enough to carry off a small dog. Damn it, that stung! I am quite sure it has its own pulse already and by

84

tomorrow will need its own zip code."

I busted out laughing. "Sorry, sorry, but that was hysterical. Not that you were bit, but your thorough descriptive narrative. Hey, Florida boy, how did you know what a strawberry fly was?"

"I did a ton of research on this place. I know more than you think I do." He gave me a quick wink, and we both laughed.

"Here comes Joe."

"Hello, kids, sorry it took me so long. Had to threaten the little monsters for a bit so they would stay in their seats while I came out. Ha, well, I already came out, you know, but I meant come outside." Joe was still chuckling at his own joke when he finally reached us. He held his hand out to G and introduced himself. "Hi, I'm Joe, Jesse's husband."

"Super great to meet you. I'm G." Joe did a head to toe, admiring his good looks and inviting physique.

"Nice to meet you, too, very nice indeed. What does G stand for? Gorgeous?"

G smiled. "Well, I would tell you but then I may have to kill you. Listen, my friends call me G, and since I know we will become good friends, I want you to do the same Joe."

Joe winked. "Well, okay, I like that answer, but you know I am already taken, right?" Uncomfortable silence ensued but only for a second until Joe laughed so hard, he was bent over grabbing his stomach. Joe loved to joke around and put people on the spot, and no one laughed harder at those moments than Joe himself. "I would love to stay and chat with you kids, but I have to get back inside before they burn the school down. Brats, entitled little brats. This generation, the ME generation, is going to hell in a handbag! Let's have dinner one night, okay? You two come over to our place, and I'll do the cooking. I am a magnificent cook you know."

And just like that, Joe disappeared back into the building. "Wow, I think I need a nap after just five minutes with him. I wish I had that kind of energy. He seems really cool, though. Thanks for doing the introductions, Stella."

"Of course, you aren't a true Piney until you've met Joe, the life of the party. He really is a great guy. Him and Cap seem extremely happy together."

"Well, that's all that really matters in life anyway, right?"

"You are not wrong, G. You are not wrong."

"Where to next?"

"Oh, Officer G, no tour of this little slice of heaven would be complete without the terrifying walk through the run down, abandoned buildings that were once home to hundreds of clinically insane patients and some criminals back in the 1940s."

"Officer Stella, you know all the right things to say to

a guy. What is the name of the place?"

"It was called 'The Knight Hospital for the Mentally Ill.' Of course, there are hundreds of stories and legends surrounding the sudden closure and missing patients. Margie says that the hospital was defunded and that the owners fired all of the employees and then stopped supplying food, medication, and services to the patients. She said they just took off, left the country with what was left of the money. It took weeks before the public realized what had happened, and by that time, legend has it, or Margie anyway, that many of them just walked off into the woods never to be found again. Some patients were killed by other patients and are believed to have been buried on the grounds somewhere. Some took their own lives. It is said that the angry souls of those who were killed still roam Pine Barrens and the abandoned structures looking for help."

"Geez, you sure tell a good ghost story. I'm really scared, protect me." G playfully leaned his head on my shoulder as if he were truly spooked for just a few seconds, and I felt a ping in my stomach.

I thought I was attracted to him not just because he was smoking hot but because he was a total flirt, and I hadn't gotten laid in too long. We both laughed, and I nudged his arm. *Oh, Stella girl, you have got to resist the urge to pull over and rip his clothes off. You have to. Where the hell would I transfer to from here? Purgatory? Just keep driving.*

After a short drive, I announced that we had arrived.

"Holy shit, you were not lying. This place looks like something out of a horror film."

The fence, that once surrounded the entire facility, was at least five acres and had since corroded, rusted, and fallen in for the most part, enabling local teens and drug addicts to enter at will. As I drove toward the entrance to the main building, the car tires bounced fiercely. The original driveway was now mostly potholes, overgrown brush, and busted bottles of every type of alcohol imaginable. I explained to my partner that the main building, which was the largest structure, housed the administration offices and also the staff member who were permitted to live there. No actual patients were kept in the main building. What remained of the structure should have been knocked down decades ago, but Cap said due to ongoing legal arguments between the families of the patients and the county, nothing could be touched. Unfortunately, it was impossible for us to patrol thoroughly. Too many holes in the fence, too many curious kids, squatters, and countless drug users considered this place fair game. No doubt that it wouldn't be too long until there was a collapse and people died, thus adding claimants to the lawsuits. It was a real mess, and I knew Cap worried a lot about it. He even went so far as to purchase, on his own dime, 'No Trespassing' signs and signs with phone numbers for drug and alcohol addiction hotlines all around the fencing. Took him weeks to complete he said.

"Do you want me to show you where the patients were kept?" My partner seemed lost deep in thought as he carefully scanned his surroundings. "G?"

"Sorry, Stella, sorry. Yes, I want to see the entire property. What year did you say this place closed down?"

"Uh, I am not exactly sure, but I think Margie told me it was in the 1970s. Are you okay? You actually look like you've seen a ghost."

"I'm not usually superstitious, I swear, but this place has such an ominous, unsettled feel to it. I don't know if it's the story you told me or not, but I can sense the despair and fear. Again, I am not usually like this, nor do I claim to be in tune with spirits, but this place is, I don't know, just wrong."

Listen, I get it. Horrible things happened here even before the owners abandoned the patients, and after. Come on, I'll show you what I mean."

We followed what was left of a brick walkway through an overgrown garden with crumbling cement benches and a wrought iron trellis that was suffocated by thick old vines. Lifeless vines, which had not seen vibrance in decades. I imagined, at one time, the garden was quite beautiful. The remnants of what looked to be an old koi pond was clogged with thick, green, pollen-looking muck. A tall statue of an angel leaned helplessly on a massive oak tree that provided refreshing yet brief shade for us from the unforgiving summer sun as we walked under. Beyond that tree, I stopped to make sure G was still behind me.

"Are you okay?"

"Yes, I'm just taking it all in. Getting myself acquainted with the area."

I knew G and I had just met, but I had such a strong feeling that something was gnawing at him. He'd just seemed preoccupied since our arrival here. Did this place trigger something in his past, or the memory of someone? An unpleasant time in his life? I made a mental note to ask him when we were together in a more casual setting.

"What were those buildings used for?" G asked, pointing to three brick structures, one of which was completely void of a roof. Time had taken its toll on the abandoned, discarded old buildings. All of the windows in the building were gone. The doors had been removed or rotted away. The thick weeds and brush that had grown on and around the one-story buildings swallowed them completely.

"The first two larger ones were used to house the patients, and the third was used for treatments."

"What kind of treatments?"

"You sure you want to see this? We don't have to go inside. For the most part, we find the vagrants in the main building where its easy access and easy escape for them when we roll up."

"I'm fine, Stella, really. I hope you don't think this place has disturbed me to the point where I can't do my job. I just find the story fascinating. Sad but fascinating, and I guess a bit shocking that this could have happened in this country, even back then."

I laughed. "Really, G, I unloaded all of my personal and embarrassing baggage on you today, and you are worried about what I may think of you? Listen, I was on edge the first time I saw this place, too. Anyone not emotionally troubled by this place cannot be human. What happened here years ago was a senseless and cruel tragedy. Come on, follow me. Last building, then we can get back on the road."

We approached the entrance to the building, which aside from the weeds, stood unprotected from intruders.

"Be careful, there are areas where the flooring isn't very stable anymore." Through the front door on our right was a small room, like a phone booth. "This is where we think the security guard must have been posted. The rooms that I want to show you are this way." I led him down the hallway. He slowed as we passed by a small office.

"Jesus, it's like people just vanished into thin air. Look, there is still a coffee cup on that desk and paper in that open filing cabinet." The papers were yellow and frail, and the room smelled moldy from years of water intrusion. A vintage-looking typewriter sat on a faded wooden secretary desk. G grabbed the single sheet of yellowed paper from the typewriter and turned to me as if he really had seen a ghost. "Oh my God, look. January 3, 1972." G handed me the paper which read just that, January 3, 1972. "Like I said, it's like these people were working one minute and then they were gone the next."

I had to admit the hair on the back of my neck tingled at that realization. This place was giving me the creeps today. "Let's step it up a bit and get back on the road." G followed me to the next room, this one still had a door, and the sign read: "ESTR#1 – Authorized Personnel Only." I turned to G. "You ready?"

"I am, let's see it."

I slowly opened the door and watched the expression on G's face as he slowly came to understand exactly what this room was used for. He looked at me with such sympathy and compassion in his eyes. He scanned the room vigilantly, as though he needed to comprehend the pain of the souls who were subjected to such utter cruelness. His eyes drifted from the soiled beds with rusted handcuffs attached to the feet restraints, then the equipment that looked like a large transistor radio from a yard sale. I could not break my gaze if I wanted to. G eyed the oddly shaped headsets, the large fork that looked as if it were used for grilling large meats, and the rusted sink stuffed with dingy, crusted brown towels. It was as if I watched him put the last puzzle piece in place. His face drained of all color, and his deep beautiful eyes glazed over, as if he were fighting to hold back a deluge of tears. The smell was putrid. Even now, it was an unrecognizable, yet familiar odor, like a dead decaying animal.

"No way, Stella. Oh my God, it stands for Electronic Shock Treatment Room."

I didn't have the heart to show him the next room of inhumane acts of horror. The room that resembled a large locker room except there were no lockers, just open showers, and large drains in the tiled floor. The entire room was one gigantic shower. Remnants of large hoses were still attached in some spots to the wall, above which a row of dials had been installed. Barely legible were the words on the dials, FREEZE and BURN. Cap said it was another form of treatment doctors used with the intent of fixing mentally ill patients.

Chapter Eleven

Augustus

I looked back over my shoulder one last time. Mom's room was still dark. I clicked the bigger flashlight on and headed toward the spot where my father had been digging. I noticed that all was dark at Javier's little house as well. I felt conflicted. I was surrounded by peace and calmness in the still of the summer night, unafraid of my father, yet I could not shake the anxious vibe in my stomach. Was I really hoping to find something awful? Something that could make my father go away forever? Well, yes, I believed that was exactly what I was hoping in that moment. I wished I had sprayed myself with the mosquito spray my mother kept on the kitchen windowsill. The bugs were relentless tonight from the stillness of the air. There was no breeze, no relief from the thick, muggy summer air, and no relief from the damn strawberry flies. The smell of the blueberries, ripe and soon ready to harvest, was a welcome scent and helped me concentrate less on the bugs and more on my purpose.

The sound of footsteps at the edge of the pine trees brought me to a complete stand still. What the hell was that? I pointed my flashlight toward the perimeter of the pines that surrounded our farm and separated us from the thick woods. Nothing. I saw nothing. I sure felt like I am being watched by someone. *Okay, Augustus, get a grip on yourself.* I knew these woods were home to a million varied species of life, most of which were nocturnal. It was probably just a fox. Hector told me and Javier that over the past ten years, several species of the fox family had tripled in Pine Barrens, concerning some that liked to camp and hike in the area. I shook it off and shone my light ahead. The big barn where my father had parked his truck was not too much further. I would head into the barn and look for shovels and any evidence that he may have left of what he had been doing.

The door was unlocked, which did not surprise me. My father scared the hell out of everyone around him, and we all knew that he forbade us to enter the barn, so why would he bother locking it. Such a narcissist. I feared him, yes, but I did not respect him, and I suspect the workers felt the same way. Inside the barn, I turned the overhanging light on just briefly, enough to realize that it was too bright, not a great idea. I clicked it back off and was relieved to see that the flashlight gave me adequate lighting to look around. Nothing jumped out at me as overly suspicious. My father kept the barn particularly tidy. Tools were hung from brackets, and larger pieces of equipment were lined in rows against the walls for easy access. Brooms, shovels, rakes, and an axe hung from the wall behind them. Everything was neat and had a specific spot. I had to be careful not to disturb anything. I pulled the shovel from the wall and was shocked to see it was caked with dried red mud. Could this be the shovel my father was digging with? He was so adamant that everything be kept neat and orderly. Why would he leave this shovel like this? Unless…? Shit, did he see me in the field? Did he forgo the usual cleaning routine in hopes that he would beat me back to the house?

Shovel in hand, I grabbed the door to head out to the spot where I saw him, but something caught my eye. In the furthest corner of the barn was what looked like a narrow door, left slightly ajar. Smaller tools and big spools of rope hung from brackets, completely camouflaging the door. I would have never noticed had it been closed completely. Was my father in so much of a rush that he neglected to close a secret door, or was this a trap meant for me? I had to know what was in there. That was my purpose tonight, after all.

The door was small enough that I had to tuck my head

down to enter through it. It was pitch black, but I knew better than to turn a light on, if there was one. I took out the second flashlight from my pocket, and by the light of both, I could make out a staircase. I never knew that there was another floor in this barn. I was quite sure no one knew. I held tightly onto the banister as I climbed each stair, cautiously scanning ahead and behind me as I progressed toward the top. I was three steps from the top when I realized that it was some sort of loft. It wasn't big, more like an office space maybe, certainly not the natural length and width of the barn. No, this was something my father must have added, but why?

I stepped onto the floor of the secret loft space, which was carpeted with some sort of a soft matting material. The kind of mat that a gymnastics team would use to do their routines on safely. It was dark gray and stained in many areas, but with what I could not tell. I walked toward the back of the room. The walls were nothing but unpainted, unfinished plywood. A small wooden table and a gray metal folding chair had been placed in the center of the floor. Above was a thin rope attached to a lightbulb and switch had been rigged. I wanted so badly to have more light, but once again, fear got the best of me, and I decided I would be safer with just the flashlights.

It was the glow of the metal that first caught my eye. Tucked back in the furthest corner of the loft was a metal cage of some sort. Not a small cage that you would use to trap groundhogs or fox, either. This cage was as tall as me and at least five feet wide. The metal door hung open, exposing a hefty, bronze-colored lock with a key still in it. Panic steadily began to overtake my sense of curiosity. Blood? It was spattered all over the mat inside the cage. I dropped to my knees, confuse, and sickened, and that was when I saw it. So small, that I almost missed it. I bet he missed it. Written in what looked like blood were just two words: HELP ME.

My initial thought was to run. Run back to the house and get my mother, but then what? We had no car and no phone, and even if we did, we had absolutely no one we could call, except the police. No, I needed time to think. I had to find out who was in that cage and where... Oh my God, the shovel, the digging! Had he killed and buried someone? Was that what he was doing under the blanket of darkness, privacy never concerning him? I stood slowly, trying to steady my legs beneath me before I made my way back down those stairs. I grasped tightly onto the wooden railing out of fear of falling. My legs so much like jelly that they could collapse at any moment. I thought I was in shock, but there was no time to talk myself out of this. When I exited the small door, I slowly scanned the barn to be certain he had not come home. Everything was quiet and dark. I closed the door behind me but remembered it had been left slightly ajar, and if this were a test of his, he would expect me to close it. I left the door just as I had found it, grabbed the muddy shovel, and returned to the fields. I knew approximately where I saw him digging, but not exactly. Although, it hasn't rained, so maybe I would get lucky and find the disturbed dirt.

I used both flashlights to light up the ground beneath me. I took slow and careful steps around each blueberry bush, making a mental note of each row I investigated to not duplicate my efforts. After what must have been at least three hours, I stumbled upon a bush that was surrounded by dirt which appeared to have been flattened by both a shovel and boots with prints still visible. This had to be it. I was not sure if it was the heat or my anxiety, but I was sweating profusely. My eyes stung from the droplets of sweat that had made their way to the corners of my eyes. I took my shirt off, wiped my face, and wrapped it around my head. I did a once around with the flashlights again, just to be certain that I was still alone, and I began removing the soil from around the blueberry bush, terrified at what I may uncover.

I dug deep under the bush to be certain not to destroy the roots and then wedged the back side of the shovel beneath the roots. The bush sprung from the earth with ease. I pulled the bush out of the hole and set it beside me. I saw nothing but dirt where the bush had stood. I had to dig deeper. He was smart. He would know that a body buried too close to the top would be unearthed by animals. I was thirsty as hell, and my mouth felt like I had been chewing on paper. I was exhausted, both mentally and physically. I was functioning on sheer adrenaline and conviction. I was about three feet below the root of the bush when I saw it: hair, long hair.

I screamed and tried to back away, but I tripped backwards over the bush and landed hard on my tailbone. Instantly, I felt the sharp pain like a sword through my skin and bones. Bile filled my throat, and I wretched hard, gagging as I tried to get back to my feet. On my hands and knees, wincing from the pain in my back and the rancid taste in my mouth, I began to question the continuance of my mission, but only momentarily. As horrified as I was, I was also enraged, in significant pain, and all but drained of energy, but this nightmare ended for mother and me tonight.

I got back to my feet, cringing from the now throbbing pain, and kept digging. It was a woman, very young. She was still wearing white high heel shoes and a very short white skirt. Her once pink shirt was stained with dirt and blood. I threw the shovel down, wrapped my arms around her and began to pull. The sick fucking bastard killed her and buried her below a fucking blueberry bush. Despite my physical condition, I gently pulled, and dragged the lifeless body until it was completely above ground, and that was when I fell apart, sobbing and barely capable of catching my breath. I was only twelve years old, and here I sat in the dirt, in the dark, next to a dead woman that my father tortured, murdered, and buried on our family farm. Oh, God, why?

The woman was more of a girl than a woman. In her twenties, if I had to guess. She was pretty before he did this to her. Her blonde hair was matted to her head with dried blood and dirt, yet I could still see the enormous gash in her skull. He had struck her with something and... what? Watched her die an agonizing death? I was right, she was in fact wearing a pink sleeveless blouse that was now completely soiled with blood and dirt. I wiped the tears from my eyes and tried to slow my heart rate before I passed out. What did I do now? My God, I had not thought this through completely. I had been so hyper-focused on finding out what he was doing that I neglected to plan on what I could logically do about it once I figured it out.

I had been out here for hours. I had no guarantee that the sick bastard wasn't coming back tonight, and I had no one to tell, and no way to leave for help. Hell, even if I could get to town safely and turn him into the police, what would happen to my mother and I, the farm, and the workers? The police would no doubt unearth every square inch of this farm, and rightfully so. My father has been here for decades, there could be countless innocent souls buried here.

Fuck! I had no choice but to put this beautiful girl back into her grave and replant the bush as if I had not been here. Disgusted with myself, I did just that, and I asked God, begged him, to forgive me and to take her soul to heaven. I hung the shovel in the same condition I found it, exactly where I found it and walked back to the house. My mother's light was still off, her room dark. I brushed the dirt off my shoes and threw them inside the hallway closet and out of plain sight. I showered and then slowly got into my bed despite my back screaming with every inch I moved. Tonight, I slept. Tomorrow, I'd figure out what was next.

Chapter Twelve

Stella

G was silent and appeared to be deep in thought as we slowly made our way out of the abandoned psychiatric facility. I felt absolutely horrible. I should have told him what we would encounter before we got there. I didn't know him or his past or if a place like this would trigger emotional distress for him. Obviously, he was shaken by what I had shown him.

"Hey, are you alright? Listen, I'm sorry. I should have prepared you before we went to that hell hole, like Cap had done for me. I'm really sorry."

"Stella, I'm fine, really. I mean, I have read about places like that and even seen a few documentaries over the years. I knew they existed. Still, it's difficult to accept that at any point in history, intelligent and educated people could actually expect that subjecting humans to such torture would somehow free them from mental illness. I know that there are incarcerated criminals and people roaming free right now that are pure evil. Murderers, psychopaths, and sadistic killers, and there is no cure for them, but mental illness is just that. An illness. I have known people throughout my life that suffer with depression, bipolar disorder, anxiety, all of which are controlled by medication. I guess we have come a long way since places like this were outlawed. Where to next, Stel? The cemetery?"

Oh, ridiculously cute, Officer G, very cute. I was relieved to see his spirits had lifted, and the tension in the car diffused. "No, next stop will be a pleasant one, comical actually."

I drove the patrol car behind Mr. Avery's shop, which actually was the name of the little place.

"Okay, let's go say a quick hello to Mr. Avery and grab some coffee before he closes shop for the day. You will love him."

"If you say so, but it's a thousand degrees out. How the hell can you drink hot coffee? Ill grab a soda instead. Same caffeine without the scorch."

Mr. Avery was behind the counter as usual, looking half asleep, but his head popped up and his smile grew wide as G and I walked in. "Hello, Mr. Avery, this is my new partner, G. G, this is the famous Mr. Avery, also known as the mayor."

"Well, I didn't know I was meeting royalty today. It is so nice to meet you, Mr. Avery. Your store is awesome." Mr. Avery, humble as usual, told G he certainly was not royalty, just a dinosaur in this village of ours.

I chimed in, "Mr. Avery, could I please get a large cup of your fabulous coffee, and you know how I like it, just cream and no sugar."

"Oh, because you are sweet enough, Officer Stella." Mr. Avery laughed and agreed with G.

"How is your day going so far, Mr. Avery? Anything exciting?"

"No, no," he replied, "but don't forget you have a committee meeting next Wednesday, and I know everyone values your input, Stella."

"What committee is Stella sitting on?"

"Stella has graciously agreed to lend us some of her valuable free time to work on the Cranberry Festival Committee. If you're not from around here, you are in for a real treat this Fall."

"That sounds great. I am looking forward to that," replied G. I held the door open, and we said our goodbyes to Mr. Avery. "Wow, he is a true icon, huh. Stel, they don't make them like that anymore. What a gentleman. He's your landlord, too?"

"Yup, turn around." I pointed to my little house a short way off in the distance. "That's my castle, for now."

"That's not bad. Can I look inside?"

Wow, that caught me totally off guard, and I guess I wore that expression on my face.

"Sorry, that was a bit forward. I know we just met but you are so easy to be around, talk to, and confide in."

"G, its fine, no worries. That look was actually my 'Jesus, did I leave clothes all over the floor and a sink full of dishes' look, but I remember that I left it in pretty decent shape today. Come on, let's go in. I'll give you the tour, but trust me, it won't take too long. I think the patrol car is bigger."

I had to wiggle the key around in the lock before I heard the lock click open. G followed me in.

"See what I mean? It's tiny. Brie will have to sleep on the sofa when she gets here, but hopefully, she will be too drunk to care."

"Am I still invited to stop by for a drink tonight?"

"Yes, of course, you are! I think she will need a lot of cheering up and a lot of alcohol."

"Can't wait to hear her story."

"So, this is the east wing, which as you can see is adorned in a rustic farmhouse motif." I tried, but I could not keep a straight face, and we both laughed hard. "The bathroom is a pretty decent size, though, right?

"It is, it is. It's bigger than the bathroom at the place I rent." We walked to the kitchen and then my bedroom. G sat on the edge of my bed. "This is not bad at all. The bed is comfortable. It's clean, and it smells good. Oh, and

I love the rustic farmhouse look."

My God, he looked so inviting, sitting on my bed in his uniform, leaning back on his elbows as if to say, 'Come and get me, Stella.' His flirtatious vibe was like hot, sexy, creative foreplay. I could feel my nipples harden and tingle slightly. My lack of a sex life and his, well, his everything were completely overwhelming, and for a second, I got the feeling that we were both having the same porn star fantasy moment in our heads. *Don't do it, Stella. Don't do it. Resist. Resist!*

Like a warning sign from my angels above, our radios kicked on loud. It was Margie, and she sounded off. She spoke in a frantic, unorganized tone. "Stella, G, I need you over at the state park, behind the Campground now. Possible homicide victim!"

"No fucking way, my first day and we land a murder!"

"Let's go!" We rushed back to the patrol car. I kicked the lights and sirens on and tore out of the parking lot. We headed back in the direction we came.

"What could have happened at a campground?"

"Really? How about a mix of alcohol, drugs, people of varying socioeconomic backgrounds, and firepits?"

"Yikes, copy that, Stella."

As we drove past the entrance to the campground and over the narrow bridge into the state park, a small group of people had gathered, and they were looking down at the edge of the waterway, which was popular this time of year for tubing and kayaking. I blew the horn and kept the siren blaring for just a minute to announce our arrival. "G, in the trunk there is caution tape. Tape off the entrance to the state park and let Margie know that we have arrived on scene but will need help with crowd control in order to preserve the integrity of the suspected scene."

"Ten four, you got it."

"Good afternoon, I am Officer Stella with the local PD. I need to know who found the body."

A young couple, maybe late teens, sitting on the bank of the water raised their hands. The female looked as if she had been crying. I nodded in acknowledgement to their raised hands. "Okay, everyone else, I need you to walk toward the other officer, over the bridge, and stand on the other side of the police tape. Do not leave! We will need statements from all of you."

The crowd of ten did as I requested, and I made my way toward the young couple. The state police would arrive shortly with their Crime Scene Investigation Unit, no doubt. Both kids looked up as I approached.

"Hi, I am Officer Stella. Can you point to where the body is please?" The young man raised his arm, hand visibly shaking, and pointed toward the water. "Are you telling me the body is under the water?" They both nodded. The poor things were no doubt in shock. "Listen, I know this has to be a horrible shock and extremely upsetting, but I need you to tell me what happened."

The young man spoke, "We were tubing and fooling around, and I knocked my girlfriend off her tube. She landed on the dead man." The girl began sobbing, and I could see she was having trouble catching her breath.

"Hey, it is going to be okay, I promise. What is your name?"

She just stared at me, tears rolling down her face.

"Her name is Penelope, and I'm Dan. We are camping at the campground across the waterway."

"Okay, Penelope, it's going to be alright. I am so sorry this happened to you. Try to calm down. Take slow deep breaths, and exhale slowly as well. Do you have anyone you want to call?"

Dan shook his head. I told them to wait for me and headed toward the water edge, which was sandy and dotted with empty beer bottles. So much for a dry state park. The water wasn't deep, but the brackish color made it difficult to see to the bottom. I only had to take two steps in before I saw the deceased's face. Definitely male, and very dead. He appeared to be wedged between a stump and a pile of large rocks. Was he wedged there on purpose? I had seen my share of homicide victims in Philly, so a corpse didn't unhinge me, but the idea that someone had intentionally stuffed this guy in the water did worry me. I didn't want to disturb anything, so I slowly walked backwards until I reach the land. I brought the kids to the patrol car and told them to sit in the back and wait for me.

Over the bridge at the taped off entrance, G was instructing the flow of people wandering over from the campground to return to their campsites. This area was for law enforcement only. In the distance, I could hear sirens. State Police, hopefully. It would be impossible for just G and I to contain this scene. It wouldn't be long before curious campers would make their way from the campground, across the water, and into the state park, possibly contaminating the scene further. I was grateful to see three state police cruisers, an unmarked SUV, and an ambulance barreling toward us. G removed the tape to let them through and I motioned for them to continue straight toward the scene. G quickly replaced the tape and continued to direct the foot traffic we didn't want away from the park.

I jogged back over the bridge in my now wet and very heavy boots, sweat rolling down my back. A handsome, more seasoned, plain clothed man walked toward me, badge in plain sight, and introduced himself as Sergeant Brendan McIntyre. I explained to him what I knew at this point and that the young couple who found the body were in the back of my patrol car. He asked that I bring him to the body, which I did. He thanked me and confirmed what I already knew, that this investigation would be handled by the state police. We exchanged cards, and he promised to call me once an identification was confirmed. When I got to my patrol car, the kids were no longer in the backseat. Another Officer had put them in the state police SUV and was speaking with them. Good. Looking at that girl broke my heart. She may never be the same again. She certainly wouldn't be tubing any time soon. At the caution tape, G was shaking hands with yet another officer. I noticed the two additional cars parked nearby as well.

I yelled to G, "Let's roll. We're out!" He shot me a confused and disappointed look. Certainly, he could not think that we had jurisdiction over the state police in a possible homicide case. He got in the front seat looking like a child who got picked up by Mommy from a playdate before the ice cream was served. I bit my lip hard trying not to break into a smile.

"What the hell? Why did you give up on handling this so quickly? This should be our case."

Wow, he was really upset about this. "G, I don't make the rules. I don't like it, either, but we don't have the resources or technology to work a case like this. However, I did get the Sergeant's card, and I gave him mine. He promised to keep me in the loop. I at least want to know the victim's identity. Was he a Barrens native or a weekend warrior here to enjoy the activities?"

"Understood, sorry, I got a bit hyped up at the

thought of working a murder."

"Would an ice cream cone make you feel better?"

"Oh, you are hysterical, Stella!" He pinched my right cheek, but not hard. Just enough to give me butterflies in my tummy.

"So, what exactly did you do in the Navy, and how the hell did you end up here?"

"I couldn't afford college, so I joined the Navy for the training and conditioning, which, by the way, was brutal. Their training camp makes ordinary police academy training feel like high school gym class. I did really well, excelled actually. I was in a class of eighty cadets and one of only three accepted into the military police force. They even sent me to Europe, to the American Embassy to recruit and train officers. I traveled a lot for over ten years and then I just decided I needed to put roots down. Florida didn't feel like home to me."

"And Pine Barrens of New Jersey did?"

"When I was five years old, my mom and dad rented a van, and we drove from Florida to right here in Pine Barrens. I was a little kid, so I can't remember every single detail, but I do remember feeling happy with my family when we were here. After my mother passed, I never got another chance to feel that way again. Anyway, despite having a military law enforcement background, a lot of police departments won't hire you unless you have graduated from an actual police academy training program. Stupid, huh? Wading Pines PD barely read my application and called me immediately, so here I am."

"Well, their loss is our gain. Perhaps you and I will both call this place home for good at some point." He smiled and nodded in agreement.

Chapter Thirteen

Augustus

My father's voice. I thought I heard his voice. I sat up in my bed, still half asleep, held my breath, and listened. Maybe I was dreaming. It was still dark. The clock said 4:23 a.m. It must have been a dream. He wasn't due home until the afternoon. Just as I laid my head on the pillow and closed my weak eyes, I heard it again, louder. He was heading up the stairs, and he sounded terribly angry. My mother's voice, trailing behind him, sounded terrified, and she seemed to be pleading with him.

"Stefan, please! No." She kept repeating over and over.

Before I could move, the door burst open and slammed into the wall behind it. The doorknob went completely through the wall. My father stood in the doorway like a rabid beast hunting prey. His face red with anger, and his dark, evil eyes wide open and full of rage, more so than usual. I couldn't move. I was completed unable to move my legs. The shock, or maybe the fear. Whatever it was, I was incapable of trying to defend myself. My mother, sobbing uncontrollably and grabbing at his arm, was unable to alter his focus. When he finally spoke, it was a rolling thunder of decibels that pierced through my eardrums like a hammer.

"Augustus, get out of that bed and get dressed! You have five minutes to get downstairs, or I'm coming back up here with a belt!" He turned, pushed my mother aside with such force that she fell to the ground, but not before hitting her head on my bedpost. He stormed out of the room and, with concrete footsteps, made his way back downstairs. I jumped from my bed, despite the sharp pain in my back, and threw my arms around my mother. She was holding her head and bright red blood was seeping through her fingers. She had a nasty gash on the side of her head. I ran to the bathroom and got a wet towel.

"Augustus, get dressed quickly before he comes back and hurts you, too. I will be fine. I am just going to sit here for a minute and get the bleeding to stop. Hurry, Augustus!"

"Mom, why is he so furious with me? What happened? Why is he home when it's still dark out?"

"I don't know. He won't tell me. Promise me that if he

tries to hurt you, you will run. And don't stop until you find help." I kissed my mother on her forehead and promised as she requested. I got dressed in seconds and ran quickly down the stairs. He was standing at the front door.

"Get your shoes on now and come outside. Don't make me come back inside and get you." His nostrils flared, and the muscles in his neck flexed with every breath he took. It was obvious that it wouldn't take much for him to become physically violent. He was already in a full-blown tantrum. Outside, he was sitting in his truck. When I reached the bottom step, He yelled to get in. For just a moment, I contemplated running for cover into the woods and attempting to make my way to help. He read my mind. "Go ahead, Augustus, try to run and see what happens." I walked slowly to the passenger side, opened the door, and got in, careful to stay as close to the door as possible. He threw the truck in reverse and slammed his foot down on the gas. My head jerked back uncontrollably and just missed hitting the dashboard when he slammed on the brakes. I thought he was going to kill me and bury me, too.

I was careful not to look at him, but at the same time, I was on guard, keeping track of where his hands were at all times, but we did not go far. At the barn, he threw the truck violently into park, got out, and slammed the door so hard that the entire truck shook. I knew. I knew right then and there that he knew what I had done, but what was he planning on doing about it? I sat motionless in the front seat. As terrified as I was, I was as equally pissed off. *This fucking psychopath is mad at me? Mad that I know that he is a murdering, evil prick?* I hated him so much. He just stood at the front of the truck glaring at me, like he could feel my hatred and anger toward him.

"Get out of the truck!"

I knew I was faster than him so running was still an option, but I actually didn't want to run. I wanted to hurt him. Hurt him for everything he had done to Mom and me. I wanted to hurt him for what he had done to that girl under the blueberry bush and any others who had succumbed to his sickness. I got out of the truck slowly, never taking my eyes off him. I slammed the door shut, hard.

"You think you are a tough guy, Augustus? You think you can hurt me? I told you never come to the barn, never. I know you were here last night. I have cameras where stupid little boys like you can't see them. Did you like what you saw? Do you want to see more? Oh, maybe little Augustus wants to hunt with his daddy, huh?"

"I'm not like you, Stefan. You are a murderer, a sick disgusting piece of shit!"

He roared with laughter. "Stupid boy! You are weak and pathetic, just like your mother. Useless! You like digging up my blueberry bushes, do you? Did you like what you found Augustus? Did you play with the little girl?"

"You are sick! I despise you! You will go to prison for the rest of your pathetic life!"

"Well, son, it looks like we have ourselves a bit of a dilemma, don't we? You see, I am not going anywhere. You however must have run off. Perhaps you got involved in drugs and gangs or went for a walk and gotten lost in the woods. So sad, we searched everywhere for you, but you never did come back to us. You are nothing, Augustus! No one will care. No one even knows you exist, except for your frail and mentally unstable mother, and she won't tell. No, she knows I'll slice her throat, just like I'm going to slice yours." He laughed again and reached behind him. He grinned, a sinister smirk, as he twirled the long metal knife in my direction, like we were playing a game.

"Why, why did you kill that girl? What could she have possibly done to you to deserve what you did to her?"

"She was a whore, a useless prostitute, just like the rest of them. Nobodies from nowhere. That slut couldn't follow simple directions, so after I was done fucking her for several nights, I had to choke the life out of the dumb bitch. Hard to believe, but she may have actually been dumber than your mother."

"If you hate my mother so much, why did you marry her and bring her here? Why did you take her from her family?"

"Poor little deprived boy, the boy with no family or friends, just desperate for human interaction, huh? Well, my boy, the story goes like this. I met your mother, and I liked how easily controlled she could be, her weakness and dependency on me were very satisfying. However, sexually, she was like bedding a corpse."

I could feel my anger build and the adrenaline surge through my body. "Fuck you! You are a pig. You say one more word about her, and I will kill you!" I meant it, too. At that moment, I could have easily killed him.

"Oh, Augustus, how noble of you. Anyway, as I was saying, I had to fill the desire that she could not, so I found a woman who just wanted to fuck me whenever I said so, a whore really, but a damn good one. Well, one night I got a bit overzealous, and oops, she died. I buried her, but not good enough. Stray dogs dug her up, and it was a major news story. A big investigation was launched. A couple of her whore friends knew that she spent a lot of time with me, so before the police could come knocking on my door, we left. I forbid your mother to have any contact with anyone in our home country. Of course, she disobeyed me, but she won't make that mistake again. Once I kill you, maybe I kill her, too. The site of her sickens me anyway."

"How many women have you killed? How many lives have you taken, and how many are buried here?"

He laughed and put his finger to his chin as if he were deep in thought, like this was a joke to him. "Hmm, I must say that after all of these years, I have honestly lost count. Let us just say, quite a few, and yes, they are all buried here. Why do you think we have such robust blueberry crops each year? Obviously, it is the added nutrients, Augustus. You should be proud that your father is brilliant enough to never get caught."

"Proud? I should be proud that my father is a serial killer? A man capable of such horrendous violence and evil? I am ashamed to be your son, Stefan. Ashamed that you are the monster that you are. I despise you. You are a liar! It is impossible for you to have killed as many women as you say without drawing attention to yourself, to us."

"Ah, see that's where you are wrong. It's all in the planning, careful planning. I hunt only whores, whores without families, whores that no one will miss, and I hunt only in the armpits of society. I am particularly fond of Atlantic City; they are always so desperate for drug money. Philly whores are a bit larger and mouthy, but so worth the trouble. I must say that Jersey Shore whores are certainly my all-time favorite, though. They tend to be prettier, smaller, and more physically manageable."

Stefan caught me off guard as he lunged at me like a wild animal, knife held over his head, eyes as dark as night and as big as coasters, grinning like a loon. It was too late to run. I held my arms over my head to protect myself and dropped to my knees, hoping once he struck and I deflected that I could make a run for it, but the blow never came. Instead, a loud crashing, cracking metal sound infiltrated my eardrums as if I were too close to a fireworks display. I looked up from my crouched position just in time to see my father drop to his knees, blood pouring from his head and ears, no longer grinning, falling face forward onto me. In a panic, I squirmed from underneath him, pushed his lifeless body aside, and jumped to my feet. There, with bloody shovel in hand, stood my mother with an expression on her face that was different. She wasn't crying, she wasn't scared or nervous. She was satisfied, proud. Yes, she looked at me with pride. My mother had just saved my life. I threw my arms around her and began to cry. She hugged me tight and then let go.

"Okay, Augustus, we have more work to do. Grab another shovel. I heard everything that your father said to you, and I believe it all to be true. We will bury him as he buried those poor women, in his precious blueberry field. After, we must decide what we will do and what we will tell Hector. Let's hurry and bury this bastard before the sun comes up." That was the very first and last time that I ever heard my mother curse, which despite the magnitude of our current situation, brought a smile to my face.

Chapter Fourteen

Stella

"Okay, that explains the past, but what about now?"

"What do you mean?"

"I mean, where are you living now? You're not in Chatsworth, right?"

"No, but I'm not far. For now, I am renting a place. It is a small house on a farm about thirty minutes from here."

"Do you like your landlord? Is he nice, nosey, an ass, or a sweet old man like mine?"

"You lucked out with Mr. Avery, Stel, for sure. Nope I have no idea who my landlord is or what he or she looks like." I must have had a pretty serious look of confusion on my face because he laughed and said, "I saw an ad online for rental properties in the Pine Barrens area from a rental agency, so they gave me the combination to a lockbox where the key is kept, and I went and checked it out. Looked good enough, so I emailed them and told them I would take it for at least six months. I told them I was a police officer in the area, so they didn't even do a background check. Rent is pretty cheap, too. I use the Venmo app to send the agency my rent each month, and the rest, as they say, is history."

"Interesting, Officer G. So, why did you tell the rental agency that you would only be there for six months? You leaving us so soon?"

"No way, you're not getting rid of me that easy. I think I'll be sticking around if that's ok with you."

Oh Jesus, that damn flirtatious wink and smile again. Oh, he so knows how to work it. I'll play along.

"Officer G, I just wouldn't know what to do without you by my side!"

We both laughed and he gently rubbed my shoulder, just long enough to make me wish he wouldn't stop. "So, I didn't want to get stuck in a long-term rental, especially not there. It's smaller than your place, and it's super creepy, especially at night. It's weird, ominous really. It's like six shades darker than black once the sun sets."

"How the hell is that possible?"

"I think it's because the property is surrounded by enormous pine trees. Unless the sky is clear with the moon and stars visible, it is complete darkness at night."

"You do have a gun, remember?"

"I know, and I am sure that once I meet my neighbors, it won't seem so desolate. Anyway, I am hoping to buy a house with a little bit of property at some point. Something I can call my own. Sound corny?"

"Not at all. I think that it is very 'American dream' of you. In reality, doesn't everyone want just that? I know I do. Although, I would miss Mr. Avery for sure."

I spent the rest of shift just driving G around, showing him some more of the nooks and crannies of our patrol area. Certainly, it would take many more shifts before he was comfortably familiar with our area of responsibility. The radio was quiet, except for a quick check-in from Margie. This time she was her usual sassy self, which was a relief.

My cell vibrated, and I picked it up quickly. G watched as I read a text from Brie.

"Everything okay, Stel?"

"Yeah, it's Brie reminding me that she will be at my house by six tomorrow."

"You look pissed?"

"I am fucking pissed! She is my best friend, and I am not there anymore when she needs me. She was my roommate in Philly, too. My roommate and my best friend. We were always there for each other. She's going through a terrible time right now, and I'm not there for her."

"Anything I can do to help?"

"Do you have an unregistered weapon and good aim?" Poor G, he looked so confused, so right or wrong, I elaborated. "She is being sexually harassed and bullied at work by her boss, and she has nowhere to turn. It's a close-knit industry, and by coming forward, she'd risk putting an end to her career. She's trying to wait it out until her boss retires, but he is relentless, and the less Brie reacts, the more frequent his unwanted, vile comments and behavior become."

"I am not an employment practices expert, but I do not get how she has nowhere to turn. A place like that must have an HR department or an attorney she can turn to, right?"

"Ah, but this is where it gets messy because *he* hired the HR staff and attorney, and he made nice with the board members as well. He is not dumb, just pathetic."

"So, I guess unregistered weapon would work best, huh?"

"I think you will like Brie. Everyone likes Brie. She is genuine and caring. Who knows, she may even open up to you about this. Just please do not let on that I already discussed this with you, okay?"

"You have my word."

I pulled our patrol car back into the station house. "Okay, first shift is in the books."

"Tomorrow I drive, right, Officer Stella?"

"Oh, buddy, you've got a few more sightseeing shifts

before I can grant you that honor."

He made the most adorable little sad face and laughed. "Understood, I'm going to run in and clock out, then hit the gym on my way home. I am looking forward to hanging out with you ladies, and I'm thankful we aren't on duty the following day."

"I shall see you tomorrow morning then!"

"Oh, Stella, thank you for making my first day so interesting and cool."

I nodded and off he went. I sat in the car for a few minutes longer texting Brie. I was so excited to see her tomorrow. I just hoped I could comfort her and at least make her forget work for a while. I was deep in thought on my way home when the ring of my cell phone startled me. I didn't recognize the number, but I picked up anyway.

"Stella, this is McIntyre from the state police, how are you?"

"Oh great, great, thank you."

"Well, I promised that I would keep you in the loop, so I wanted to let you know that we got an ID on the victim."

"Definitely a victim, huh?"

"Oh yes, once we got him out of the water, cause of death was obvious. Back of his head was crushed with something very heavy and by someone with great strength. Coroner says he's probably been in the water for a few days, maybe longer, but she can't determine exact time of death until she gets him back to the morgue. Anyway, NJ license says his name is Kurt Jacobs, thirty-one years old, and he's got an address in Hammonton. I got a unit heading over there now. Records show he is not married but has a couple of domestic disturbance charges recently against him from the same woman, Sandy Brown, twenty-seven, also of Hammonton, but different address. I am headed there now to talk to Ms. Brown. Would you like to join me? Address is 26A Maple Leaf Court. It about twenty minutes from your station house."

I was so caught off guard that he asked me to join him that I missed my turn off. "Sure, absolutely. I will be there in twenty."

I arrived at the address McIntyre gave me sooner than I had estimated. He had not yet arrived, so I stayed put. The area appeared to be home to an ethnically diverse, financially struggling community. A quick Google search, and that suspicion was confirmed. Hammonton was about forty square miles big and home to about 30,000 residents. Maple Leaf Street consisted of mostly row homes, like apartments, old apartments. Front yards were no more than dirt and weeds. Air conditioning units buzzed and clunked from the windows of the old homes as they struggled to ward off the never-ending humidity. Across the street from Ms. Brown's apartment, a crowd of about six children played in an empty dirt lot where, I assumed, a home must have stood at some point in time. They took turns kicking a red ball that was almost completely devoid of air against an old wooden fence that had been spray painted with just about every curse word I had ever heard, and even some I didn't recognize. Although the kids looked to be having fun, I could not help but feel sad. Sad that this was their childhood, their environment, and unfortunately, most likely their future as well. So hard to break a cycle like this without politicians stepping up and lobbying for a better community life. I certainly did not grow up in a wealthy family, but being here and watching these children today, reaffirmed how blessed I was.

I heard a car door shut behind me, and the children turned in my direction and then all ran off in the opposite direction. I looked in my mirror to see that McIntyre had pulled up behind me. Heartbreaking that the young children had obviously been cautioned by adults to run from law enforcement. I opened my door and greeted McIntyre.

"I guess the welcoming committee was not welcoming me, huh?" He motioned his hand in the direction the children had run.

"It's really a sad situation, McIntyre. This community could certainly use some help."

"I agree, but that's not our mission today. You ready

to speak with Ms. Brown?"

Apartment 26A was the bottom apartment of a two-story home. The fact that this house was legally occupiable was questionable. It was a very faded, pale yellowish color and almost completely engulfed in green vines of ivy that had obviously been left unattended for many years. The ivy stretched all the way to the roof, which was missing a good portion of its shingles. The sidewalk in front of the apartment was buckled and broken and nearly impossible to walk safely on. The porch steps had rotted away, and in their place, cinder blocks had been staged to gain access to the front porch. On the porch, a rusted aluminum chair and an old Folgers coffee can were the only décor to be seen. The can was filled with cigarette butts, and the smell of nicotine in this heat made me lightheaded. A small cardboard box had been nailed next to the front door, and in black marker it read "Brown, S. 26A," which I assumed was a mailbox. This was the right place. There was no doorbell, so I gave a hard knock to the flimsy screen door and then cautiously took a few steps back. McIntyre stood to the left of me. He was sweating pretty heavily from his temples. I counted to thirty and was just about to knock a bit harder when the door opened slightly, but not enough to see a face.

"What the hell do you want?"

"Are you Sandy Brown?"

"Who's asking?"

McIntyre stepped closer. "Listen, ma'am, we aren't here to play games. I am Sergeant McIntyre, New Jersey State Police, and this is Officer Stella. Please step out of the house." His voice was stern but not threatening. The door opened very slowly, and a thin, haggard looking woman stepped onto the porch.

"Yeah, yeah, I'm Sandy."

I could not believe what I was seeing. How the hell could this woman be just twenty-seven years of age? Her oval shaped face was tan, and her skin weathered as if she had spent her whole life working in a field, under a brutal sun. She had prominent wrinkles around her mouth, courtesy of heavy smoking for a prolonged period of time. She had thin, long, mousy brown hair that already revealed gray strands throughout. Her eyes were brown and sad. She was so very thin, too thin, malnourished even. The white tank top she wore hanging off her shoulders was stained and much too big for her frame. She wore what looked like men's boxer shorts which she had tied at her hip so not to lose them. Her feet were bare. Life has obviously not been kind to this woman.

McIntyre spoke again. "Ms. Brown, we would like to ask you a few questions about a friend of yours, Kurt Jacobs."

"Ha, get it right, man. He ain't no friend of mine. He's a scumbag that likes to beat on me when he's drinking."

Sandy plopped herself down in the aluminum chair, pulled out a cigarette that she had tucked behind her ear, and lit it with a lighter she had stashed in her shorts.

"Ms. Brown, were you and Mr. Jacobs in a romantic relationship? Did he live here with you?"

She looked me up and down and grinned, revealing her badly stained teeth. "You are too damn hot to be a cop, honey. You like girls? I'll start battin' for the other team, baby doll, you in?" She winked at me and licked her lips, and it made me nauseous and pissed me off all at the same time.

"Please answer the questions, Ms. Brown."

"No! He ain't never lived here, and I ain't in no relationship with him no more. Not since a week or so ago when that motherfucker grabbed my hair and smashed my face onto the bar just 'cause I was looking at a hot piece of ass that had walked in. We ain't fucking married! I can look at whoever I wanna look at. Anyway, I ain't seen or heard from his sorry ass since. Listen up, you two officers. I mind my own business. I work, and I pay taxes, and I don't break the law, so what has that useless piece of shit done now? Why are you here on my porch, on my only day off in three weeks?" She blew a large cloud of smoke in our direction and flicked the butt below into the coffee can.

McIntyre shook his head in disgust. "Ms. Brown, I need the name of the bar where this incident happened, and I need to know exactly what night this occurred."

Sandy dropped her head into her hands and pulled her feet up under her like a child sitting in a time out chair. "Well, now, let me think. It was karaoke night at the Wander Inn Bar over on Fairmont Avenue, so it must have been a Wednesday, but not this past Wednesday 'cause I was working a double at the diner. It was the Wednesday before that for sure."

"What happened after Mr. Jacobs assaulted you?"

"Bunch of the regulars at the bar threw his stupid ass outside and beat the hell outta him. I watched from inside, laughing like my ass off, even though my head hurt from the knot the asshole gave me. He laid in the parking lot moaning for a long while till he crawled off like the rat he is and got in his crappy car and left. I ain't seen him since. Oh, and the good thing about it all was that nice piece of ass I told you about bought me a drink after and listened to me bitch about Kurt and all the shit he'd done to me."

"Did the nice piece of ass have a name?"

"Ya know, baby doll, I never did ask. I went to use the restroom at one point, and when I got back, he was gone, but he left enough money for me to have three more beers. He was a class act. I wish I knew where he was. Boy, I could do some damage to him, but he wasn't from around here anyway. No way. He was too classy like."

McIntyre pulled out a business card from his shirt

pocket and handed it to Sandy. "Call me if you think of anything else."

I followed McIntyre off the porch and onto the sidewalk. "Have a lovely day, Ms. Brown, and thank you for your time."

"Oh, you come back anytime, baby doll, without Officer Stuffy Pants. Wait, wait, you never said what Kurt done!"

McIntyre yelled over his shoulder, "He's dead." Oddly enough, Sandy Brown had no smartass comeback to that. She looked like she had just watched a train wreck in slow motion. She never uttered another word as I got into my patrol car. "Let's get out of here, Stella. I'll call you tomorrow."

"Thanks, McIntyre, and thank you sincerely for including me. I know you don't have to, and I very much appreciate it."

He nodded, and I watched as he got into his car. I rolled out first and involuntarily let out an obnoxious snort when I caught once last glimpse of Sandy Brown still in the same position with that dumb look on her face. Priceless, this experience was truly priceless.

I was anxious to get back home and shower. My deodorant had minimal effect at this point in the day, and it made me feel disgusting and tired. The humidity in Pine Barrens was ridiculous, maybe because all of the trees and vast forests hovering over the steaming hot ground. Whatever the case, I needed a shower.

Chapter Fifteen

Augustus

We did it together, my mother and I, under the dim light of the fading summer moon without a minute to spare before the sun would rise. We buried my serial killer father, face first, dead smack in the middle of his blueberry field deep under a large bush and then carefully replaced the soil. I took the shovel from my mother and told her to go back to the house and take a shower. I told her I would put the shovels back and clean up before I came home. I hugged her tight and kissed her on the forehead.

"Thank you for saving my life, Mom. I love you, and I am so proud of you." She looked up at me and smiled, then turned toward the house. I watched her walk home for a few minutes. I really was proud of her. Even after so many years of living in fear of that man, her love for me brought her the courage to end his reign of terror and protect me from him when my life depended on it.

I returned to the spot where my father took his final breath. A large area of bright red blood stained the cement floor where he had fallen headfirst. I hung the shovels up and looked for something to clean up the mess. Under a makeshift sink in the back of the barn, I found bleach, scrub brushes, and old torn rags. For a moment, I thought how incredibly lucky I was to find everything I needed in one spot out in this barn and then I realized that the bastard kept these supplies handy for the same reason I needed them. To clean up bloody messes after a kill. On my hand and knees, I scrubbed as hard as I could. My knuckles were white from the pressure applied to get the job done, and the smell was nauseating and made me dizzy.

I had no remorse. I wasn't sad. I wasn't worried. I was free. The chains of terror and fear were broken, never to restrict us from a normal life again, but we had a lot of decisions to make. Funny, I wasn't the least bit concerned about getting caught or attracting law enforcement types. No one ever came here. Never. The harvested blueberries were taken by my father to a large distribution and processing plant not too far from here, or at least I didn't think it was far. The company sent my father a check for his blueberries. My father fixed all of his own machines with the help of Hector. We could handle this.

Me and Mom could handle this.

I finished scrubbing and wiping up the blood until I was satisfied that it could not be seen by the naked eye. I put the rags and the scrub brush in an old metal bucket that had nails and garbage in it and carried it back to the house with me. As I reached my front porch, I turned to see that the sun was just about up, and it was incredibly beautiful. I felt grateful and peaceful. I sat down on the top step, bowed my head, clasped my hands together, and spoke to God.

"God, it's me again, Augustus. I know that what we have done is a sin, the taking of another life, but please forgive my mother. She killed him to save me, and she had no choice. She saved us Lord and probably many others that he would have killed. Please keep us safe and away from any further harm or evil. Please watch over us, God, and help us make the right decisions. I could really use your help right now. I pray also that my father has gone straight to hell. A murderer and sadistic, soulless man that I pray will be punished. Please forgive us, Lord, Amen."

I walked through the front door, exhausted and filthy, but the smell of my mother cooking breakfast drew me to the kitchen. She had showered and had a sun dress on that I had never seen, and she was humming along with the radio she played all day, every day, for as long as I could remember. "Oh, Augustus, I didn't hear you come in. Is everything in order at the barn?"

"All clean, all good, but we will need to burn the stuff in the bucket on the front porch."

"Okay, good! Run up and shower. Breakfast won't be ready for a while, but you will love it, another of my mother's recipes."

The house had a different feel to it, not so dark and sad. On my way to my bedroom, I realized what was different to me. Mom had pulled the curtains apart and lifted all of the blinds in her room. The sun shone brightly through the old glass-pane windows. I was pleased to see she had done the same in my room and in the bathroom. Such a simple pleasure that people took advantage of every day without a second thought was a priceless new gift for us. I took a quick shower, grabbed my blood-stained clothes, and headed back downstairs. Oh, the sweet aroma of breakfast was hypnotizing. I opened the front door, threw my clothes in the bucket, and returned to the kitchen. Mom had piled a plate high with the heavenly treat she created, and I dove in quickly.

"Augustus, you are going to choke if you don't slow down. There is plenty more."

"What is this, Mom? It's incredible."

"It is called Brotchen, a German sweet roll with raspberry marmalade, and a hearty German style omelet with mustard sauce, and of course, potatoes. Eat slowly, and enjoy every bite, Augustus. When your belly is full, we have a lot of decisions to make, you and me. Come sit with me on the porch when you finish, but slow, Augustus, slow!"

I think I enjoyed that meal more than any other in my life, but not just because it was delicious, but because I wasn't all twisted up inside waiting for him to walk into the room and bark orders or sling insults at us. Yes, eating without being under duress was something we had never experienced, and it was utterly fabulous.

Mom was sitting in her usual chair on the porch, head back, eyes closed, and a smile on her face so sweet that I could not help but smile, too. I touched her shoulder lightly so not to frighten her. After all, years and years with him had taken its toll and made her jumpy, on edge, but she just ever so calmly opened her eyes and told me to sit next to her. I did as she requested.

"Augustus, I am going to tell you what I think we should do now, but only if you agree." I nodded, and she held my hand firmly. "I think we should tell Hector that your father passed away early this morning after they returned from their trip from a massive heart attack. I will explain to him that the ambulance came, without sirens, at my request, but that they were too late to save him. They pronounced him dead and transported his body to the morgue at the hospital. I will tell him that he will be cremated. We have no family or friends, so there will be no announcement in the local newspaper, nor will there be a service. I found your father's phone in the truck, and in a few hours, I will call my parents in Germany and tell them the same story. Augustus, I want to go back home with you. Home, to Germany. I want you to know the loving family that your father robbed you of all these years. I want you to know love and happiness, and of course, eat all of the traditional food you want. I want you to go to school and decide what you want to do when you are finished with your schooling. Augustus, we can start over. We can be happy. We are free, but I want to know what you think. Does that sound like something you would like?"

Tears dropped uncontrollably from my eyes, and my mother pulled me close and hugged me tight. We sat just like that for quite a while until I could speak. I told her that the plan sounded wonderful to me. "Let's leave here and never come back," I said. "Let Hector have the farm. He and his family can live in our house and continue to harvest the blueberries and handle all the chores. He can have the truck, too. Tell him that he is to pay the bills with the money from harvest time and the rest is his to care for his family and the upkeep of the house."

I stopped myself from telling my mother that I needed to go back into the barn to the secret room where Stefan kept his other prisoners, to disassemble the cage and clean the blood. We could have nothing left behind that could cast suspicion on us.

"Mother, do we have money to travel?"

"We have plenty of money. Your father did not trust banks, so all of his money is here in the house. We don't have to take much, just some clothes, some books, and what few pictures we have. Everything else can just stay right here. We don't need it because we are starting a new life."

"Well, this is a perfect plan. When will you tell, Hector?"

"I will go see him later today."

I nodded and headed back to the barn to make sure we didn't leave anything that would draw suspicion behind.

Chapter Sixteen

McIntyre

Stella was right. This community and the Sandy Browns who lived here deserved better than this. I had always hated responding to calls out here. It was disheartening to see hard working people with limited educations due to their financial and socioeconomic situations stuck in a hamster wheel of poverty and oppression in this, the richest country of all. My mother always said, "There but by the grace of God go I. Never forget that, Brendan." Growing up Catholic, it took me more years than I'd like to admit to actually understand what she meant. Seemed sort of hypocritical to me given the whole Catholic Church, upper class snobs vibe I always felt on Sundays. Some of the best people I had ever met didn't have a dime to their name but would give you the shirt off their back if you needed it, and on the flip side, some of the most selfish and judgmental people I'd ever met went to church every Sunday but would still step over you if you lay dying on a sidewalk. Needless to say, I did not go to church on Sundays, but I did talk to God every day. I knew that He had my back. Twenty-four years and six months on this job, and I was still breathing, with just six months to go until retirement. I was in the homestretch now, so a homicide that brought me out from behind my desk and into detective mode again was the last thing I wanted.

The Wander Inn Bar, that was what the sign above the door read. Typical neighborhood dive bar. I personally handled my fair share of calls here back in my patrol days. Looking at the parking lot, it was obvious that this was the neighborhood happy hour hot spot. I took a deep breath and stepped inside, which triggered a blanket of complete silence and confused stares.

"Hey, McIntyre, is that you? Man, you got old! What the hell are you doing still working, my friend?"

"Jimmy, is that you? Man, you got even older. What the hell are you still doing pouring watered down drinks in this dive?"

The crowd seemed satisfied that there would be no excitement and returned to playing pool and darts, talking, and consuming booze. Jimmy did look a lot older, but hell, I knew I did, too. At least he didn't mention the extra twenty-five pounds I put on sitting behind a desk. Jimmy was one of those guys who was just another generation from this community, but Jimmy was smart. He went to community college after high school, got his degree, worked his ass off, saved his money, and bought this bar. I always respected him for that. He didn't use his situation as a reason to fall into a bad way.

"McIntyre, seriously, how long has it been? Oh, and hey, you know I look better than you. Don't you know black folks age at half the rate you white folks do?"

"You got me there, Jimmy. That is absolutely true. How the hell are you? How is business?"

Jimmy shook his head. "Look around, even a recession can't stop these fools from bellying up and spending all of their unemployment and disability money, but that isn't why you are here, is it?"

I motioned for him to follow me to the end of the bar that was currently empty. "Listen, Jimmy, I have some questions. You know a guy named Kurt Jacobs and his friend Sandy Brown?"

Jimmy chuckled and once again shook his head. "I know both of those bottom dwellers. Kurt is in here every day, except I haven't seen him in at least a week. Thought maybe he got arrested. Sandy, she's a sad story. Just another impoverished, forgotten generation living the dream right here in hell. She works hard over at the diner, though, long shifts, but she still barely makes ends meet. That girl is in her twenties, man, but she looks older than you and me. Nice girl, but just a mess. Took care of her mother up until a few months ago when she passed from lung cancer. Now I hear Sandy lives alone in the house over on Maple Leaf."

"Yes, she does. I spoke to her earlier today. She said her and Kurt were in here a week and a half ago for karaoke night, and they had a fight."

"Not much of one. Drunk asshole put her face first into my bar. One minute they were drinking and laughing, then the next, he smashed her head down. She had a knot the size of my fist on her forehead. Luckily, her state of intoxication kept her from feeling the full reality of that blow, but I'm sure she hurt like hell the next morning."

"What happened next? Did anyone call 911?"

"Didn't get a chance. Everybody in the place saw it happen. It was crowded that night. Only thing these drunks like more than alcohol is alcohol and a little karaoke. Bunch of regulars pulled him off his stool, started whaling on him, and then threw him out the door. After a while, a few minutes, I went to check on him, but he was gone. I haven't seen him since. Thought maybe she turned him in. What's going on, McIntyre?"

"He's dead. Found his body in the water at the state park over in Chatsworth."

"Oh man, you serious? Did he drown?"

"That's what we are trying to determine now. You

think any of these losers would want him dead for what he did to Sandy?"

"No way, they were always fighting. There are squabbles in here all the time. These morons throw punches and then they are buying each other beers, talking about how much they love each other. Listen, I feel for Sandy, but truth be told, nobody is going to put themselves out for her."

"I appreciate your time, thank you. It was good to see you, old timer." Jimmy howled at that. "Oh wait, one more question. Sandy said there was a guy in here that night that bought her drinks after Kurt got thrown out. You remember him?"

"Yeah, yeah, I do. Strange, though, I had never seen him before. He just sort of showed up that night and was sitting at a table all by himself back there by the pool table drinking a beer and looking at his laptop. Hasn't been back in here since, but he must have been just passing through. Definitely not a local guy."

"Any chance you caught any of his conversation with Sandy? He sat at the bar with her, right?"

"Yup, she did most of the talking. She complained about Kurt for a long time, complained about her job, her life, you know, just complained. You know, I did hear him ask Sandy if Kurt was local and where he worked, but it was super busy that night, so that's really all I heard."

"You catch this guy's name?"

"Nope, never asked, and he never offered."

"What did he look like?"

"Like he didn't come from here. He had brown hair, average height, I guess, had all his teeth, too. Like I said, not from here."

We shook hands, and I left. I wondered if Sandy gave this guy Kurt's address. Waste of time asking Sandy. Between the booze and the blow to the head, anything she said now would be questionable. Time to head home. Hopefully, Jill made something good for dinner and not one of her healthy vegan dishes.

Chapter Seventeen

Stella

Six in the morning, and I was wide awake. Wide awake an hour before the alarm was set to go off. I guess that was what happened when you went to bed at 9:00 p.m. like a senior citizen. I should probably do that more often, actually. I sat on the edge of my bed feeling really good, rested, and energized. I must have slept like a rock. I didn't even get up to pee thirty times during the night. I grabbed my cell phone, which I faithfully kept by my bed out of habit. I missed a text message from my mom saying she was just checking on me. I laughed. It had to have taken her over ten minutes to type that since she refuses to get a new phone and those "jitterbugs" don't have full keyboard capabilities. I replied to let her know I was fine and that I was on duty later today, but that Brie was staying with me for the weekend. If I didn't reply, she would call nonstop until I answered. If I didn't respond, I had no doubt she would then call Mr. Avery, followed by the precinct. I learned the embarrassing way that it was best to reply to my mother quickly.

I was feeling really excited about tonight. I knew Brie was in a major funk, courtesy of the pervert, but once we talked it out, she would feel better. She always did, but it was just another temporary fix. Afterwards, we would grab some food and a few drinks at the bar, and I would introduce Brie to G and the gang. We could all use a night out. My stomach was growling loud, likely because I never ate dinner last night. I threw on a t-shirt and jeans, slipped my beat- up flip flops on, grabbed my phone, and headed over to Mr. Avery's shop. The humidity slapped me in the face like a heavy wet blanket. Even this early in the morning, the humidity was almost intolerable. I should have put shorts on. Oh, well, I was not turning back now. As always, Mr. Avery's face lit up when he saw me, and he gave me that adorable Norman Rockwell smile that made him so endearing.

"Stella, I am so glad to see you, dear. How is work going? Are you hungry?"

"Good, and yes, I am starving. I am craving your scrambled eggs and home fries this morning."

"You got it. Sit down and relax, and I will bring you coffee."

He did not have to tell me twice. I plopped down at

the corner table against the back wall. It was pretty busy in here this morning. The usual table of old timers were deep in gossip and did not notice me come in, which made me happy because I certainly wasn't in the mood to get into heavy conversation about the damn cranberry festival committee right now. I already promised I would be here Wednesday evening to join in. Hopefully, I could get out of here unnoticed as well.

Afterwards, I walked back to my place feeling twenty pounds heavier. I ate every single crumb on my plate and threw back two cups of Mr. Avery's fabulous, like no other, coffee. I really should put shorts on and go for a walk. Nah, too damn hot. I decided to tidy up my place for Brie's visit. I cleaned the bathroom and vacuumed and put the dishes that had been on the counter away. I didn't have much food in the fridge, but I had frozen pizza, popcorn, and plenty of wine. Brie and I didn't need more than that. Thankfully, my cleaning frenzy was cut short when my cell rang. It was McIntyre.

"Stella, hey, it's McIntyre. I had an interesting conversation with the bar owner at the Wander Inn after we spoke to Sandy. He confirmed pretty much what Sandy told us. He also confirmed that Sandy was talking to a guy he had not seen before, who was not a local. Apparently, after Kurt slammed her face on the bar, she unloaded all of her baggage on this guy, and the bartender recalled hearing the guy ask where Kurt lives and works, too."

"Really? Well, that is remarkably interesting. Sounds like it could be more than just a coincidence to me, but then again, why would this guy kill Kurt over a woman he didn't know, over Sandy?"

"I don't know yet, and the bar has no security system, and it is a cash only joint, so we are still in the dark as to his identity. I sent a unit to Kurt's address, but the place was locked up tight, and the officers reported no suspicious activity and nothing that looked like a break in had occurred. I'm going back over there now, and I'm letting myself in. This is now an official homicide investigation. There could be evidence in the house that may lead us to whoever did this."

I tried to mask my enthusiasm, but I was super stoked. "Okay, I'll jump in the shower quick and meet you."

Radio silence.

"McIntyre, are you there?"

"Yeah, I am here. Listen, Stella, I'm on the fence about working with you any further on this. You know we've got jurisdiction, and technically, that means we stop sharing info with the LEOs."

I tried not to sound like a high school girl who just got dumped by her boyfriend a week before prom, but I knew he could hear the disappointment in my voice when I told him I understood.

"Listen, I really like you, kid. You have more potential

and common sense than some of the guys I have been on the job with for twenty years. Problem is that there are plenty of newbies in the state police that I should be mentoring. However, problem with that is I am six months from retirement and do not want to be a babysitter. So having said that let me ask you this. How would you feel about working with me on this case but off the record? Meaning my people are not advised of our partnership and neither are yours, and that includes your partner. You would only be able to work with me when you are off duty. Honestly, I could use your help on this. Are these conditions you can live with?"

Without hesitation I responded. "I am in, McIntyre, yes."

"Good, I'll see you in an hour. The address is 179 Farm Road, use Wharton for GPS, and remember this is just between us."

"You have my word, and hey, thank you!"

This time McIntyre beat me to our destination. He was on his phone, and from his mild tone, I suspected that it was his wife he was talking to. Even though I just met him, I could tell he was an honorable guy, probably married forever and actually still in love, maybe even with a couple kids. Even though I didn't know all the facts, the life I imagined as McIntyre's in my head made me jealous. I gave him his space, and within minutes, he ended his call with an 'I love you, too.'

"Checking in with the wife already, McIntyre," I said in a smart-ass tone.

"Very perceptive of you. Yes, that was my wife. Jill. I get about ten of those calls a day, each with a new chore she has added to my honey-do list when I retire. I figure I'll spend the first year of my retirement completing her list, and not on the golf course or beach, but that's okay with me. She hung in there with me all of these years. That woman has earned her wings."

"You got any kids?"

"Yes, a boy. Ian just graduated college, and I just paid it off."

"Sounds like you had a pretty amazing life plan that you stuck to so far. I am really happy for you."

"What about you, any significant other, kids?"

"Ha, me not a chance. I am single now after a horrific, embarrassing breakup back in Philly. This is a fresh start for me, and I am concentrating on me and my career for now. Besides, story book romances like yours are one of a kind, rare."

"Hey, listen, I didn't say it was perfect. There were plenty of times I would have left me if I were her, especially back in my heavy drinking days, but Jill rode out every storm with me. I don't deserve her, but we've been married for thirty years now, and I haven't driven her away yet."

"Don't get ahead of yourself. She may decide having

you at home every day is the last straw, if you know what I mean." I smiled.

"Yeah, she thought about that already and decided that she would continue working her teaching job for another year or so."

"Smart lady."

"Agreed."

"So, what's the plan here? I see the mailbox, but where is the house?"

"From what my people have told me, the house sits way back from the main road here, on a significant number of acres, and there are several other barn type structures decaying as well throughout the property. Apparently, Kurt and his brother Roy inherited all of this when their father died about three years ago. Looks like their father only owned the place for about ten years or so. I didn't go back any further, don't think it matters at this point. Records indicate the brothers are the legal owners, taxes are paid up to date. Oh, but Roy is currently on the tail end of his five-year prison sentence for aggravated assault, something to do with a disagreement at work that turned ugly quick. Roy beat the guy unconscious, but he lived. I am assuming if we follow this dirt road we will eventually end up at the house. Leave your car here and jump in mine."

McIntyre and I followed the road very slowly for quite some time, mostly because the road was a mix of potholes, overgrown brush, garbage, and large jagged stones.

"What was this place, what did they farm here?"

He pointed toward a large field that looked to go on for miles. "Those look like blueberry bushes in an overgrown field of weeds to me." He drove closer to the edge of the field, careful not to get stuck. "Yup, looks like blueberries are still growing on most of them. Hard to kill a blueberry bush once it takes a solid root."

"You think the brothers were harvesting blueberries?"

"Not a chance, these fields haven't been tended to in years. That old barn over there is barely standing. Looks like most of the roof fell in. Can't harvest without the proper equipment. These morons could have sold this property and made a small fortune. Big money in blueberries and cranberries out this way."

"Look, there's the house." We were on the right dirt road. In the distance, well beyond the field and the barn, stood a large structure. Really couldn't make out much more than that from a distance, though. The sun was blinding to say the least. Finally, McIntyre was close enough to the house to ward off the effects of the bright sun. "Wow, this is a lot better than I expected."

"Me too, I thought for sure it would look just like the barn. It's actually in decent shape for an old farmhouse. Needs some paint, and a new roof, but aside from that, it's got a lot of potential. Again, the morons could have gotten enough money for this place to last them a lifetime, especially since they probably wouldn't live to see forty-five. Well, I guess thirty-two for Kurt, but that's my point."

The front porch was wide and completely covered, even had those outdoor ceiling fans. The flooring was rough from lack of care, but the porch wrapped almost completely around the house. It was old but solid. The curtains reminded me of an Italian restaurant, very lacey and ornate. Peering through the front door I could see now that they had begun to yellow. Probably hadn't been changed or cleaned in decades.

McIntyre pulled out his pocket-knife and made quick work of the old lock. "Let's go in and see what we find."

The smell of must, mold, and moth balls hit me like a tidal wave. "Oh God, that smell is horrendous. How the hell could Jacobs stand that?"

The interior was a far cry from the exterior of the house. To the right was a living room of some sort, but most of the furniture was covered in plastic, which despite the attempt, failed to prevent the sofa from decaying. The walls in this room were white, or were white at some point, now they were just stained and dirty. The carpet had holes throughout and was badly stained and water damaged as well. There must have been a roof leak or pipe burst that was never addressed. In front of us was a magnificent staircase. The sort of staircase that actors from the 1950s would catwalk in their stunning ball gowns with a sexy, pouty look on their faces.

"Let's start in the kitchen. I think it's through here."

I followed McIntyre through the doorway to the left of the grand staircase. The kitchen was smaller than I expected for a house of this size. It was more outdated than the living room. The walls were painted a moss green kind of color and a small wooden table with two mismatched chairs apparently served as the kitchen table. McIntyre opened the fridge, and already feeling unsettled from the mold, my stomach just couldn't tolerate the additional putrid odor he released. I ran for the front door and just made it to the stairs when I puked up everything I had eaten for breakfast. I immediately felt better but decided to stand outside for a while longer to be certain I was done. I heard McIntyre open the front door.

"Stella, are you okay?"

"Jesus, I am now. How do you not puke from that?"

"I know better. I never eat before I investigate inside a victim or a perp's house, but I admit that I learned that the hard way."

"Duly noted, McIntyre, duly noted. I'm okay now. Let's go back inside, but not in the kitchen. I am sure we both concur that since Jacobs has been dead over a week, the food in his fridge is rotten, right?"

"Agreed. I did open the backdoor that leads from the

kitchen to the backyard, and there is a vehicle parked out there. I believe the old shit-brown Camaro was Jacob's car, but I will have to confirm that."

"I thought you sent your men out here. Why didn't they see the car out back and report back to you?"

"An exceptionally good question indeed, and the exact reason why I am working off the radar with you and not the just out of the academy wanna be's. They don't want to do the grunt work. They don't want to get dirty. They want to investigate via computers. They have no social skills because, since the time when they figured out how to use their thumbs, they have communicated exclusively via texting on a cell phone. Can't send them to interview a suspect or a victim because they are incapable of face-to-face communication. No, they graduate the academy and expect to be assigned to head the cybercrimes unit or the anti-terrorism task force. It's the entitlement generation, Stella. These kids genuinely believe that they are owed a high paying job, a nice car, and a big house."

"Boy, are they in for a rude awakening. Well, I like doing the grunt work with you as long as you don't mind me tossing my cookies from time to time."

"It's a deal. Let's head up that crazy fancy staircase. Jacob's bedroom must be up there."

The first few rooms were bedrooms that looked abandoned, stuck in a different time, a different decade. The bathroom on the other hand was a disgrace. Piss all over the toilet seat, a shower that has never seen a scrub brush, clothes thrown on the floor, and gobs of toothpaste in the sink. The worst bachelor bathroom I had ever seen. Nothing more to see in here. I hadn't noticed McIntyre was no longer behind me.

"Stella, come here, last room on the right." McIntyre's voice was diffcrent, his tone deep and serious. I exited the bathroom and not more than six feet away, the door of the room was only half open, but I could see McIntyre bending over the bed.

"Sweet Jesus, what the hell happened in here? The blood, there's so much blood. My God, McIntyre, do you think Jacobs died here and was driven to where we found him?"

"Yes, no one loses this much blood and lives. Look at the blood spatter on the wall behind the headboard. You don't see spatter like that unless tremendous force was used to shatter the skull. Follow the blood trail. You can see where he was most likely pulled from the bed onto the floor and away from the bed, but the blood ends there. I would bet that whoever delivered that surprise final blow wrapped him up in something that wouldn't leak and carried him outside to a vehicle."

"You think he saw it coming?"

"Nope, I think due to the fact that he was probably drunk, he never knew what hit him, probably died instantly. Must have been sleeping on his stomach because when he was removed from the water, it was obvious that the back of his head was demolished, but with what I don't know yet. The killer more than likely took whatever he used with him."

"Now what," I asked.

"Now, I drive you back to your car and call the Crime Scene Investigative Unit. They have a lot of work to do out here. After I drive you back to your car, I am going to check out that barn we passed, as well as a shed behind the house I noticed when I opened that backdoor. Something awfully bad happened here. I have a gut feeling that this is going to get worse before it gets better."

McIntyre dropped me at my car and promised to update me as soon as he had any info to share. It was going to be a long day for him out here, an exceptionally long day. It didn't take me long to get back to my place. I still had plenty of time to take another shower and relax for a bit before my shift started, maybe read the book I had been wanting to read since I moved in.

Chapter Eighteen

Augustus

The expression on Javier's face the morning he and Hector dropped Mom and me off at the airport would forever remain embedded in the better memories folder in my head. I was not sure what Hector told him, but his expression of pure compassion and genuine empathy was one that I would always cherish. I wished I could tell him now, all of these years later, just how much his friendship meant to me. Just knowing that someone other than my mother cared about me filled me with hope that day.

Life in Germany made my mother happy. She flourished. We got our own apartment not far from my grandparents in the village of Bamberg. The streets were mostly cobblestone, and a fast-moving river ran almost all the way through it. People were kind to each other, and they greeted each other with smiles and conversation on the streets. It was as if this tiny village got stuck in a time warp a hundred years before. Mom took a job in a daycare as a teacher, and she said she was blessed to be doing what she loved. She found true joy in empowering kids to think on their own and to explore their imaginations. "Always stay curious," she would tell them. "When you stop being curious, you stop learning."

My grandparents were kind to me, and I could see the love they had for me in their eyes, in the way they looked at me, feel it in the way they hugged me. Despite that, not being able to communicate made me feel just as lonely as I did while I was growing up in America, held prisoner by my father. I attended school at a special international charter school one town over for children from other parts of the world. My teacher spoke perfect English, and he was a great guy. He was impressed with how much I had already learned as a home-schooled kid. I enjoyed being at school and learning, but again, other than my teacher, no one spoke English. I was lonely, but I was free.

Time marched on pretty uneventfully, and finally, I completed my last year of high school. Many of the students at the school were going on to college or to work in family businesses, and some planned to travel before making commitments. I, however, had no plans, which made me feel sad and hopeless. However, that summer after I finished school, I was invited to work for my mother's cousin, Hans. Hans owned a small winery just outside our village, nestled on a lush, green, postcard-perfect hillside. It was the most beautiful sight I thought I had ever laid eyes on. Hans was a pretty cool guy. Sort of that 'love, peace, and granola,' laid back type. He spoke a little bit of English, mostly curse words, though, and he smoked a ton of pot every day. So, as far as bosses went, he was a pleasure to work for. My job was to help pick the grapes from the vines when they were ripe and drive the tractor that pulled the partially enclosed trailer full of tourists each day, who were paying for the sightseeing tour.

The place was a gold mine. Between the tours, the wine tasting, and the gift shop, he had to be pulling in major cash. His wine was sold in restaurants and liquor stores all over Germany. Not too bad for a complete stoner. I spent most of my summer with Hans. He had a big house that overlooked the vineyard with four bedrooms, so instead of taking the train back and forth every day, I just stayed with him. On Sundays, I did take the train back home to spend the day with my mother. I missed not seeing her every day, but the money I was making was crazy good. At night, Hans would light a fire, and we would sit outside listening to music and talking. He let me drink beer, too, as much as I wanted. I was starting to really comprehend the German language, and

Hans made a point to learn words that were not profane. He was actually a really interesting guy.

Hans explained that when he was a young man, he decided to enlist in the German military. He lied to the recruiter and told him he was nineteen because he knew they would not accept a kid. He said the first few years were relatively boring. He saw no real action. It was mostly physical training and learning how to work on the military equipment. They were allowed to leave the base one weekend every month. Hans said he and a couple of his buddies planned to head to town on their free weekend, get drunk, and hopefully, meet some ladies. They stopped in a pub that was in a less than desirable part of town and began drinking heavily. It was ladies' night, so the ladies could drink for half price. They were buying a few girls drinks and, eventually, convinced the ladies to head back to their hotel with them.

Hans thought he was going to get laid until two thugs with guns shoved them all into an alley way and demanded money, jewelry, and their identification. One of the girls fell to her knees and started crying and begging for her life. The thug pointed a gun at her and told her to shut the fuck up, but she cried harder and puked all over herself and the dirtbag's shoes. He got so pissed that he held the gun to her head and released the safety. He was going to shoot her point blank in the face. Hans, without hesitation, dove head-first at the girl and knocked her backward off her feet, but not before the shooter pulled the trigger, leaving a bullet lodged in Hans's shoulder. The thugs took off, and Hans was hospitalized and underwent surgery to remove the bullet. Unfortunately, due to the injury, he could no longer serve the military. However, that girl whose life he saved, had a father who was a billionaire that owned banks all over the world, and wineries, too. Thus, Hans's current and lucrative situation. Yup, guy was so thankful that his beautiful princess was alive that he just signed the entire place over to Hans. Hans never married or had children, but he seemed happy and at peace with his life.

That was by far the best summer of my life. Summer turned to autumn, and the grapes were all picked and the vines ready to hibernate. The tourists all went home, and Hans would only keep the store open for wine tasting on the weekends. The night before I was leaving to go back to my mothers, we had one more night at the fire. There was a distinct change in the weather, and the warm summer breeze I had become accustomed to turned to a brisk chill, but that did not stop us from enjoying nature. We put our coats and gloves on and sat close to the fire, drinking, and reminiscing about the summer and making fun of some of the more memorable tourists. For a long time that night, we did not speak. We just sat quietly in our own thoughts, appreciating our surroundings, and admiring the perfectness of the round moon above us.

Finally, Hans looked up at me and asked what my plans were for my future now that summer was over. I thought I wanted to travel, I told him. I saved pretty much all of the money I made, so I wanted to see more of the world before I decided where I would settle. He nodded and sat staring, seemingly mesmerized by the dancing bright red flames. What he said next came completely out of left field and left me stunned and speechless.

Hans wanted to make a deal with me. He promised that if I enlisted in the military service and learned everything I could about working on machinery and the meaning of honor, bravery, and respect, he would give me half ownership of the winery when I completed my tour of duty. To my surprise, I shook his hand and told him that we had a deal.

Chapter Nineteen

Stella

G was waiting at my desk for me when I got to the precinct. Margie had pulled a chair over and was chatting him up. She was wearing a very low-cut pink blouse and tight white pants with pink heels that I could not walk a city block in. She was giggling and conscious, I was quite sure, that she was bent forward just enough so he could get a full view of what was under her blouse. She certainly was a trip. I gave her a lot of credit for her effort. G appeared to be playing right along. He was an incredible flirt.

"Hey, you two, hope I'm not interrupting anything important here at *my* desk."

Margie looked startled, never even saw me coming she was so caught up in the moment. I couldn't blame her, though. I mean, after all, he was not hard to look at. G looked up at me and winked.

"Stella, nice of you to join us. What's on our agenda today?"

The phones starting ringing, and Margie jumped up from her chair. "I gotta get those, ladies and gentlemen, carry on. Oh, and hi, Stel!"

"Good morning, Margie! Well, she was certainly saved by the bell, huh? Did I interrupt you two having a moment?"

"Oh, you know I only have eyes for you."

Damn, he caught me off guard again with his smooth comeback and sexy ass smile. "You ready to work, Officer G, or do you have more contestants waiting in the wings to drool over the bachelor in the barrens show here?"

"Ha, ha, ha, you should do stand up, Stella. Nope, I am ready, willing, and able." Again, the smile.

I was so screwed. He followed me out to the front desk where Margie had already left our keys for the patrol car we were assigned. She was deep in conversation on the phone and gave a quick wave as I grabbed the keys and headed out the back door to the parking lot. Before G could even ask and give me the pouty face, I reminded him that I would be driving.

"I wasn't even going to ask!"

"Yes, you were."

"Okay, so maybe I did think about it. Where to

today?"

"Well, I figured I would take you to the spots that seem to generate the most calls. First stop is Lake Oswego. Lake Oswego is a hotspot favorite for local teens to drink, light fires, and swim at night. All of which have ended in tragedy in recent history. Cap said about five years back, a bunch of teens snuck back to the lake at night to drink, fool around, and stay under the radar. Problem was they lit a fire during one of the driest Julys on record. Ended up burning 3,600 acres of land, including homes, a campground, and countless wildlife. Margie told me a few years back they got a call in the middle of night reporting a swimmer who had gone missing. Same situation, group of teens back there drinking and carrying on. They decided to jump into the lake to see who could swim the furthest. A sixteen-year-old high school kid never made it out. They found his body the next day on the other side of the lake, near the waterfall. Tragic night, real popular kid, football star. We try to swing back here every shift as a deterrent, so we can avoid any future tragedies."

We arrived at the lake within twenty minutes.

"Wow, really cool place. They let you fish back here?"

"Yup, from what I hear, there are monster bass in these waters that have eluded fisherman for decades."

"Sounds like local legend to me."

"Yup, right up there with the Jersey Devil and the

buried mobsters. Anyway, this is part of our routine now."

"Ten four, Officer Stella."

"Next few stops will be the top five."

"What the hell is the top five?"

"You know, top five crazies that call anywhere from three to five times a week."

"Ah, got it."

"You still coming out with us tonight? I am going to ask Margie, too, and maybe Cap and Joe will stop in as well. Should be fun."

"Yup, I am in. Looking forward to it. Like I said I have been pretty much of a loner since I got here."

"I think we could all use the laughs and the drinks." I pulled off of Route 563, just shy of the Petersons house. "Okay, you see that yellow house, just beyond the chicken coops. That is the Petersons' place. They call every other day to report that the Jersey Devil has yet again killed one of their chickens. We stopped coming out for obvious reasons. We just tell them that we will add it to the complaint, so that when the Jersey Devil is brought to justice, his sentence is longer. They always seem pleased with that."

"Jesus, Stella, are you making this shit up?"

"Nope, my imagination does not reach that far, my friend."

We spent the next few hours driving around, and I

showed him the remainder of the top crazy callers, then we headed over to do a loop through the state park, the schools, and then back to the station. Margie was still at the front desk tapping away at her cell phone.

"Margie, don't forget about tonight. Seven at the bar."

"Girl, you know I don't turn down an invite to have some cocktails and social time with my favorite people. I will be there."

"Great, me and G are going to finish up some quick paperwork and then I am out of here. Brie should be here in a couple of hours, and I want to be home when she arrives."

"Poor baby, how is she?"

"I honestly don't know, but please remember not to bring it up. I am sure she will, but I don't want her to know that I already talked to you about it. I am just so worried about her. I know she is not in a good place right now."

"Well, then, cheering her up and making sure she has fun tonight is our mission."

Cap was in his office when we got back, so I stuck my head in and invited him and Joe to join us. "Well, that's really nice, Stel. I will try my best, but tonight is our standing date night, and you know how sensitive Joe can be when you sway from the plan." We both laughed, and I told him to let Joe know I would really like him to come and meet Brie.

Chapter Twenty

McIntyre

My cell rang.

"Hey, Jill, I can't talk right now, babe. I'm out here in deliverance NJ, also known as Pine Barrens. Unfortunately, the case I was telling you about is now a homicide investigation, so I am not sure when the hell I will be home. Eat your tofu ala healthy slop for dinner, and I will grab something greasy and delicious on my way home later. I love you, and yes, I will be careful. Bye, bye." I hung up, turning to the others behind me. "What are you idiots giggling at?" The Crime Scene Investigation techs, who were so young that one still had pimples, laughed even harder. "Just do your jobs, guys. Remember, I want every inch of this bedroom put under a microscope or whatever you call that fancy equipment of yours. I want every fingerprint lifted and run through any and every database we have access to."

From the bedroom window, I could see that the cadets had arrived to begin the grid search I ordered. I headed back downstairs, and outside, which was where I ran into Kevin Johnson.

"Hey, buddy, how the hell are you?"

"McIntyre, shit. When the hell do you retire?"

"Ah, six months, just six more month."

Johnson was FBI, a good guy. We went through the academy together and started in the state police together, but Johnson was brilliant. He had a real knack for profiling, so it wasn't long before the FBI swooped him up and sent him to earn his masters and doctorate in behavioral sciences. Now, he was the top guy on the east coast. The specificities of his profiles resulted in the capture of three serial killers before his fifth-year anniversary with the bureau, which was why I called him out here today. There was just something ominous about this place, and I could not shake the feeling that horrible things had happened here on Kurt's property, aside from Kurt's death.

I filled Kevin in on the situation and told him about my gut feeling. "Well, I have known you a long time, and that gut has never been wrong, but why the jump to the grid search?"

"Between you and me, something is just off. This place is, well, wickedly seething with a darkness I cannot shake. It is an unsettling feeling that I have never experienced before."

"Jesus Christ, now you're giving me the chills, and I am used to this sadistic shit. You expect to find bodies buried out here, don't you?"

"Yes, I think so, but I really pray I am wrong."

"Okay, get your cadets moving, and I will meet you around the back of the house."

The cadets were young and antsy and already soaked in sweat from the thick, summer haze. "Okay, cadets, listen up. I am Captain Brendan McIntyre of the NJ State Police. You are here today to conduct a grid search of this specific area. You are to maintain a distance of two feet from the cadet on your left and two feet from the cadet on your right. It is imperative that you walk slowly, in a straight line until you have reached the end of the field. At that time, you will wait for further instruction. Any questions so far?"

Fuck. Up went three hands, idiots. I shook my head and pointed to the cadet nearest me who looked young enough to still be in high school.

"Captain McIntyre, what are we looking for?"

"I was getting to that cadet." I pointed at the other two cadets with their hands up and told them to put them down. "You are looking for signs of disturbed earth, bushes, brush, or weeds. You are looking for areas that appear as if they may have been dug up. You are looking for areas that seem greener than others. You are also looking for evidence. If and when you find any of what I have just described, stop, blow the whistle we gave you, and raise your hand. At that time, the entire line must stop. An officer will come to you to investigate and collect the evidence if he deems it necessary. Okay, let's get going before we run out of daylight. Good luck."

I motioned for the officers who would be watching over the cadets to join me and instructed them to make sure they kept the line straight, and the cadets focused.

"Let me know if they find anything. I'll be around the back of the house."

I walked around the west side of the house, it was more overgrown and harder to maneuver through, but I wanted no stone left unturn. Nothing suspicious, couple of broken windows, but from the looks of them, they had been in distress for years. I spotted Johnson behind the house, past where the cars were parked, peering into the old wooden shed I had looked through earlier.

"Nothing, right?"

"Nope, so far just looks like a run-down car and equipment, but like I said, I have always trusted that gut of yours, and we've got more places to look." Johnson pointed toward the large, buckling barn. "I think we should take a walk toward that pathetic monstrosity."

"I'm in, God knows I need the exercise."

Johnson and I stopped in our tracks when the first

whistle blared. The cadets had found something already. "You want to head over there, McIntyre?"

"Nah, they can call my cell if its big. Remember, these are inexperienced cadets, eager to find a critical piece of evidence that will catapult them to the top of their class."

Johnson chuckled. "Yeah, I remember those days. You and I have come a long way, buddy, and now you are on the verge of retirement!"

"I am honestly looking forward to it. You know this job slowly eats away at your soul. After so many years of seeing the worst of the worst offenders and what human beings are capable of doing to each other, I am ready to hang it up. Besides, Jill is ready for me to become her fulltime personal handy man."

"Well, despite this job costing me my marriage, and the prospect of having children, I am not ready. Too many fucked up people out there to quit now."

"I totally get that, and with that brain of yours, you could save countless lives, my friend. Stick with it. We need you for as long as you can take it."

My cell phone rang. I pulled it out of my pocket to see Stella's number. I didn't want to answer it in front to Johnson, so I let it go to voicemail. I really didn't have anything new to tell her anyway.

"McIntyre, you see that?"

"See what?"

"The tree line past the barn. I saw someone run into

the woods."

"You sure, Johnson?"

"Oh, I am sure. Dark hair, medium build, not real tall."

"You think he was in the barn and saw us coming?"

"I don't know, but now my radar is stoked."

We stood outside the barn trying to assess the stability of the structure. While the roof had all but collapsed in a section or two, the walls and beams looked strong, or at least safe enough for a quick look. We walked cautiously through the side door, which was not locked, actually it was barely on the hinges. Front and center view revealed a completely rusted pickup truck without plates. A closer look revealed that the vehicle identification number had been scratched off with some sort of sharp tool.

"Jesus, this damn thing has got to be forty plus years old." I slowly opened the driver's door which made a horrific squeal, the nails on a chalkboard kind of sound that made your teeth ache. It was empty. Nothing in the glove compartment or under the seats, either.

"Beds empty, too," Johnson called.

"Okay, I vote that we look around and then get the hell out of here. Would hate for both of our stories to end here, if you know what I mean."

"No arguments here." The entire barn was filled with years of debris, dust, animal skeletons and dropping. Tools, shovels, hoses, and empty crates were strewn about the place. "McIntyre, look at this." I met Johnson near the far side of the barn where there was not too much damage to the roof. "This entire structure is in complete chaos, except this area. Look, someone brought a fairly newer chair and a radio in here. Oh shit, look. Whoever has been hanging out in here also hooked up a mini fridge. Perhaps the person I saw running for the woods."

A barrage of whistles blaring in the distance left us both startled, staring at each other like deer in headlights.

Chapter Twenty-One

Augustus

I kissed my mother and my grandparents goodbye, picked up my duffle bag, and headed for the train station feeling both excited and a bit saddened. As much as I preferred the United States to Germany, the simpleness and beauty of this small town provided me with a sense of security and freedom that I would be forever grateful for. I was not sure how Hans would feel about me having enlisted in the United States Navy in lieu of the German military, but it just felt right. If, when I returned from duty, he had changed his mind about including me as a partner in the winery, well, then so be it. I was, after all, an American citizen, and as such, felt a sense of loyalty and duty to serve for the United States. So, home I went.

After a total of nearly twenty-four hours of travel, I stood second guessing myself, right there on the sidewalk of Cotman Avenue in Philly in front of the recruiter's office. Shit, did I really want to give up four years of my life? What would I do if I didn't go through with this, though? Mom had given me a debit card to a bank account she opened for me with $25,000 in it, which surprised me. I didn't realize she had saved so much money, or maybe my grandparents were the generous ones. In addition, I had saved $16,000 from working with Hans. I could easily get an apartment and a job. I didn't know if there were any wineries in the area, but if so, that would be perfect, yet seasonal. I decided to walk for a while to try and clear my head and reflect on my life thus far. Thinking back to those years, those critical childhood years, in which my mother and I were basically hostages in our home, ruled by an evil bastard of a father who did horrible things to us, to women, and his subsequent demise. It seemed like something I may have read in a book in lieu of actually experiencing it. Once Mom and I arrived in Germany, we promised each other never to speak of him again, and we stuck to that promise.

I walked for quite a while, taking in all of the sights. Philly was a pretty cool place, but terribly busy. People passed me by without a glance. Strange, really. People seemed to intentionally ignore each other. Back in Germany, it could take you over an hour to walk a half mile because people, friendly, smiling people, were always ready and happy to greet you with conversation, a handshake, or even a hug. This non-contact society I was experiencing in Philly seemed contrary to the way humans were supposed to be. After all, we were social beings in need of human contact.

As I turned to walk up Comley Street, a beautiful, larger than life cross caught my eye. It was absolutely stunning. The sunlight reflected from the cross upward toward the heavens, as if Jesus Christ himself had planned it that way. Maybe he did. Maybe I was supposed to be right here, right now, and maybe I was meant to go inside. The church was simple brick, not lavish nor enormous, but that cross was mesmerizing and inviting for sure. An old, heavy-looking wooden door without a window was ajar at the top of the steep cement steps leading to the church. The steps looked as if they had seen better days, and most certainly were in dire need of repair, as was the roof at closer look.

It took a moment for my eyes to adjust to the dim lighting inside, but the coolness of the air was a fabulous relief after walking for so long in the heat of the last bit of summer. The church appeared empty as I made my way further in. The aroma was bizarre but not bad. It was sort of a mix of sage, old books, moth balls, and once dampened carpet. It was not an awful smell, or one that would prevent someone from staying, not at all. I thought it was the way a long-standing house of worship should smell. I walked toward the pulpit slowly. The wooden pews I passed had incredibly old and a bit battered bibles placed strategically on each row. The stained-glass windows depicting various religious events were incredibly detailed and just so beautiful. I was lost in the alure of the window depicting Jesus at the Last Supper when I heard a subtle yet friendly voice behind me. I suddenly felt very awkward. Was I trespassing? Was I in trouble?

"Good afternoon, young man. My name is Pastor Dan. Welcome to Marathon Baptist Church. What brings you by today?" The pastor had just a hint of a southern twang and the kindest face I had ever seen. Looking at him, I felt like I had a direct line to God himself, just behind those pale blue, genuine eyes.

"Oh, hello, Pastor Dan. I hope it is okay that I am in here. I felt drawn to this place. The cross atop of your church just sort of called me in. Is it okay?"

"Well, of course, it is!" he said with a huge smile and a friendly chuckle. "Actually, during this time of the day, I am usually over at the Children's Hospital making my rounds, but today, I decided I needed to be here. Call it God's will, I suppose. Son, you seem like you have the weight of the world on your shoulders. Let us sit down and talk for a while. How about a drink and a donut?" He motioned for me to sit in the pew that I had been standing in front of, and I obliged.

"I would love a drink and a donut, if you don't mind."

"Heavens no, I'll be right back."

I felt very much at peace sitting in the little church. I didn't even feel nervous about speaking with a man of God, despite what Mother and I had done years before. I had already begged for God's forgiveness on that terrible day, and in my heart, I had always felt that His forgiveness and His mercy had been granted to us.

"Ah, here you go. Say, what's your name?"

"Oh, sorry." I held my hand out and shook Pastor Dan's hand. "Augustus."

"Well, that's a fine name, son."

I ate my donut and drank the water Pastor Dan had given me. We sat and talked for four hours that day. I told him everything, well, I told him my father died, but I didn't tell him exactly how, and he did not ask. I told him about my childhood, about life in Germany, about Hans, and about my current dilemma regarding the Navy. I asked him if God would be angry with me if I backed out of my enlistment with the Navy.

He was quiet for just a moment and then said, "Augustus, we are all sinners, even I. We sin every day because only the Lamb of God was pure and without sin. Jesus gave his life on the Cross of Calvary so that our sins may be forgiven. So long as you acknowledge and welcome Jesus as your Savior, your sins are forgiven. Sometimes a conversation with Jesus is all I need to figure out a complicated situation."

"I do know about Jesus, and of course, God," I told him. "Back when I was a kid, my father had farm workers that taught me a little bit about that, and I am a believer."

"Listen, follow your heart. Actually, I have an upstairs apartment here right above the church. You are welcome to stay and perhaps help out with some of the much-needed repairs in exchange for room and board if you decide you do not want to be shipped out, okay?"

I left my backpack and bag with Pastor Dan and told him I needed to think a bit longer, but that one way or the other, I would be back. It was ridiculously hot, but not carrying everything I owned while I walked the streets was a relief. Philly most assuredly was not a place where I would want to put down permanent roots, but the thought of a temporary situation in lieu of giving the Navy four years of my life seemed like a good decision.

It was late afternoon, and the sidewalks were once again crowded as were the bars. A man and a woman were having a very animated argument in front of the Philly Bodega. Half the argument was in English, but the other half was in Spanish. People had everything you could imagine for sale. You could buy keychains, jewelry, artwork, socks, pocketbooks, and even have your fortune told. Each vendor as I passed begged me to stop by and look at their incredibly unique merchandise, at the absolute best price in the city. Some got mad, some even yelled curse words at me for not stopping. I guessed when you were trying to make your living hustling on the streets you had to be aggressive, bold. The constant blaring of car horns from drivers was enough to make anyone miserable and on edge. It was no wonder people walking the streets of Philly looked so angry. A place called Daly's Irish Pub was standing room only, as was a bar called Stevenson's Place.

I kept walking but was really in the mood for a cold beer. Finally, I stumbled on a watering hole, a local hole in the wall called the Locust Bar, and there were plenty of empty barstools. The bartender was half asleep and half watching *The Ellen DeGeneres Show*. Now, to get that beer without an ID saying I was 21 years of age would be my next hurdle.

Chapter Twenty-Two

Stella

I pulled in my driveway, jumped out of my car, and jogged to the door. I was so excited about seeing Brie. I was going to take a shower and actually put makeup on and do something with this head of hair. Perhaps I'd even break out the curling iron. I knew sweet Brie was sick with worry that I was going to become so depressed living here that I may consider ending my life. The weeks following my breakup with Thomas left me in a dark place, and for a moment, I did consider ending my life. Brie probably expected to find me in tattered clothes, smelling of perspiration with a lifeless ponytail on top of my greasy head. Honestly, I wasn't far from that mess a month or so ago. I felt as if I truly had nothing to live for, like the only things important to me were, in fact, lost. It took a lot of soul searching, brutal self-honesty, and some absolutely wonderful and caring people here in the barrens for me to realize that my journey wasn't over. I had a new pathway to the next part of my adventure, the opportunity to realize my purpose in this crazy life.

I made a quick sweep of the house to make sure everything was neat. I washed all of the extra blankets and pillows for Brie. I had wine, snacks, and plenty to talk to her about. After I showered and shaved my legs, I headed for my closet, remembering that I really didn't have much of a wardrobe. I had work clothes and weekend cleaning clothes, then I remembered that I had put some clothes I didn't think I would wear in the old wooden trunk in my living room. A flood of memories hit me hard when I opened the trunk and saw the sun dresses I had bought when Thomas and I had decided to sneak away to the beach for a weekend. I stopped myself from tearing up. Nope, no fucking way am I going to shed one more tear for him. In fact, this yellow sundress looked amazing on me the day I had tried it on in Macy's, so I am most certainly wearing it tonight. I threw the dress on and was grateful that I still loved it. I guessed it took me about an hour or so to put makeup on, dry and curl my hair, and find the sandals I wanted to wear. I stood in the mirror feeling good about the reflection, about Brie coming, and about the night ahead.

I heard a car door shut and sprinted to the door. Yay! It was Brie. She made it. I ran outside, arms wide open and hugged her as tight as I could.

"God, Brie, I am so, so, so glad to see you. I have missed you desperately, girl."

Brie was beautiful, but she looked tired, stressed too. She had her long, straight blonde hair in a ponytail, and she was wearing jeans and a white t shirt. She always looked hot in jeans, but with that body, she could wear a potato sack and look hot.

"Oh, Stella, I have missed you so much. You look beautiful." Brie started to cry and held her face in her hands. I wrapped my arm around her, grabbed her bag and guided her inside.

"Sit, Brie. Sit. Let's talk. I know things are much worse at work. Tell me please."

I left Brie for a moment to pour us each a glass of cabernet. When I returned, she was wiping away teardrops and smiled when I handed her the glass. "Now that's the remedy I need, a glass of wine and my best friend. Okay, I am going to tell you everything and probably cry again, but after that, I am done. We are going out with your friends tonight and having a good time."

"It's a deal, sweetie," I told her.

"Okay, well, the last month has been awful, Stel. So much so that I have my resume out to headhunters."

I did not say it out loud, but my inner voice screamed thank God!

"He is making me feel awful about myself. He makes me feel cheap and stupid. I was once so confident about my career and my abilities. I was always so excited to head to work. You remember right, Stel?"

I nodded. I certainly did remember. The happiest fucking morning person living with the worst fucking morning person.

"Now, I feel dread and fear in the pit of my stomach when my alarm goes off. A few weeks ago, Will Bayo had sent a meeting invite to me, Jane, and Melissa to meet in the conference room to discuss the upcoming budgets and department salaries. All three were already seated when I walked in and were chatting about something in the news, I think. He looks up at me, smiles, and then asks me if I were ever a bra model!"

"Brie, are you fucking kidding me? What did Melissa and Jane do?"

"They just sat there, jaws dropped and speechless. Will half-assed apologizes and says he was only kidding. Then, he starts the meeting like it never happened. You could cut the tension in that room with a knife. After the meeting, he stops in my office and tells me he cannot believe he said that in front of them but still wants to know if I was ever a bra model. He is vile, Stella. He is old, creepy, and ugly on the inside and out. The sight of him turns my stomach. Why the hell does he feel entitled to say these things to me? He is escalating, and he scares me."

I took Brie's hands in mine. "Sweetie, what he is doing to you is illegal. You have to take a stand. Report him to the board."

We sat for a few minutes just sipping wine, and then Brie looked me in the eyes and said, "That's not all. It gets worse, much worse. Monday night, I was leaving the office late. I took the elevator to the lobby, which was empty, or so I thought. I was almost to the heavy glass door, ready to head outside when the bastard reached over me and held the door closed. I was in shock, terrified. I didn't know who it was at first. I thought I was being mugged. I would have preferred being mugged, actually. I turned to look and realized that he had me pinned. I held my hands to his chest to keep hm from making bodily contact with me and told him to get the fuck off me or I would call the police. He laughed in my face. The fucking pervert laughed in my face. He looked me in the eyes with a numbing, ominous expression and told me that if I had any plans to go to the board or record our conversations, I would regret it. He said he already spoke to Melissa and Jane, and he told them if they ever repeated what they thought they heard in the conference room, he would make sure they were blackballed in the industry from Philly to California. He even had the balls to tell me that he gave them both promotions and raises to seal the deal, as he put it. Stella,

I was never more scared in my life. I was paralyzed with fear. I couldn't move, and he wasn't moving. Then, out of nowhere, some guy walking down the street opens the door next to us and asks me if I am alright. Will tells him to mind his own business and to leave. I guess the guy could tell from my expression that I was not okay. He put Will in a headlock, threw him to the floor, and kicked him in the face twice. Will laid there moaning in pain. This guy walks toward the door, holds it open for me, and says, 'After you, miss.' I walked out the door, and when I turned to thank him, he was gone."

"Brie, I don't even know what to say except that I want him to die a horribly painful, long death, and thank God above for that stranger who came to your rescue. Had you ever seen this stranger before? What did he look like? What happened to old man Bayo?"

"Jesus, I was in such a state of shock that I have no clue what he looked like, and as far as the pig, I haven't seen him since, or at least I don't think I have. HR says he took an undisclosed amount of vacation time and cannot be reached by phone."

"Wait, wait, wait! What do you mean you don't think you have seen him since then?"

Brie started to tear up again and hung her head low. "Stella, I thought I saw him in my rearview mirror on my way here. It wasn't his fancy sports car that he is way too old to drive. It looked like a Ford Explorer, black. I think he followed me from my place."

"Was this car behind you when you pulled into my driveway?"

"Yes, it flew by me when I pulled in. Stella, maybe I am just seeing things? Maybe I am losing my mind?"

"I don't think so. He is a sick old pervert who is obsessed with you, and he doesn't like not getting what he wants. Listen, you are safe here with me, okay? Besides, I do have a gun or two, you know."

We both laughed, and she held up her empty glass, which was my que to get us a refill. I didn't want to appear worried in front of Brie, but truth be told, I was. This creep was obsessed and obviously not thinking straight.

Chapter Twenty-Three

McIntyre

"McIntyre here." I had the call on speaker so that Johnson could listen as well. I knew this was not going to be good news. The voice on the other end of the phone was that of the supervisor in charge of the cadets.

"McIntyre, I think you better get over here quickly." Johnson shook his head in disbelief, and we wasted no time getting back to the field. So much for the perfectly spaced straight line. Every idiot cadet was standing together behind the supervisors that were kneeling on the ground looking at something. Johnson startled them all with his very loud announcement.

"Cadets, get your asses back in the line you were supposed to stay in. Any evidence around whatever you found is surely compromised because you cannot follow simple orders!"

They all looked embarrassed, but they quickly got back in line. One of the supervisors had a shovel in his hand but was no longer digging. He looked rattled. I asked them what they found.

"See for yourself. It looks like human remains. That is a human skull. I am almost positive." It only took me a moment to realize that it was, in fact, a human skull. I was just wrapping my head around what I had just seen when a cadet blew his whistle about 100 yards from us and held his hand up.

Johnson glared at him. "Your hand better not be raised because you need a bathroom break, Cadet."

The cadet looked mortified but replied, "No, sir, no. I think we need a shovel over here, too. The ground below this bush is exceptionally soft and the bush is almost twice the size of the ones around it."

"Good call, Cadet. We will be with you in a minute. Everyone remain where you are!" Johnson looked at me with a curious expression. "You know, McIntyre, I was really hoping that damn gut of yours was off today. I have a feeling this is only the beginning of the story that will one day be a *60 Minutes* episode."

The second location was a grave as well. We didn't have to dig too deep, maybe less than a foot, and that was exactly what we uncovered: the remains of a human left foot. Some sick son of a bitch had buried this person headfirst beneath this bush. From the size of the foot, I estimated the sex to be male, but we needed a coroner or seven out here immediately. I addressed the cadets as loudly and clearly as I could.

"Cadets, what we have uncovered thus far today appears to be the burial site of multiple victims. At this point, I need you all to turn and face the route in which you came and slowly and carefully make your way back to the edge of the field and wait for further instruction. If I see any cadet with a phone in his or her hand, they will be immediately expelled permanently from the academy. You are not to discuss this situation with anyone. Do I make myself clear?"

In unison, they replied, "Yes, sir."

I instructed a supervisor to follow them back to the edge of the field and collect every cellphone. "I do not want them to have access to anyone or any social media outlet. This generation can't take a shit without posting it on Facebook. Morons."

Johnson snickered.

"Johnson, I think we are going to need a bigger boat, man." Johnson knew what I meant. "What do you need, McIntyre? Whatever you need, just say the word, and you got it. The FBI is at your disposal, my friend."

"Well, we could spend three months out here with whistles and shovels and still not uncover all that needs to be found. I think we are going to need some fancy, expensive FBI ground penetrating radars, as many as you have."

Johnson pulled his cell phone from his pocket and made the call. I took the opportunity to call Stella. She picked up after a few rings.

"Hey, McIntyre, what's up?"

"The question should be what's down," I told her.

"Okay then, what's down, McIntyre?"

"So far, Stella, two bodies are down, but not too far down."

"McIntyre, what the hell are you talking about? I know I have had a glass of wine, but I don't think it's me not making sense."

"I am back out at the Jacobs place. I brought some Academy cadets out here on a hunch, and right out of the box, they uncovered two bodies buried beneath blueberry bushes about 100 yards apart. I am sending them back to the academy, and a friend of mine, who is an FBI profiling genius, is here with me, and he is calling his people to get ground penetrating radars out here."

"Holy shit, that is incredible. What do you want me to do?"

"Nothing right now. Go enjoy your evening, and we will regroup Monday. I should know more by then, and please remember this must stay between us, Stella."

"Of course. Please call me Monday, okay?"

When I hung up with Stella, Johnson motioned me over. "Okay, buddy, so far we have four radars and technicians coming, but unfortunately, they are coming from Langley, so we need to station officers here 24/7 until that time."

"Understood. Hey, Kevin, thank you so much. This was the last thing I needed so close to retirement, but if it has to be, I'm glad we are in this together."

The first coroner was pulling on site as the cadets were boarding their bus back to the academy. I had to laugh. Some of them looked super excited, and some looked like they were minutes from vomiting. This year's graduating class may have just gotten a lot smaller.

I knew this would drag on into the night and me getting home before my normal bedtime was not going to happen. Jill was not thrilled when I called her. It had been a number of years since I had to make one of those calls. I must admit, although I was tired, hot, and uncomfortably sweaty, the adrenaline rush had me fired up. Riding a desk for too many years wasn't good for the body, the mind, or the soul. Situations like this were the reason I wanted a career in law enforcement. I was careful not to share my enthusiasm with my wife. After all, that honey-do list was carved in stone now.

I recognized the coroner right away. Although I had not seen her in years, Diane Smith and I had worked together since the beginning of both of our careers. We even dated for all of five minutes when we were young. Despite having a job that kept you surrounded by more dead than living, she was one of the most upbeat, positive people I knew. Time had been kind to Diane. Her dark curly hair and piercing green eyes were still prominent, although she looked like she had gained a little weight, just like me. It was called the dreaded fifties. She waved and smiled as soon as she saw me.

"McIntyre, I missed you." She gave me a big hug and a kiss on the cheek.

"Diane, you look fabulous. It must be working with all those corpses, huh?"

"Doesn't stop me from eating," she said, pointing at her ass. Always the joker, always fun to be around. She had not changed much.   "So, how are Jill and Ian?"

"Everyone is good, and Ian just graduated college, so I actually get to keep some of my paycheck. You thinking about retiring soon, Diane?"

"Hell no! Retirement is the kiss of death in my family. Every family member I can remember died shortly after retirement. I am going to work until they load me into the back of my van. Heard you are cashing out, though?"

"Yup, I am ready. Jill is ready."

"Good for you, you deserve it. So, what is the story out here? All they told me was to bring a bus but be ready to dispatch additional units."

I explained the situation to Diane from the beginning. Even though the words were coming out of my very own mouth, they sounded like highlights from a murder mystery. We headed over to the first grave. Diane took pictures from every angle possible and then motioned for the crime scene techs to continue digging. She instructed them to begin digging three feet from the body and slowly and carefully make their way toward the remains. She told them to stop when they were halfway so that she could take additional photos and ascertain proximity to avoid compromising the body or the surrounding soil, all of which would need to be taken back to her office.

"Oh, and I need the actual bush transported as well. That will aid in determining when this person was buried." The techs nodded in agreement, and we set off for the next burial site. "Jesus, McIntyre, you didn't tell me that whoever did this had a sick sense of humor. This one is buried head-first? What the hell is wrong with people. This is a first for me, and I don't see many firsts at this point in my career."

"First for me, too, Diane. That's why I called Kevin Johnson in to help get a handle on this guy or girl's psyche. Like I told him, something unbelievably bad, evil perhaps, happened out here at this place, and we need to find out who, when, and why."

"Okay, well, let me get to work, and I will keep you posted. Good to see you."

"Thank you, Diane. Good to see you, too."

Chapter Twenty-Four

Augustus

The old barkeep never even looked at me when he asked me what I wanted. I told him that I'd take a very cold Budweiser. This guy was so engaged in watching *The Ellen DeGeneres Show* that he poured a beer and slid it down to me without ever looking away from the television. Now, that was a devoted Ellen fan for sure. After about thirty minutes, it dawned on me that I was glued to the tube, too. My mother always watched this show. She loved Ellen's energy and sense of humor. Today's show was actually a rerun. It was a Christmas episode, and Ellen was giving away cars, motorcycles, vacations, and money to the studio audience. People were going nuts, and Ellen was singing and dancing and having a blast. She just oozed coolness. The episode ended, and soon after, the bartender looked over at me and the four other guys bellied up to the bar.

"Anyone ready for another round on me?" He didn't seem like the giving type, but I assumed we had Ellen DeGeneres to thank for his current, out of character state of generosity. I ordered another beer and watched the late day news with the rest of patrons, and of course, the bartender. This joint was more like a library than a watering hole, which was simply perfect for me.

I refrained from ordering a third beer and paid my tab. I certainly don't want to smell like booze when I headed back to see Pastor Dan. I thanked the old barkeep and headed out. He didn't reply. Probably didn't hear me. This guy loved that idiot box. Despite it being six in the evening, the sun was still strong and the humidity still thick. The sidewalks smelled like urine. I pretty much made up my mind that I was going to take Pastor Dan up on his offer, but I wasn't quite ready to head back to the church yet. I thought about calling my mom and Hans but decided to hold off on that until I had a complete plan in place for how I was going to support myself and what my future looked like. I wandered around Philly as the sun started to set. Although I preferred peace and quiet, I had to admit that this town was actually kind of cool, despite the occasional smell of urine. This crazy double decker tour bus that was painted bright colors and playing loud music passed me several times, and each time it was packed with people laughing, drinking, waving to everyone, and just having fun. I was going to put that on my to-do list for sure.

A man in a suit stopped me at the next corner and handed me a pamphlet that mentioned the top ten things to do in Philadelphia. I thanked him and walked on flipping the pages. *Wow, you can tour an old penitentiary, participate in a historic walking tour, and a twisted history tour, too.* The pages were filled with museums, nightclubs, restaurants, and coupons to about every attraction. I folded up the brochure and stuck it in my back pocket. As the darkness of nightfall began to surround me, I noticed that the atmosphere became a bit "seedier" than I had anticipated. I spotted a lot of prostitutes, at least I thought they were prostitutes, dressed in clothing that barely covered their private parts. Some of the girls looked much younger than me, and some of the women looked older than my mother. Lines of animated twenty-somethings lined the streets waiting to get into the bars. I passed a few fist fights, which at quick glance seemed to be alcohol-related incidents. I avoided eye contact, minded my own business, and decided it was time to find my way back to the church.

I arrived back at the church with the beautiful cross just after eight and hoped Pastor Dan was still around to show me the room he talked about. I entered the church and said a silent prayer just to thank God for blessing me with so much opportunity. I spotted Pastor Dan right away. He was seated in the very first row with a man and a woman. They were praying together, but she was also sobbing loudly. The man with her had placed his arms around her and was trying to comfort her, but she seemed very distraught. I sat in the last row so not to interrupt their privacy. I picked up one of the old bibles that was laying on the seat beside me. I opened the book to Samuel 1:24, Hannah's prayer.

"Then Hannah prayed and said: My heart rejoices in the Lord; in the LORD my horn is lifted high. My mouth boasts over my enemies, for I delight in your deliverance. There is no one holy like the LORD; there is no one besides you; there is no rock like our God. Do not keep talking so proudly or let your mouth speak such arrogance, for the LORD is a God who knows, and by Him deeds are weighed. The bows of the warrior are broken, but those who stumbled are armed with strength. Those who were full hire themselves out for food, but those who were hungry are hungry no more. She who *was barren has borne seven children, but she who has many sons' pines away. The LORD brings death and makes alive; he brings down to the grave and raises up. The LORD sends poverty and wealth; he humbles, and he exalts. He raises the poor from the dust and lifts the needy from the ash heap; he seats them with princes and has them inherit a throne of honor. For the foundations of the earth are the LORDS; on them he has set the world. He will guard the feet of his faithful servants, but the wicked will be silenced in the place of darkness. It is not by strength that one prevails; those who oppose the LORD will be broken. The most*

High will thunder from heaven, the LORD will judge the ends of the earth. He will give strength to this King and exalt the horn of the anointed."

I quietly closed the bible and thought about the prostitutes I passed on the streets tonight. Surely, God must be angry with them. I wondered if there would come a time when they realized they must come to God for forgiveness and pray for a new life. One that doesn't involve selling flesh for money. I prayed that they would.

"Augustus, I am so glad you came back." I was so deep in thought that I had not noticed Pastor Dan standing in front of me.

"Hi, Pastor Dan. Yes, I hope it's okay that I came in when you were with people. The woman and man you were speaking with looked terribly upset."

"Yes, unfortunately, their hearts are broken, and they are desperate to come to terms with the tragic loss of their young daughter, Scarlett. Her body was discovered just two nights ago. The poor child was only nineteen."

"I am so sorry. That is terrible. Just awful. What happened to her? How was she killed?"

"Well, I guess I am not breaking a confidence since the story will be on all of the media outlets by morning. Scarlett was a troubled girl, as far back as I can remember. She just had a wild side that could not be tamed. She was an exceptionally beautiful girl and always looked much older, more mature than her natural years. She ran away from home numerous times, but her parents and I, and sometimes her therapist, were always able to convince her to come back home. However, this last time was different. There are parts of this city that are nothing but Satan's playground after dark. Scarlett began using drugs and became addicted to their evil hold on her soul. With no money to continue buying drugs, she turned to prostitution. Her handler kept her high and working all night, every night. Her parents, the police, me, we all tried to get her to come home, but she wasn't the same Scarlett anymore. No, the streets had swallowed the Scarlett that was born to this world, pure and loved. The drugs took control of her and rendered her incapable of making sound decisions. For the past year, we were unable to find her on the streets. Her pimp was questioned by detectives on numerous occasions, but he stuck to the same story: that she met a man and ran away to be with him."

"Pastor Dan, what happened to her?"

The pastor, with tears in his eyes, hung his head and asked for God's mercy on her soul. We sat in silence for a few moments until he was emotionally ready to proceed with the story. "Well, two nights ago, a couple of detectives from the city knocked on her parent's door and told them that the NJ State police discovered a body buried in a shallow grave in the woods over in New Jersey. Based on the age of the victim and the gold necklace with the name Scarlett written in diamonds, they were quite sure it was her. They took her parents to the morgue the same night where their worst fears became reality. It was, in fact, Scarlett." Tears rolled down the pastor's face, and I put my hand on his shoulder and told him how sorry I was. "She was murdered, Augustus. She suffered a brutal, violent death and then was just tossed into a shallow grave. Lord, please forgive her for her sins. Please open the gates of heaven and welcome this child home."

"Pastor, can I do anything to help?"

"Have you decided to stay?"

"Yes, I have made up my mind. I can't explain it, but I sort of feel like I am needed here, like I am supposed to be here at this moment in time. Does that sound crazy?"

Pastor Dan chuckled. "No, it sounds like divine intervention, God's will. It has been a long day. Let me show you to your room. I had a feeling you would be staying, so I made up the bed with fresh linens and hooked the cable and phone back up, too."

"Pastor, I cannot thank you enough. I can pay you for the room."

"Nonsense. I will need help now and then with some things around here. That's how you can repay me."

"You got it, Pastor, thank you so much." Pastor Dan left me to get settled, and I noticed that he had placed a brand-new bible on my nightstand. Perhaps I was right, that this was all supposed to happen this way.

Chapter Twenty-Five

Stella

Brie and I arrived at Piney's Bar right at 7:00 p.m. After that second glass of wine back at my place, Brie started to relax and enjoy herself. I spotted Cap and Joe and Margie and G already at some high-top tables they had pulled together. The place was pretty packed. If I had to bet, I would say Margie got here an hour ago to get those tables. I noticed right away that G looked delicious in a pair of fitted blue jeans and a button down, light pink shirt. He was smiling ear to ear when he saw us. We made our way through the masses, and I introduced Brie to everyone. I noticed G look her up and down a few times and then made eye contact with me. Not sure if he did that more for my benefit, but I admit I felt the ugly green monster stir just a bit inside of me. I had not thought about the potential of G and Brie being attracted to each other. However, I had known Brie forever, and I would have known in an instant if she liked him. She probably assumed that I have already repeated my injurious behavior, the behavior that landed me here.

Joe instinctively jumped from his chair and gave Brie a big hug. "Brie, you are gorgeous baby, just gorgeous." Brie immediately turned bright red and looked to me for help. She always hated being the center of attention. Cap could see Brie was embarrassed and jumped in.

"Okay, Joe, remember what team it is that you bat for, honey." We all laughed like hell. Margie then announced that she had ordered wings, nachos, clams, and mozzarella sticks for everyone to munch on as she motioned for the server to come over for drink orders. Margie asked Brie to play a round of pool with her, and Brie gracefully accepted.

Joe jumped up and said "Oh, oh, me too, gals, me too," and off they went into the next room where the pool tables and dart boards were. I had not expected to have an opportunity to be alone with G and Cap, but I decided to take advantage of it.

"Listen, guys, I need to talk to you very quickly about something serious that must remain between us, okay?"

They both nodded in agreement, both looking concerned.

"Cap, G knows a bit about this situation, but I need you both to know. Brie works in Philly and has a successful career at a marketing firm. For some time now, she has dealt with a boss, who despite being way too old for her, sexually harasses her and is escalating to violence."

G held his hand up, "Stella, what do you mean violence?"

I explained to them what Brie had told me about Will Bayo threatening and cornering her and about the stranger who handled it.

"Jesus, Stella, why the hell hasn't she called the police," Cap asked.

"It's not that simple. He threatened to blackball her in the industry and make certain the board of trustees thinks she is mentally unbalanced." He opened his mouth to speak, but I held up my hand. "Wait, let me finish before she comes back. I don't know if it's the enormous stress, fear, anxiety, whatever, or her mind playing tricks on her, but Brie swears he followed her to my house from Philly in a black Ford Explorer."

G was visibly pissed off. "Are you fucking kidding me? Let's go find the son of a bitch."

"Guys, please play it cool. I do not, cannot, let Brie know that I have confided in you two. She is mortified enough. Please let's handle this between us. She is my best friend. I can't lose her."

G put his arm around me. "Stella I'm sorry, I'm sorry. Of course, you can count on us and our confidence. I just hate men that use positions of any sort of power to take advantage of women."

Cap said, "Stella, we are in, and this stays between us, but I am going to call in to Volpe and Garguilo, who are on duty tonight, and tell them that someone at the bar told me that a black Ford Explorer kept driving by their home, and it's making them nervous. Is that okay?"

"Yes, yes, thank you."

"Wait, this guy knows where you live, right?" G asked.

"Yes, if he really did follow her, then he saw her pull into my driveway."

G shook his head. "Then, you two can't stay there—"

Cap cleared his throat loudly and just in time for G and I to see the gang coming back from the pool tables.

"That was quick," I said.

Margie waved her hands in her usual dramatic fashion. "Oh, they have a marathon game going on back there. The guys playing promised to come by and get us when it's our turn."

Cap excused himself and said that he needed to step outside to check in with the on-duty crew. I knew what that meant and felt relieved and grateful.

I looked across the bar at my best friend laughing and flirting adorably with the bartender, who, by the way, was very handsome, and very into Brie. He must be on a break because he and Brie had tucked themselves into a small corner booth and looked deep in conversation. I was pretty sure she gave him her phone number. She looked extremely happy. It made me feel really good to see her enjoying herself. I truly was a blessed and grateful gal in this moment. I was lucky to have people like this in my life. G and I exchanged a few lingering glances at each other throughout the evening, the kind that gave me a flutter in my stomach, and the kind that were a dead giveaway to anyone paying attention. Luckily, everyone was feeling carefree after a few drinks and involved in their own conversations. Would it really be that awful if G and I's relationship became more than just partners, more than just friends? Aside from working together, neither of us were married or even involved with anyone else, and as far as I knew, Cap didn't have any rules against dating coworkers, or at least he never mentioned it. I guess we would just have to see what happened and where this went. Only time would tell.

Around midnight, Brie was feeling no pain at all. She needed a night like this, and I knew in advance that I would be the designated driver. It was the least I could do. Brie and Margie were deep in conversation when Cap asked me and G to walk him and Joe out. Cap had a look of concern on his face. We stood in the parking lot under the streetlight. The humidity, despite the late hour, still had not let up, and the bats were diving left and right at the enormous insects buzzing just above us.

"Cap, what is going on," G asked.

"Volpe and Garguilo reported back to say that prior to receiving my information, they actually did spot a black Explorer parked on 563, not far from the entrance to Batsto Village. They pulled up beside the driver to see if he needed assistance. Volpe described the driver as male, in his sixties, and impeccably dressed. The driver informed them that he had pulled over to take a call and that he was fine. Once they got my call about the Explorer, they circled back, but the car was nowhere to be found."

I shook my head. "This is unbelievable. That monster really did follow her down here."

"Stella, we aren't certain of that yet, but nonetheless, I want G to follow you home, just to be safe. And please call me the second anything seems off, and I mean it, Stella!" Cap's tone was both stern and fatherly.

I did not want to worry Brie, so I told G to follow me but to let me get Brie inside and to bed before he came up. She was pretty intoxicated, but I did not want to take a chance of freaking her out while she was drunk. That was no fun to manage at all. I went back inside and got Brie. We had all thrown money in toward the bill, and Margie had just finished paying the tab. We all said our goodnights and headed home. I could see G's headlights quite a distance behind me, but aside from that, the roads were empty. Brie fell asleep, which made me happy. Hopefully, she didn't get a second wind when we got home. Looking at her next to me sound asleep, unaware of the fact that her stalker could very well be near, my heart just broke for her. She looked so peaceful. I started to tear up, but my moment of sadness quickly turned to anger at the man who dared to treat this beautiful, giving, genuine human being like a piece of property. A flurry of thoughts fluttered in my mind. *Maybe I pay his wife a visit? Maybe I pay him a visit? Maybe I shoot him between the eyes? Problem solved for good!*

I looked back in my rearview mirror as I slowly pulled in my driveway. G had pulled over behind me about 100 yards from my house and turned his lights off.

"Brie! Brie, sweetie, let's go inside and get you to bed. We're home."

I was both surprised and thankful at how easy it was to wake her up. She never said a word. We walked inside, and I guided her to the bedroom. She sat on the bed, took everything off except her underwear, rolled on her side, and she was out. I threw a blanket over her, turned out the light, and then turned it back on. Although my closet was small, it could still hide a pervert. No pervert in the closet. I made certain the window was locked, and I pulled the shade all the way down. I turned the lights out again and closed the door behind me.

I opened the front door and walked toward G's car. He was outside of his car and walking toward me. "Let's do a perimeter check together. I already drove around

Mr. Avery's store and down the road about a mile to be certain the Explorer was not in the vicinity." We walked around the property twice. Nothing but darkness, a warm breeze, and a shit ton of bugs.

"I really appreciate you doing this. I know you must be tired and eager to go home. We will be fine. I'll lock up the house and sleep with my gun. This guy is in his sixties. He should be the one who is worried."

G laughed, "Yeah this is true. Officer Stella is on the job tonight."

I hugged him and whispered thank you in his ear. It felt wonderful to be in his arms. He pulled his head back, looked me in the eyes, and then pressed his soft lips against mine. His tongue slowly made his way inside my mouth, and I pulled him closer. He kissed me with such tenderness and passion as he stoked my hair. He paused for a minute.

"By the way, you look incredible tonight, and I've wanted to do this all night."

We were again locked in a kiss that I didn't want to end, ever. So many physical sensations that I had not experienced in a long while filled my mind and body. I pulled away slowly, kissed him on the cheek and said goodnight. He was slow to release my hand from his as I began to back away, heading to my front door. God, he was so beautiful. I wanted him, all of him, now. He smiled as if he could read my thoughts and slowly walked backward toward his car, still watching me.

"Officer Stella, I think I love you."

Chapter Twenty-Six

McIntyre

I hated calling Stella this early on a Monday morning, but I needed to speak with her now. Stella picked up on the second ring.

"Hey, McIntyre, how was your weekend?"

"Fabulously boring, just the way I like it. I'm waiting for the coroner's report on the Jane Does we uncovered at the farm, but that's not why I am calling you."

"This sounds serious. What's going on?"

"Stella, last night a couple of troopers found an abandoned car parked just off the road near Lake Oswego. The vehicle was unlocked, no sign of the driver, and no identification recovered. The vehicle is a rental, but we haven't been able to get anyone from the rental agency on the phone as of this morning, bankers' hours, I guess. Here is the strange part. On the passenger seat of the car was a yellow post-it note with your name and address on it."

"Was it a black Ford Explorer?"

"Yes… how did you know? Whose car is it, Stella?"

"Can you meet me at my house as soon as you can get here, please? Obviously, you have the address."

"Okay, on my way now. See you soon." I couldn't wrap my head around what the possible connection could be and why my news hadn't shocked and horrified her.

Stella was sitting on her little front porch when I pulled up to her place. She was wearing shorts and a tank top, and her hair hung softly over her shoulders. I noticed for the first time just how beautiful she actually was without the manly cop uniform. I did not think she will have any problems finding her 'forever after' like I did. I tossed my phone and radio on the passenger seat and took a seat next to her.

"Okay, McIntyre, what I am about to tell you will sound like a bad after school movie on one of those sappy networks. "My best friend Brie, who I lived with in Philly, still lives and works in Philly and spent the weekend with me. We had an amazing time drinking too much, eating, talking, walking the trails, but I digress… Brie works for a super high-end marketing firm in Philly. Her boss, Will Bayo, is old, horribly unattractive, narcissistic, degrading, pathetic, perverted, aggressive, a sexual harasser, a liar, and all-around volatile. Concisely, he is a *dark triad*!" McIntyre grinned and nodded his head. Everyone in law enforcement new the term. "He threatened Brie's job and promised to destroy her reputation in the industry if she told anyone about the endless sexual harassment he has violated her with for far too long. He became physical last week with her. Trapped her in a corner inside her building's lobby after hours when everyone had gone home. She was beyond terrified. He was steadily escalating but suddenly leapt off the deep end of reality, it seemed. Brie was certain he was going to rape or kill her. Thank God, a stranger witnessed this from outside on the sidewalk and quickly came to her defense. The guy beat the hell out of the asshole. Brie did not report this, nor did she call anyone to come help Bayo. She hasn't told anyone but me. Apparently, Bayo was so beat up that he had to take extended time off from his position in the company. Brie was fairly certain that he had followed her from Philly to my house on Friday in a black Explorer. A similar Explorer was seen by my coworkers, pulled over on the side of the road, driven by an older, well-dressed man."

Wow, I was blown away. I didn't see that coming. "Stella, yes, as I said, the vehicle we found was a black Explorer, but the driver is missing. Did you let anyone else know about this?"

"Yes, my captain and my partner. My partner followed

Brie and I home from the bar Friday and did a perimeter check. He waited in his car, lights off, down the street for about an hour before he headed home himself."

"What do you think happened to him?"

"I have no clue, but I hope he stopped on the side of the road to pee and was eaten by a pack of wild animals, the Jersey Devil, killed by the mob. But really, any horrible, painful demise would do."

"I get why you feel that way. He sounds like a disgrace of a human being. Let me try the rental agency again. They should be open now."

"I'll go in and grab us some waters. Hot as hell again, but what else is new here?"

The woman at the rental agency quickly confirmed that the license and credit card provided were those of Will Bayo. He really had followed her here from Philly, possibly to inflict bodily harm. Stella stepped back out on the porch just as I was thanking the agent and providing her with my phone number and email to forward a copy of the license and credit card to. I assured her that the car had been impounded by the state police and would be returned post investigation. She was not too happy about that, but she understood.

Stella looked completely stunned. "Oh my God, it was him, wasn't it? It isn't that I doubted Brie, but she was so stressed and so overwhelmed by him that I thought, well, I thought she may have imagined it. Jesus, McIntyre, he may have been looking for an opportunity to kill her, run her off the road, maybe…"

"Stella, listen to me. You cannot say anything about this. Brie cannot know. Think about it, she may very well have been one of the last people to see him alive, worst-case scenario."

"I know, I know, but I hate keeping this from her. She is my best friend and has been living in fear of this maniac too long as it is. What's next?"

"I am heading to my office. I'll pull his information and his cell records. Maybe we can get a location from that. Is he married?"

"Yes, the pig has a wife."

"Okay, then I'll get her info as well. I promise I will call you later. Just remember, for her own good, do not call Brie."

Stella nodded in agreement, but the look on her face told me she didn't like it.

It took under an hour to get the info I requested from our tech nerds. Bayo's cell phone was off but last pinged at the location in which the Explorer was discovered. This meant either he voluntarily turned his phone off, he was forced to turn his phone off, or something bad happened to this man. I left a message for his wife, Bonnie, to call me. As I headed back to the spot where the Explorer sat unoccupied, my phone rang with her call. I anticipated a very hysterical and confused woman on the other end of the line anxiously awaiting my hello. Surprisingly, I found quite the opposite. I explained to her that we found a vehicle rented by her husband, Will, in the Pine Barrens section of New Jersey, but that we were unable to actually locate him. She calmly proceeded to inform me that she had no idea why he would be there or why he would have rented an alternative vehicle. She further, and without emotion, explained that she and Mr. Bayo have been separated for over six months, divorce pending, and that she is currently living in Boca Raton with her sister. She advised that she has not spoken to Will in at least a month.

Wow, this woman obviously didn't care whether this guy was alive or not. Perhaps he was in fact the pig Brie claimed him to be. I told Bonnie that I would keep her posted. "If you feel the need to, sure. If not, that's fine as well," and with that she ended the call.

My cell buzzed again, and this time it was Kevin Johnson. This should be interesting. "Hey, buddy, what's the good news?"

"Not sure if its good news, but we just completed the area search with the imaging equipment, and we found the remains of eleven more females, and one additional male, all badly decomposed. It appears that these victims have been deceased for many years, but I'll know more when our coroner gets here. You understand that at this point FBI must take the lead? Obviously, this is a serial killer situation, my friend."

I couldn't grasp what he was saying, not fully. Fourteen bodies in total? This was completely insane. Was Jacobs a serial killer who finally got what was coming to him? But by whom? My head was swirling. Johnson asked again if I understood that the FBI must take over, and I was able to put the words together finally.

"I understand, Johnson, but please keep me in the loop, let me help you out. I am working on a sort of mystery myself. We have a missing man, abandoned car, a wife that doesn't care, and a fellow officer who is the best friend of the woman that this guy has been sexually harassing in the workplace."

"Anything I can do to help, McIntyre?"

"Yes, keep your eyes peeled for a pathetically ugly, perverted, old guy wandering Pine Barrens please."

Johnson laughed, "Well, you will have to be more specific. You just described a pretty significant percentage of the population in these parts."

Unfortunately, Kevin was right, but I just needed one old, ugly, perverted guy in this area. The Explorer had been impounded, but I decided to go take a look around the area in which it was discovered anyway. The boys had left a marker with caution tape to identify the possible crime scene. There was no blood, no evidence of a struggle,

and no sign of this character. I walked toward the

wooded area next to the marker. It was an area not easily maneuvered. The thick brush consisted of weeds and large thorny bushes that looked extremely unpleasant. There was no evidence that anyone had walked through here. I walked a bit longer parallel to the overgrown terrain until something shiny caught my eye. Damn it, now I had to make my way through this crap. I was wearing jeans and hoped it would help.

Four feet in, I pulled latex gloves out of my pocket and picked up a cell phone. *Talk about needle in a haystack. Maybe I should stop on my way home and buy lottery tickets, too.* The phone was completely dead. I just hoped that this was actually Bayo's phone. After all, dreadful things had happened in the barrens, a historical fact. .

Next stop, headquarters to drop this phone off to the lab for prints and trace evidence and then over to the techs again for any digital evidence. I missed the days of just pressing *69 on a home phone to see who a suspect last talked to or simply calling the phone company, actually having someone answer, and requesting phone records, which was precisely why I needed to retire. Everything had changed, most of which was not for the better.

Chapter Twenty-Seven

Augustus

I awoke the next morning before sunrise to the sound of loud, thundering skies. Rain pelted angrily at my windows, and every few minutes, a bolt of lightning lit up the world outside. A fierce storm, indeed. I wondered if this was God's way of cleansing this city from the sins of the night before. I imagined the beautiful cross standing guard, protecting the church and all who worshipped here. Nevertheless, I wasn't wandering off to continue my sightseeing adventures until the storm had passed. It was early, not even 6:00 a.m., but with the time difference, Mother should answer my call. She picked up the phone immediately.

"Augustus, Augustus, is that you?"

"Yes, it's me, Mother. I am fine, please stop crying. Really, I am okay, but I wanted you to know that I had a change of heart."

"What do you mean?"

"Well, I decided not to join the military, after all. I am in Philadelphia, and I found a beautiful church with a pastor that had a room for me, at no charge. He refused to take money. Instead, he asked that I give him a hand around the church when he needs physical jobs done. He is a wonderfully warm and caring man. I think I am going to be happy here for a while until I save up enough money to get my own place. I am going to look for work this week."

"Augustus, Philadelphia is a big city. A scary place where someone like you could easily get lost or be taken advantage of, or worse."

"No worries, Mom. I can handle myself, and I am well aware of the evils of city life, but it is also a beautiful city. One with a rich, fascinating history, museums, parks, churches, schools, and opportunity. I want to see it all, all of it. I promise that I will be careful and smart. After all, I managed to survive my childhood, right?"

"Yes, you did, and you are right. You are a strong, smart young man with honorable morals and values. I love you, Augustus!"

"And I love you. I will call again soon."

I decided to rest some more. I surely wasn't going anywhere until the rain stopped. Besides, I was exhausted, mentally and physically.

A loud knock at my door shot me to my feet. For a brief moment, I wasn't sure if I really heard it, but then I heard Pastor Dan.

"Augustus, are you okay?"

I was relieved to hear his voice. I must have been in the deepest possible sleep, which meant I was rested and refreshed. I opened the door and told Pastor to come in. I explained how I had fallen back to sleep after awaking to the storm.

"Well, you must have been exhausted. I started to worry when noon rolled around, and you still had not come downstairs."

"Wow, noon, really? I don't think that I have ever slept that long or deep. Oh, and look the sun is out again."

"I was wondering if you had plans today?"

"No, no plans yet."

"Okay, would you like to accompany me on a bit of a road trip?"

"Sure, of course, where to?"

"Scarlett's parents have asked that I meet them at the spot in which Scarlett's body was discovered to pray for her soul and ask God to forgive her."

"Of course, I will go with you. Where is this place?"

"Southern New Jersey, in the area of Pine Barrens."

My heart jumped into my throat. *Of all the places in the world, she had to have been discovered there?* Truth be told, I had not planned on ever going back there, but now I had no choice in the matter. Only God knew the sin of Mother and I, and I wanted to keep it that way. But Pastor Dan needed me, and I wanted to be there for him and for Scarlett's family.

It turned out to be a truly magnificent day. The rain had hindered the crippling humidity, and the air was fresh and pleasant. The view as we drove over the Ben Franklin Bridge was absolutely breathtaking. Pastor and I chatted the entire ride. I did most of the talking. I told him all about Germany and my time with Hans, how friendly and personable people were. We were on Route 70 in New Jersey, and the traffic was light for such a beautiful day.

"We should arrive soon, Augustus. If I'm not mistaken, the next right is Route 563, and poor Scarlett was discovered about 12 miles in. I did some research and found that Route 563 is actually 43 miles long and named one of the most beautiful, scenic drives in New Jersey, especially in the fall. Unfortunately, it is also a burial ground to many unknown and undiscovered souls. I thank the good Lord that Scarlett's parents will at least have the opportunity to provide their daughter a proper burial." I nodded in agreement.

Despite spending my childhood in this area, nothing

looked familiar to me. Not surprising, after all, it wasn't like I had consistently travelled these roads to school, friends' houses, or stores as a kid. No, Mother and I were not permitted to leave our property, unless with my father, and even that was a rare occasion. My old house could be a mile from here or ten miles. It would take some research on my part. I did wonder what ever happened to the property. Was Hector and his family still there? Was it still a thriving blueberry farm? Had anyone unearthed the sinister secrets of my father?

I admitted I was curious for answers, but not today. Today was not about me and my demons. No, this was about Scarlett and her family. Boy, the scenery was incredibly green. The tall trees that seemed to brush the clouds reminded me of the trees that surrounded our farm, as if keeping guard, and the state of seclusion they provided. We passed a few cranberry bogs, two campgrounds, a lake, and a canoe rental business when Pastor cleared his throat.

"I think we are here."

I had been deep in my own memories, not realizing the distance we had travelled on Route 563. Just up ahead on the right, cars had pulled off the road onto the sandy, weed spotted terrain. Scarlett's parents were standing with another couple. We parked as well. We approached the group, and Pastor made the introductions. The other couple was Scarlett's aunt and uncle. I didn't know what to say to her parents, so I just nodded and smiled.

Pastor Dan asked that we form a small circle with hands held and spoke. "*Matthew 5:4, Blessed are those who mourn, for they will be comforted. Psalm 23, The LORD is my shepherd, I shall not be in want. He makes me lie down in green pastures, he leads me beside quiet waters, He restores my soul. He guides me in paths of righteousness, for his name's sake. Even though I walk through the valley of the shadow of death, I will fear no evil, for you are with me; your rod and your staff, they comfort me. You prepare a table before me in the presence of my enemies. You anoint my head with oil, my cup overflows. Surely goodness and love will follow me all the days of my life, and I will dwell in the house of the LORD forever. Amen.*"

Scarlett's mother was sobbing hysterically, and large tears welled in her father's eyes as he held her tightly to him. Pastor Dan bowed his head again, as did we, and he began to speak again in a soothing tone that I believed only the true messengers of God were blessed with. He spoke of Scarlett, the child of God who had lost her way in this troubling world. He asked forgiveness for her and for comfort for her family. His words were beautiful. His sorrow genuine. We didn't speak much on our way home. I suspected Pastor was emotionally drained.

Chapter Twenty-Eight

Stella

As soon as we heard Cap coming through the door, and Margie's cheerful, high pitch greeting, G and I bolted toward him. G got to him first and like an excited child said, "Stella and I have to talk to you in your office."

Cap replied, "My goodness, is something on fire? You two look like you've both seen the same ghost. Okay, okay, follow me."

I shut the door behind us, and we all sat. "Cap, a friend of mine, McIntyre, that I met over at the state park during that body discovery, stopped by my house. He is a sergeant with the state police, and he informed me that a black Ford Explorer was found abandoned by one of his patrol officers. This is the really odd part. The vehicle was found unoccupied, no identification, no signs of a struggle, but what they did find was a note with my name and address on it."

"Please tell me that they know who the registered owner is and that it's not Brie's boss," Cap said.

"I wish I could, trust me. It was a rental, and the agency confirmed that it was by Will Bayo."

Cap shook his head. "Well, it sounds like we have some investigating to do."

My cell rang. "It's Brie," I announced.

"Answer it, Stel," G said, so I did.

"Stella, it's me. Something weird is going on. The receptionist, Sue, just told me that Will is missing. Apparently, his wife called this morning and told Sue, who she has always been friendly with, that the police found his car but not him. Do you know anything about this? I also got an email from the board chair advising me that I was needed at an emergency meeting tonight."

"Wow, Brie. Let me do some digging and see what I can find out. I will call you later. Love you." God lying to her felt like I was ripping my own heart out, but for her own good, I had no choice.

Once again, my phone rang, and this time it was McIntyre.

"Update. Mrs. Bayo could care less that her husband is missing. They are in the process of finalizing their divorce. Also, found a cell phone close to where the Explorer was left. Techs confirm it belongs to Bayo."

"Okay well where the hell is he?"

"I wish I knew. Think about the possibilities, though. He could have staged his own disappearance, met an untimely demise, wandered off in the dark and gotten lost, or succumbed to wild animals. Really, Stella, the possibilities are endless."

"Well, that is what scares me, McIntyre. What if this is all staged, and he plans on returning to the city to harm Brie?"

"Highly unlikely, but I understood your concern. I think we have no choice but to loop Brie in and provide security while at work and at home. You speak with Brie, and I will handle the rest."

"Thanks, McIntyre."

I decided to wait a bit before I called Brie. I knew she was in her office and safe, at least until after her meeting tonight. McIntyre would make certain she was protected thereafter. G and I decided to head out to 563 to see if we could locate our missing unwanted visitor. G was pretty quiet as we drove. He seemed a million miles away, and I wondered what or who he was thinking about. It wasn't uncomfortable silence, just unusual silence, but I left him to his thoughts. Route 563 was pretty quiet. Most of the weekend camping crowd headed back home on Sunday afternoons, which meant most of the tourist spots and activities were relatively quiet.

"Do you think if anyone killed him and buried him somewhere out here off of 563, he would ever be found?" G asked in a serious tone.

"Is that what you have been deep in thought over?"

"Yes, I am just thinking that if no one finds him, he is probably dead, right? But on the other hand, if no one finds him, Brie will never have peace of mind."

His thoughts were accurate, but his demeanor was different. His words seemed cold, harsh. "Unfortunately, you are right. She will be looking over her shoulder for the rest of her life, and I don't think she could handle it. It would destroy her."

G noticed the tear that, despite my best efforts, had escaped from my eye and dropped onto my cheek. He ever so gently wiped it away with his thumb. He took my hand in his and kissed it with such compassion and tenderness, and I thought it was this exact moment when I realized that I was falling in love with him. He held my hand a few seconds longer before letting go.

"It's going to be okay, Stella. I promise."

"I really want to believe that, G."

Chapter Twenty-Nine

McIntyre

It had only been a couple of days since I last spoke to Johnson, so when I saw that he had called while I was in the shower, I knew it must be important. I didn't even listen to the voicemail he left. Kevin picked up on the first ring.

"McIntyre, you aren't going to like this, but I think our cases just became linked."

"Not sure what you mean, Johnson?"

"I got a call late last night from one of my agents assigned to the Jacobs property. He informed me that he was investigating suspicious activity."

"What the hell does that mean?"

"You remember when you and I were out there and we found evidence that someone had been in the barn and thought we saw someone running in the tree line, right?"

"Yes, I do."

"Well, the agent noticed the glow of a light along the tree line near the same barn last night. He identified himself and ordered the trespasser to stop, but the light went out, and whoever it was took off back through the woods. I have guys out there now looking for any evidence that may have been left. However, that isn't the bombshell. Whoever was out there with the flashlight left us a package. He left us the dead body of your sexual harasser. Fingerprints confirm the deceased is Will Bayo."

"Are you absolutely certain? How? Shit. Cause of death?"

"Someone beat this guy to death. Coroner's preliminary exam shows he sustained multiple blunt force trauma injuries to the head and body. Coroner is still counting broken bones. Oh, and one notable thing, his penis was removed, cut clean off, which indicates this was personal."

Before I could even form a sentence, Johnson said he had to take a call coming through, but he would call me later. I sat on the edge of the bed trying to absorb everything I just heard. I had a sick feeling in the pit of my stomach. Stella. Could she have done this? No! No way, she wouldn't, and besides if she did, she wouldn't have dropped him out at the Jacob's place, but whoever did murder Bayo knew about the pervert's history. Removing genitals is a clear indicator that this was a very personal revenge.

I decided to take a ride out to the Jacobs property. I didn't know what I was looking for, but my gut told me that I should start there. I thought about calling Bayo's wife, but despite my curiosity as to her reaction to the news, I decided to leave that task to the Feds. I thought about calling Stella but decided to wait until I was on my way back home. I needed a clear head right now. This was a bizarre twist that no one could have anticipated, other than the killer.

An agent was parked at the end of the driveway. I flashed my badge quickly, and he motioned me through. Several agents had parked near the old farmhouse and looked pretty deep in conversation. At the tree line, crime scene investigators dressed in white coveralls were looking for anything that may help identify the killer. I recognized one of the agents and made my way over to the huddle.

"Hey, Adam, how are you? It's been a long time."

Adam Womack and I went way back. He was my first partner on the force. We rode together for quite a few years. Great guy. Great cop. Although I was proud of him, I was bummed when he left to work for the FBI.

"McIntyre, you're still on the job, too, huh?"

"Six more months, and I'm out."

"You're shitting me. Me too, man. End of this year, and I become an official pension collecting, golf playing, old timer." We both laughed, and he gave me a big hug. "You looking for Johnson? I hear this case and yours just became one and the same."

"Yes, that's exactly what Kevin told me this morning. Anything new since then?"

"Crime scene techs have been out here for about two hours, but so far, nothing. Except mangled footprints due to the muddy conditions. Rained out here last night, so nothing useable unfortunately. I will say, though, that in my opinion this unsub is no stranger to this area. These woods are thick, dark, and dangerous. As you know, people get lost in Pine Barrens, and sometimes they stay that way. Not this guy. He carried a body from somewhere and was able to escape into the pitch-black night."

"I agree, makes perfect sense, but why carry the body here? Unless…"

"Unless what?"

"Unless finding the body was exactly what he needed us to do."

On the way home, I decided to update Stella. She answered on the first ring.

"Stella, you busy?"

"Nope, I'm home, getting ready for my meeting tonight with the Cranberry Festival Committee. Don't ask!"

I chuckled. "Okay, okay I won't ask for now."

"So, what's up? Anything new?"

"Well, you could say that yes. Bayo is dead."

Total silence, crickets. I gave her a few seconds to take the news in and then I repeated myself. "Stella, did you hear me? Bayo is dead."

"Jesus, you might have prepared me before you drop a missile like that on me. How did he die? Where?"

Body was found out at the Jacobs property. He was beaten to death, and brace yourself, Stella. His penis was removed."

"Are you serious? That screams personal to me, but who? Who did it?"

"No suspects yet. FBI noticed a flashlight in the tree line past the barn last night, but by the time they got to the spot, the perp had taken off and left the body of Bayo."

"Well, obviously, he knows about the investigation at the Jacobs place. Why else would he bring the body there? He could have buried it anywhere never to be found again."

"Agreed, thought process is that this guy knows this area very well. At least that's something, but unfortunately, it's the only something we've got right now."

Chapter Thirty

Augustus

Saturday night service, and church was packed with Pastor Dan's faithful worshipers. The musicians at the front of the church were incredibly talented. Everyone was clapping, singing loudly, and praising the Lord. The vibe was so positive, so uplifting. I had never attended a Baptist service before. In Germany, we attended a Catholic church, but I never understood anything that the priest said. Tonight, I was totally overcome with emotion. I was not sure why, but tears rolled steadily from my eyes. Not really tears of sadness or loss, though. No, these were tears of gratefulness and joy. The congregation settled down, and Pastor Dan asked that we all be seated. He led us in prayer. His voice and his words so genuine and full of love and hope. He spoke of Jesus and his followers. He taught us about the disciples and their importance in the mission that God had commanded. For a solid hour, I hung on Pastor's every word. He didn't just read from the bible. No, he explained every verse to us in his own words. The service ended, and I found myself disappointed that it had. A crowd had formed around Pastor near the front exit. All wishing to shake his hand or to speak with him. I decided to slip out the door around the crowd and take a walk. I really would like to find a job soon.

The air felt a bit cooler tonight, even though the sun was still an hour from disappearing for the day. It was a pleasant change from the stifling heat that showed no mercy the past month or so. I grabbed a newspaper and a coffee at the corner market and headed for the library that I had passed on my last outing. It was only a few minutes from the church, and I wanted to read the paper and look at the local online postings for jobs. The library was pretty much a ghost town, except for a few stragglers here and there. The room with the computers was completely empty, so I grabbed a chair and Googled jobs near me. The search quickly popped a total of 1,612 help wanted opportunities in Philly and the surrounding areas. *God, that's incredible,* I thought, until I started scrolling and realized many of them seemed like scams or money for flesh opportunities. There were quite a few postings from the Philadelphia Police Department looking for new academy recruits, no college degree necessary. Not surprising, the thought of policing this city was terrifying to say the least. Between the shootings, the prostitutes, and the drug pushers, the police were fighting a losing battle and risking their lives doing it. I admitted that the thought of a career in law enforcement did pique my interest, but certainly not here, not now. I decided to search security career opportunities instead. Results showed 636 opportunities near me. I jotted down the contact information from a few postings that looked promising on the newspaper that I had brought with me and logged out. The smell of this old library was starting to give me a headache. Who knew books could smell like a locker room?

Outside, the streets were busy with people enjoying the cooler temperatures. My stomach started to growl, and I realized that I had not eaten yet today. A beer and a burger would be perfect. I remembered passing a bar the last time I walked around exploring with a decent bar food menu called Hannah's. I was getting rather good at maneuvering the streets of Philly, and within twenty minutes, I was sitting at a high-top table at Hannah's. The server, who was absolutely gorgeous, came right over with a menu and a stunning smile. Her eyes were so green, so pretty, and I found myself staring. She must have noticed too because she turned bright red.

"I am so sorry. I don't mean to stare, but you have the most beautiful green eyes. I am sure you hear that all the time, right?"

She laughed and shook her head. "No, actually I don't, but thank you for noticing. I'm Lilly, what can I get you?"

"Hi, Lilly, I'm Augustus. It's nice to meet you. I'll take a cheeseburger, well done, with an order of fries and a bud light, please."

She smiled and nodded. "You got it, Augustus; I'll be right back."

I made it a point not to watch her walk away. I didn't want to seem aggressive or desperate. She sure was pretty, though. I never had a girlfriend before. Then again, my best friends were my mom, Hans, and a Baptist pastor. I chuckled to myself and thought, *Sad Augustus, really sad.*

Lilly came back quickly with my beer. "Your burger will be right up. You live around here?"

"Not too far. What about you?"

"I am a student at Temple University, so I'm not too far from here, either. I live off campus in a super small apartment for now."

"Where are you from originally?"

"Believe it or not, Oregon."

"Wow, this is a huge change of pace for you."

She laughed and headed for a table of five that had just come in. My food came out shortly thereafter, but a different server brought it over to me. I was not sure if it was because I was starving, but the burger was excellent. Lilly came back to check on me a couple of times, and we exchanged some more small talk. I left her a really big tip, and when I was leaving, she was waiting on another table but waved and told me to come back soon.

Like someone flipped a switch, the streets were once again packed with loud party goers, prostitutes, shady vendors, and disturbing looking characters offering to get anyone high. I knew with certainty, right then and there, that I could never make this place my permanent home. I hate this seedy atmosphere. It just felt so wrong to me. I wanted no part of it.

One of the prostitutes approached me and asked me if I wanted oral sex. *Jesus,* I thought, *this is ridiculous.* I stopped dead in my tracks and looked at the girl, who was probably no older than me, dressed in a skintight short dress with most of her chest exposed, and asked her why she was doing this. She looked at me with the oddest expression, put her hand on her hip, and told me to fuck off. I watched her walk away, back to her fellow prostitutes, turn and then give me the middle finger. I guessed the streets here in Philly, in the night, really did swallow people up and then spit out a darker, addicted, immoral, soulless version of their former selves. I just couldn't watch this for the rest of my life. It was incredibly depressing to watch people throw their entire lives away for this short-lived miserable existence.

I headed back to the church with a heavy heart and a lot of life decisions to make.

Chapter Thirty-One

Stella

Brie answered on the second ring. "Hang on, Stel, let me close my office door."

My heart was in my throat worrying about Brie's reaction to the news I was about to give her. I heard her pick the phone up. "Brie, honey, listen I have something to tell you. It will be upsetting, so try to stay calm and let me talk."

Radio silence.

"Brie, Will Bayo's body was recovered last night down here in Pine Barrens. He is dead. Coroner confirmed that he was beaten to death by someone extraordinarily strong. There is one more thing. The killer removed his penis, cut it off... Brie, do you understand what I am telling you?"

After a hefty pause, Brie spoke in a calm and

contained manner. "What happened to it?"

"What happened to what, sweetie?"

"His penis, did you find it?"

"Brie!" It was actually a good question, and I didn't recall McIntyre mentioning if it was found near the body. "Why the hell do you care about that? He is dead. Someone murdered him. The state police and the FBI are handling the investigation."

"Why?" Brie asked in a snarky tone.

"Because his body was dumped at the scene of a recent crime involving numerous casualties, so that gives them jurisdiction."

"Did they call his wife yet?"

"I am not sure. That, too, would be up to the Feds. Are you alright? I didn't anticipate you handling this news with such grace. You understand that the investigators will want to speak with you, as well, because of the harassment, right?"

"Why? How the fuck would they know anything about that?"

Oh, she was pissed. She rarely dropped the f-bomb. I had no choice but to tell her everything. I explained that she was correct. Bayo had rented a car and followed her down here. He was spotted by the police at least once that night. I told her that I confided in G and Captain Jesse and about McIntyre finding the Explorer abandoned. She still hadn't uttered a word. I knew she was fuming mad at me.

"Oh, and McIntyre called his wife when he realized that he had rented the abandoned Explorer. She pretty much told him not to bother her as she was anxiously awaiting the final divorce papers while living the life in Boca."

"Maybe she hired someone to kill him, like a hit man for hire or something. Maybe she wanted the penis as proof that the job was done."

I couldn't help but giggle. She was right.

"Brie, I think you chose the wrong career path. That definitely is a possibility. Like I said, the investigation just started, but you have nothing to hide, so just tell them the truth."

"Stella, last night at the emergency board meeting, the president offered me Will's job and I accepted. Do you think that makes me look guilty?"

I told her that I didn't think so and that I had to go, but I would call her later. Truth be told, it certainly could cast suspicion on her, but Brie was no killer. Any decent investigator would realize that within two minutes of an interview with her.

I plopped down on my sofa, contemplating whether or not I should let McIntyre know that Brie had replaced Bayo at her firm but decided to wait until later. I decided to get some fresh air and some exercise. I was reaching for my sneakers when I heard tapping at my front door.

Probably Mr. Avery checking on me. I hadn't been in for coffee in a couple of days, and I was sure he got concerned. I opened the front door without peering through the peep hole. Send in the butterflies again. It was G. He was standing on my porch smiling, wearing a pair of khaki shorts, a black tank top, and his aviator sunglasses. His arms were tan, toned, and beautiful. From behind his back, he handed me a bouquet of sunflowers, which were my absolute favorite. Did I tell him that? Rarely was I speechless, but there I stood like a concrete statue.

He was still smiling when he took my hand and walked me back inside, shutting the door behind me. He took the flowers from my hands and placed them on one of my end tables. He ever so gently took my face in his hands and placed his lips on mine softly. I pulled him closer, and he slid his tongue slowly down my neck, pausing every few seconds to kiss my lips again. I ran my hands tenderly over his chest as I kissed his neck.

He whispered in my ear, "Stella, is this okay with you?"

"Yes, please don't stop."

He pulled his tank top over his head and threw it on my sofa. God, he felt so good, so warm. I could feel his hardness pulsating against me, and as much as I wanted this to last forever, I wanted to feel him inside me now. I took his hand and led him to my bedroom. I stopped in the doorway and pulled my t-shirt over my head, revealing my full breasts and my nipples, which had hardened from the sexual excitement that had eluded me for far too long. He kissed me hard and then bent to his knees in front of me. He took his time pulling off my shorts and then my pink g-string. I stood in complete nakedness before him. I could barely contain myself. I was so incredibly horny.

He started at my knees, kissing and sucking my flesh ever so slowly, climbing his way with his wet tongue toward my upper things. The sensation was enough to make me collapse, but I held tightly to his shoulders and moaned in pleasure as his mouth finally cupped and sucked the lips of my vagina. He gently laid me on the bed, caressing my nipples first between his fingers, then finally with his tongue. I didn't know how much longer I could wait, but I didn't have to.

He stood up to release his throbbing penis from his shorts, and I leaned over and ran my tongue over his belly button and toward his manhood. With that, he was on top of me, inside me, thrusting in and moaning in mutual pleasure. After a few minutes, he pulled out and flipped me easily over onto my stomach. I got to my hands and knees and moaned in ecstasy as he slid himself inside me again, and again, and again. His hands placed on my buttocks, thrusting himself in and out. Both of us moaning in the overwhelming pleasure, my body shaking as I orgasmed in perfect synchrony with him. As he gently pulled out from inside me, I felt the warm reward of his efforts flow onto my back. I collapsed under him and sighed loudly. My body, completely drained of energy, I rolled onto my side.

Afterward, we lay still, his arms around me as we tried to catch our breath. "Stella?"

"Still here, yes?"

"I love you."

"God, I love you, too, G."

He kissed me again, softly, and we both drifted off to sleep.

I awoke an hour later, but G was no longer beside me. I hoped that he had not left, that would really hurt. I threw my shirt, undies, and shorts on that I had tossed to the floor of my bedroom in the heat of the moment and headed for the kitchen. My front door was open, and G was sitting on the top step. I stepped outside and sat beside him. He kissed me softly on the cheek and laid his head on my shoulder. We sat quiet for a moment, and he took my hand in his.

"Stella, I love you, and I do not want to hide that from anyone. If Captain Jesse has a rule or an issue with our relationship, I will resign and find a position with a department close by. I do not want to live a lie. Life is too short. I want to let the entire world know that I am in love with the beautiful, brilliant, perfect, Officer Stella

Mack."

I squeezed his hand tightly. "G, I think that may be by far the most beautiful thing that anyone has ever said to me. I love you for being you, and I agree. I don't want to live a lie, either. I did that already, and it ended in disaster. Let's tell Cap together. I know he will understand and approve. I swear he treats me more like a daughter than an employee, and he made it clear that family comes first. Let's tell him tomorrow. Oh, but poor, poor Margie, who will she flash those boobs at now."

G took me in a headlock and tickled me until I almost peed myself. "Come on, funny girl, let's go see Mr. Avery. I'm hungry."

Chapter Thirty-Two

McIntyre

I decided to give the coroner a call to see if he had any updates. Technically, he didn't have to tell me anything, but he's been on the job longer than I'd been, and we had always had a good professional relationship. Dr. Robert Earl picked upon the second ring. He sounded like he was out of breath.

"Dr. Earl, it's Brendan McIntyre. How are you?"

"Ah, Brendan, I'm good. Suddenly very busy, but I have a suspicion that is the reason for your call."

"You always were perceptive, Doc. Yes, this case is a doozy, one I would like to see put to bed before I retire at the end of the year. Any chance you could bring me up to speed? I'm sure Johnson won't mind. We go way back."

"Well, I can tell you this: the two male victims have

been deceased at least twelve to sixteen years. The tissue is too degraded to hope for a DNA match, no chance of fingerprints, either. You already know the specifics as they pertain to the deceased Will Bayo. Preliminary exams reveal that most of the female victims were also killed well over a decade ago. I sent tissue sample to the lab. Results are pending."

"Thanks, Doc, I appreciate it."

I was about to hang up when Doc said, "Oh, oh, wait, Brendan, one more thing. Preliminarily, I can also tell you that all of the victims died from blunt force trauma."

"Good to know, interesting, Doc. Thanks again. Very much appreciated."

I had a thought, so I rang Johnson's cell. He picked up after few rings. Before he could get a word in, I unloaded my theory.

"Kev, I had a thought. What if we are looking at this all wrong? What if the unsub doesn't travel to dispose of his victims, but instead, he comes home to bury them?"

"I'm not following, McIntyre."

"Listen, we already know that someone recently spent time in that barn out there at the Jacobs farm. Twice now a so-called trespasser was spotted. What if he's not a trespasser at all? What if he considers that barn his home? What if he leaves his home, chooses a victim, and then returns to the property to bury the body?"

"Jesus, McIntyre, that's good, really good. Meet me

back out at the barn in two hours. I'll bring more crime scene techs to look for prints and biologicals inside the barn. They can print the items we found in the barn."

"I'll see you shortly." I had another revelation after I hung up with Johnson. Had Kurt Jacobs known this person living on his property? I decided to head over to Camden County Prison to have a little chat with Kurt's brother, Roy.

After about a thirty-minute wait in the tiny, hot interrogation room, a muscular black guard with a bald head led Roy Jacobs through the door and shoved him hard down into the seat across the table from me. Both the table and the chairs were bolted to the floor, and when Roy held his hands out and motioned to the guard to uncuff him, the guard laughed and squeezed his shoulder so tightly that Roy yelled out loud from the pain. Then, the guard patted him on the back, nodded to me, and gave us the room. Roy was still rubbing his shoulder when I finally spoke.

"My name is Sergeant McIntyre with the New Jersey State Police. I need to ask you some questions about your property and your brother."

Roy crossed his arms, let out a long sigh, and said, "Yeah, I know he's dead. They already told me. You gonna find out who murdered my baby brother, Mister Officer, or whatever your name is?"

"It's McIntyre, and yes, that's why we are sitting here."

He laughed and shot me a dirty look. "Fine, what do you want to know?"

"Aside from you and your brother, was anyone else living on your property?"

He scratched his greasy looking long, thin hair and grabbed his chin as if he were thinking really hard. "Well, now, let me see. Last time my baby brother came to visit he did mention that he thought we may have some squatters in one of them old barns. Said he thought he could see lights on out there, but he was always drunk so who knows. I did tell him to get his drunk ass out there and collect some damn rent if these losers were staying. Baby brother ain't too smart, ya know. I'm the one that gots all the brains in the family."

"Well, Roy, that's simply terrifying to hear."

"Oh, you're one of them funny cops, huh?"

"Just keep talking, asshole."

"Well, I told Kurt ain't nobody gets nothing for free. That's just the American way, man. We ain't been out there since before Dad died. No reason to be out there."

"Do you know if he confronted the squatter?"

"Hey, Officer, duh, you fucking listening? I just said the last time he was here, I told him what to do."

Man, I wanted to punch this moron in the throat. What a waste of creation. "I heard you, smart ass. Do you know who your brother's friends are or who he was dating?"

"Dating, ha, man, you are old, huh? He was banging that ugly chick that works at the greasy spoon in town, but I can't remember her name. Looks like a crack whore. Oh, and friends? I guess you could say his friends were whoever was belly up to the bar with him on any given night." He thought that was hysterical, so I let him cackle like a loon for a minute or so before I reached over and slapped his sore shoulder. That shut him up quickly. "What the fuck is wrong with you, man? I'm answering your stupid questions, trying to be a good citizen."

"Yeah, you're a stellar human being, Roy." I called for the guard and Roy flinched when the guard reached to get him of his seat.

I was glad to get outside again and breathe the fresh air. Temperatures and humidity weren't too awful today. I gave Jill a quick call to let her know that I wasn't in the office and to call my cell if she needed me. She was just starting her yoga class, so it was a quick conversation. I tried Stella's phone, too, but it went straight to voicemail. I got to the Jacobs farm about thirty minutes late, and Johnson was already inside the barn with the crime scene techs.

"Sorry I'm late, Kev. I made a quick stop at the prison to have a heart to heart with Roy Jacobs."

"Really? Well, did he have anything helpful to say or was he just a dick?"

"Both, actually. He confirmed that the last time his

baby brother came to visit he mentioned that he thought they had squatters living in one of the barns. Said they hadn't been out there since their father died years back. Roy also told me he sent baby brother back home with a mission to confront the squatters and get rent money if they want to live in the barn."

"Shit, he may have signed Kurt's death warrant with that order. Dumbass! Certainly, may explain why Kurt's head was bashed in. Well, the good news is that the crime scene techs have recovered several finger prints and fibers from the barn. They are heading back to the lab now. Maybe we will get lucky."

"Your lips to God's ear, Johnson. Okay, I am heading back to my office. Keep me posted please."

"You bet, McIntyre."

I was trying to wrap my head around what would connect a dirtbag like Jacobs to a Philly corporate professional like Bayo. There must be one. It was obvious that neither Stella nor Brie killed him. I guessed it was plausible that the wife could have hired someone to follow him and take him out, but that doesn't explain why his body was carried back to the Jacobs farm. The trespasser had to be the bow that tied this mystery together. Hopefully, the lab would get a hit on those prints.

Chapter Thirty-Three

Stella

G held my hand on the short walk over to Mr. Avery's place. His face lit up when he saw us walk through the door.

"Ah, hello kids, come on in. Sit anywhere you like. I'll bring some menus over." We took a corner booth, and within seconds, Mr. Avery was over with two cups of coffee and menus. "Now, don't you two forget, tonight is your first meeting with the Cranbury Festival Committee. I know they are excited that you've both agreed to join and offer your expertise." Mr. Avery left us to ring up some kids who rode their bikes over for candy.

G laughed. "Stella, did I agree to this committee?"

"Ah, well I sort of confirmed for you."

"Okay, but it will cost you." He winked at me.

"I look forward to paying that tab."

"So, what time is our meeting?"

"Seven sharp tonight."

"Well, that leaves plenty of time for us then."

"Whatever do you have in mind, sir?" I asked in the sexiest southern accent I could offer.

He reached under the table and slid his hand up my thigh. "You really have to ask?"

I didn't think I could be happier than I was right here, right now, flirting with this amazing man, who loved me. I felt truly blessed.

We took our time eating and talking. G again held my hand on the way back to my house, stopping a few times to kiss me. It just felt right.

"I'm going to jump in the shower. Try not to miss me."

I wasn't in the shower thirty seconds before the shower curtain opened, and G stepped in and under the water with me. He kissed me, circling my mouth with his tongue. His hardness pressed against my stomach, throbbing. He reached for the soap and ran his lathered hand over my wet breasts and slowly down and into me. It was incredibly sensual, orgasmic. He lifted me and pressed my back against the wall of the shower, and once again, we were thrusting in harmony and in climactic pleasure. I couldn't help but moan loudly. Never had I experienced sex like this. So erotic, yet so loving. It wasn't too long before we both exploded in the passion. He slid me down the wall slowly, licking my naval and then lightly nibbling on each nipple. My legs were like jelly. We kissed for a few minutes longer.

After we both finally agreed to get dressed, we decided to go for a walk. Perhaps do a little exploring of the trails nearby. I picked up my cell phone and noticed that I missed a call from McIntyre. I didn't want to call him with G still here, just in case he wanted to talk about the Jacobs farm victims. I gave my word to McIntyre that I would not discuss my involvement in the case with anyone. I'd call him tonight when G went back to his place after our meeting.

It was easy to see how quickly hikers could end up lost in these woods. The trail we decided to follow from my house split off in two other directions, not 500 yards into the thick woods. I took my phone out and snapped a picture of the trail in the direction we decided to head. After about a half an hour of walking and talking, G said, "It's so peaceful and green out here. I understand why people flock to this area to camp and vacation. Spending an hour out in the wilderness brings about an inner calmness that feels revitalizing. We should do this on all of our days off."

I giggled. "Okay, so, even in December when it's zero degrees and snowing?"

"Yup, as long as we get to go back to your place and bring about the heat."

"I just may take you up on that. So, I never did get a straight answer from you, what is the G short for?"

He looked at me, so I knew he heard me, but he did not respond. "Oh, look, Stella, over there. Two baby deer with their mom."

Was I reading too much into this, or was he avoiding my question? But why? I knew his last name was Wagner because it was on his uniform. I didn't know for sure, but the blatant manner in which he ignored the question seemed deliberate. *Okay, Stella, enough. You have a great guy here who loves you and is obviously majorly embarrassed by his given name. Let it go. Don't mess this up.*

I grabbed G's hand and kissed his cheek. "I think I hear waterfalls lets walk this way." After a short distance, I said to G, "See, I was right!"

"Yes, you were. These woods are filled with surprises, huh"? We were both startled and a little concerned when we heard loud laughter from just ahead.

"Hi, you two!"

Finally, just beyond a line of very thick brush, we could make out several kayakers that were waving and hollering to us as they maneuvered a tight turn before disappearing into the thick again.

"Now, that looks fun," G said.

"Oh, no, not a chance. I hate snakes and getting lost on the water. There is an exit called Alligator Ally that comes up on you quickly, and if you blink, you miss your only opportunity to get off the river close to civilization. We've had people missing for days, found by search parties Captain put together with law enforcement and locals."

"But they were eventually found, right?"

"Yes, miles and miles away. They were located but scared, dehydrated, and completely exhausted, but yes, located just the same. So, to reiterate, no kayaking."

"Deal, lets head back before we end up lost."

My cell rang just as we got back to my front porch. It was Mr. Avery. He was calling to tell me that the meeting was postponed because one of the committee members had a death in the family. I thanked him and put my phone back in my pocket. I was actually glad about the postponement, not the death of course, but I was super tired. G decided to head back to his place to do laundry and pay some bills. We were both on duty for the next three days. As much as I hated to see him go, I was anxious to call McIntyre back and check in on Brie. I kicked my sneakers off and plopped down on the sofa. I tried McIntyre first. Straight to voicemail. Brie picked up in the third ring.

"Hi, Stel, what's up?" She sounded in good spirits.

"Did anyone from law enforcement talk to you yet?"

"Yes, a couple of FBI investigators stopped at my office to ask me about Bayo. I told them everything I knew, even the sexual and physical harassment that I endured for so long. I told them I thought he followed me but that I never did see him. They seemed satisfied. It wasn't a long interview. I'm only glad it's over."

"Well, it's not over on my end. I'm waiting for a friend of mine to call me back with updates."

"On a brighter note, I had a date the other night."

"What, with who?"

"The bartender John from Piney's. He's a great guy, Stella. So sweet and polite. I really thought there was no chance in hell after I unloaded all of my problems on him at the bar in my drunken stupor that he would call, but a couple of days ago, he did. He took me to the Capital Grille. I don't even know how he was able to get a reservation. Usually, they are booked for months straight."

"That is so wonderful, Brie. I am so happy for you. You deserve to be happy. Tell me about him."

"Well, he is originally from North Jersey, never been married and no kids. He worked on Wall Street in New York and was successful in his investment firm. One day, he just decided he was done. He said he realized that his entire life focused on just making money. He had no real friends, just moochers, no real relationships, and then his mom passed away. That was it for him. He left the rat race and moved to South Jersey and bought some property. The night we saw him at the bar was his first night there. I really like him."

"Oh, I am so happy for you. I cannot wait to meet him."

"I gotta go, Stel, I have a meeting in a few minutes.

We were just about to hang up when I heard Brie say, "Wait."

"I'm still here, sweetie."

"I debated telling you this, but I feel not telling you is the same as lying to you. I saw Thomas with some girl at the Capital Grille. He was sitting just a few tables away." My heart sank. "Stel, he had the nerve to come over to my table to say hello and ask about you. I told him to go to hell."

"Then, what happened?"

"He walked back to his table, head down, and never looked our way again. I, of course, had to explain why I acted the way I did to John. I didn't want him to think I'm just a bitch. Oh, and by the way, the girl he was with, she was really ugly. Okay, gotta go, I'm late for this meeting. Love you, talk later."

Just like that, Brie was gone, and I, well. I didn't know how I felt about that news. I guessed it stung a bit to hear that Thomas has moved on already, but so had I. I was a bit pissed off that Thomas had the nerve to ask Brie about me but never the balls to find me. Lastly, I was a little shocked that Brie would divulge the specifics about the lowest time in my life to a guy she just met. He must have thought that I was total trash without even meeting me yet.

Before I could dwell on my conversation with Brie too much, McIntyre called me back. He brought me up to speed on the two cases that now seemed to be connected, but he was not exactly sure how. He told me that Roy Jacobs stated that Kurt told him that they had an uninvited squatter on the property during his last visit to the prison.

"Oh, and, Stella, the crime scene techs are back out to the barns looking for fingerprints and traces on and near the chair, the fridge, and the other items we discovered. I am beginning to think that our bad guy spent quite a bit of time in that old barn until Kurt Jacobs confronted him at the insistence of Roy. I think the unsub killed Kurt. I also think he considers that farm his home base. He goes out, kills, and returns home to bury."

"That doesn't add up. Why would he dump Kurt's body in a public place where it would certainly be found? Why not bury him on the farm?"

"Think about it. Placing his body in a public place draws any investigation to that spot and away from the farm. I told you that when I sent my guys out there to look around, they initially advised that there was nothing of suspicion to report. That would have been the end of it if you and I hadn't dug deeper."

"Okay, but what about the victims and the lack of connections?" "Too early to tell. A number the bodies have been there well over ten years, some not so long. The coroner is working on that now."

"And Bayo, how does he fit in?"

"That remains a mystery as well, but we are making progress."

"Oh, what about Bayo's wife? Is she a suspect?"

"Feds don't think so. When they called to tell her that her husband was found murdered, she replied, 'good riddance,' and hung up. If you murder someone or pay to have him murdered, you don't play it that way. You play the distraught, grieving widow."

"Yeah, I guess you're right, McIntyre. Okay, I'm on duty tomorrow, but keep me posted."

"As always, my friend."

Chapter Thirty-Four

Augustus

The walk to the train station was pretty uneventful. It was early, so the city had that nine-to-five busy vibe. The weather was perfect. Not a cloud in the sky and zero humidity. Summer was winding down, and the air was brilliantly perfect. There was a young kid with a beat-up Eagles hat on a bike selling newspapers and bottled water. I bought one of each. The train pulled up slowly and stopped in front of the little booth where tickets were sold. I took a seat in the front row and watched as a decent sized crowd continued boarding.

There were people dressed in business attire, a group of girls that looked to be in their early twenties and who appeared very hung over, and then there was a handful of guys that looked like they were up to no good. One of them in a sarcastic tone yelled, "All aboard the crack train," grabbing at his crotch as he boarded.

I made certain to avoid eye contact with him, and he kept walking until he found a seat alongside his buddies. I flipped through the newspaper I bought to the classifieds section. I had been searching for a good but cheap, used car for weeks now. Although I believed my destination today, Rogers Used Car Depot in Burlington, New Jersey, on Route 130, had exactly what I wanted, it didn't hurt to take another look at the classifieds. I didn't get much of an opportunity to look too long. Within twenty minutes of boarding, the conductor announced that our first stop, Burlington, was three minutes away.

I gathered my stuff up and prepared to get off quickly. I had no idea what sort of area I was getting off in. I didn't tell Pastor Dan where I was going because I didn't want him to worry, and I knew he was very busy preparing for his board meeting. He would have insisted on driving me, and I couldn't inconvenience him. I could see the past week or so something had been weighing heavy on his mind and in his heart. He had been spending more time than usual praying alone at the foot of alter. I, too, prayed that everything would work out for him.

The train stop in Burlington was exactly that, just a stop. There was no ticket booth, no vendors selling goods, nothing. The tracks ran alongside several large commercial buildings. I got off quickly and walked with purpose toward the highway. Luckily, it was Route 130. I walked about two miles or so before the sign came into view: Rogers Used Car Depot. There were hundreds of cars on the lot. I took my water out of the sling bag I had been carrying and drank every drop. I was now ready to pick out a car.

I knew I didn't want a truck or a van. No, I wanted a car. Nothing fancy, though. I was hoping they still had the 2011 Honda I saw online. It had 90,000 miles, no accidents, and just one previous owner. The ad said the car was selling for $6,000 without a warranty. It was a pretty substantial chunk of the money in my account, but if I were going to find a place to live and a job outside of Philly, it was a must. I wasn't looking long when a salesman came over and introduced himself.

"Hi there, my name is Brian. Can I help you find a car today"?

Two hours later, Brian handed me the keys to my black 2011 Honda, which he had filled with gas, and wished me luck. I was a bit nervous that I would be unable to purchase a car at all when Brian seemed hesitant to continue because my license was not US issued. Something I needed to work on. I was sure I could find a vendor in Philly and buy a fake license with a fictitious name. Nevertheless, the wad of cash I pulled from my bag quickly changed Brian's mind. He even helped me find insurance and pay for that up front, too.

I sat in the parking lot for a while familiarizing myself with all the distinctive features. It had a sunroof, which I absolutely loved, and a nice stereo system, too. Aside from a few scratches on the driver's door, the car was in perfect condition. It felt really good to have a car of my own. It was yet another new sense freedom for me. I no longer had to rely on Pastor Dan or public transportation for rides.

I pulled up Google maps on my phone and plugged in the address for the church. The car rode smooth. My only issue was having to constantly remind myself which side of the road I had to be on. In Germany, it was the opposite side. By the time I got back to the church parking lot, I had it mastered. I parked the car in the spot closest to the stairs that led to my room. There were several other vehicles in the parking lot that I didn't recognize. Usually, during the weekdays it was just Pastor's car here in the lot.

I decided to walk through the back door to make sure Pastor Dan was okay. I could hear loud voices, not yelling really, but raised and in firm tones. Pastor Dan was seated in the front row, and there were seven other people in the row directly behind him. It didn't take me too long to realize that it was the board of trustees for the church. I ducked into the very last row, nearest the door. I picked up the Bible next to me and pretended to read.

Pastor sounded upset. One board member, a woman,

was relentless. She wouldn't shut the hell up. She was complaining that church membership was down, as were revenues. When this annoying woman finally came up for air, Pastor Dan raised his voice.

"What the board refuses to acknowledge is that the people of this community are, for the most part, lower income, uneducated, but industrious men and women who love God and want to worship with us but cannot always contribute an offering. You must realize that it is especially difficult right now, and as you know, even in this post-recession economy, people are still trying to recoup from being unemployed. Go take a walk around the neighborhoods and count the number of businesses that were thriving just a year ago but are now boarded up for good. Lastly, as I have stated during previous meetings, if the board's goal is to attract new members from affluent communities in alternative parts of the city, they must agree to invest in upgrading the exterior of the church, as well as sections of the interior. I am willing to help, but I will not stand by and let you blame the lack of member contributions on me. Thank you for your time, and God bless you."

And with that, Pastor turned and walked toward his office. I decided to wait a bit longer, at least until after this group of crappy people left, before I went to talk to him.

Chapter Thirty-Five

McIntyre

I was in my office still trying to understand how Bayo tied into this. It just didn't make any sense. How would the unsub even know him or what he had done to Brie? Maybe her coworkers did know more than she thought. Could they have "taken care" of him on her behalf? I knew she was loved at her firm, but that was a hell of a leap to murdering for her. I closed my eyes and rubbed my forehead. *What am I missing?* A soft knock at my door broke my concentration. It was the receptionist, Careyanne.

"I'm so sorry to bother you, Sergeant McIntyre, but there is a woman here who insists on speaking with you about the Kurt Jacobs case. Her name is Sandy Brown."

"Oh, this should be interesting. Send her in please."

With that, Careyanne disappeared from my door. She

returned a few minutes later with Sandy Brown in tow.

"Thank you, Careyanne, please shut the door behind you."

"No problem, Sergeant."

There she stood, Sandy Brown, wreaking of cigarettes and chewing gum like a cow. Oh, this woman was such a train wreck, but I smiled at her and asked her to take a seat. She was wearing jeans and a t-shirt that read "Real bitches drink beer." Very classy. I asked her why she stopped by and what I could do for her.

"Get it straight, it's what I can do for you," she said in a sarcastic tone. I wanted to tell her to fuck off and get out of my office, but before I could, she continued, "I saw that guy yesterday. You know, the hottie I told you about from the night Kurt tried to kill me."

"Where did you see him?"

"Well, I was working a double at the diner, and damned, if he didn't stroll right on by and get into a dark blue… Well, I think it was blue, coulda been black, it was dark anyway, small car. Before you ask, my eyesight ain't that good, so I couldn't see the make of the car or the license plate. I do think that he was coming outta the liquor store across the street, you know, Rosie's Packaged Goods. That place been there forever."

I didn't want her to know how excited I was about this information, but it could actually be critical. I could just feel it. I stood from behind my desk and shook her hand.

I thanked her and told her to keep me posted if she saw him again.

"There some kind of reward for information leading to his capture?" She was chewing away at her fingernails when she asked.

"I will surely let you know." I opened the door to my office and out she went, mumbling under her breath like a fool, stinking of stale cigarettes. I wished I had air freshener to spray, and Lysol for that matter. I resumed my position at my desk and thought about what Sandy had just told me. I didn't believe she was lying. She wouldn't waste her time coming up here if it were bogus. So, what would this guy have been doing at the small-town liquor store? Sandy said he didn't fit in and was just passing through. Same info I got from Jimmy at the Wander Inn Bar, too. No, there was more to this story. Could this be the elusive unsub twice sited at the Jacobs property? That would explain the connection to Kurt, but not Bayo or the other bodies buried out the Jacobs farm. I was missing something. I felt it in my gut.

I was still mentally beating myself up when Kevin called.

"Hey, Brendan, it's me. So, I just heard back from the coroner. The two male victims that we uncovered are John Does. Coroner also believes that his initial estimate was incorrect. He now confirms that most of the female bodies have been buried for at least twenty years. He said that based on trauma to the vaginal cavity, as well as the uterus, these girls were sexually abused, and tests show they all have one form or another of STDs. I'm thinking they may have been prostitutes, which is why no one ever looked for them. We went back twenty years, and there were no outstanding missing women reports from that time period."

"Okay, well, I have news for you as well. Sandy Brown stopped by my office today to tell me that she saw the man who came to her rescue when Kurt smashed her face into the bar that night. Said she saw him getting into a blue or dark colored smaller car. Said he had just come out of the liquor store across from the diner she works at."

"I thought that guy was an out of towner, just passing through?"

"Apparently not, Kev."

"Oh, and lab techs ran the prints they collected from the barn. They were all from the same person, but unfortunately, he isn't in our system or any other system, so that's a dead end."

"Maybe not. Have the lab techs go to the liquor store, talk to the clerk, recover prints form the door and anywhere else the clerk remembers him touching. If this guy is as good-looking as Sandy says, the clerk will remember him. I know it's a long shot, but if we at least got prints that match the ones recovered in the barn, we will know if it is the same unsub."

"I'm heading over to the liquor store now. I will call you later, McIntyre."

I decided to head back out to the Jacobs farm. That place was the key to solving these murders. I gave Stella a call to catch her up, but it went straight to voicemail. She did say she was on duty today, and because I insisted that she not speak to anyone else about it, it may be an impossible time to talk.

I made good time getting out to the farm. Not a soul out on the roads today. The weather was more than likely to blame. Overcast, light drizzle now and then, and stifling humidity. I was looking forward to the colder weather and a vacation somewhere with Jill, maybe Ireland. The drive back to the barn was once again brutal on my car, and my spine. I was surprised to see just one undercover vehicle parked at the farm. We exchanged head nods as I drove past him. If I were calling the shots, I would make certain I had someone stationed on the tree line at all times as well, but I was not. We already knew that the unsub traveled through the woods. Woods that he was extremely acclimated with. I drove toward the tree line and parked about twenty feet back. Unless the unsub had a twisted psychological need to dispose of another body here, he would be a complete idiot to return to the farm.

I sat for a while debating on my next move. I doubted

any of the agents had been back into the woods since we last spotted our murderer, dumping the body of Will Bayo. I decided to take a look for myself. The brush was pretty thick, even for this time of year, but I made my way through the worst of it and onto a path. Nothing to see, an occasional deer or snake, but not much more than that. After walking for about forty-five minutes, the path opened up to a clearing with a dirt road leading west. I could see tire impressions in the thick sandy terrain. Someone had been here recently. The aftermath of a campfire, a plastic chair, and empty cans of Miller Lights were all that remained. Could this be how our killer traveled? By car, then by foot? I picked up one of the empty cans for Kevin to print and for possible DNA evidence. The only way I was going to know where the dirt road led was to follow it. I wasn't much prepared for a hike like this, but we needed a lead to finding out who this guy was.

The sun finally broke through the cloud cover and was bearing down on my neck. There was no tree cover on the dirt road, and I didn't want to walk through the brush. Never knew what was lurking beneath. Ahead, I spotted what appeared to be a tiny house. It was reddish, but as I got closer, I realized that it was an abandoned travel trailer that was all but destroyed. It looked as if it had been here longer than some of these tall pine trees. It gave me the creeps. I pulled out my phone to call Jill, but I had no bars, no service. The silence was deafening. Like a scene from a movie, I felt as if the world had ended and I was the only human being that remained. I would welcome a bit of civilization right now.

Not too hard to imagine mobsters back in the day driving on this exact dirt road to dispose of a body, the unfortunate result of a squabble with the wrong family. Lots of mystery surrounding these woods, lots of tall tales, too. I estimated that I walked close to four miles before I saw what appeared to be pavement ahead, a real road. The opening couldn't be more than four feet wide, meaning whoever used this road must have scratched the hell out of the paint on their car getting in and out. Standing out on the roadway, it took me just a few minutes to realize that I had absolutely no idea where I was. I was most definitely on an actual road, but at the same time, I was surrounded by thick woods on both sides.

I started walking east. I still had no signal on my phone. The heat and lack of water finally started to affect me. My head was pounding, and I felt dizzy. I sure as hell wasn't going to die here in the middle of nowhere. As I walked, it amazed me to see so many small dirt roads that there were leading into the forest. Finally, after about a half hour walking this road, my phone rang. Thank you, God, it was Kevin.

"McIntyre, where the hell are you? I am standing by

your car. My agent said you arrived here at the farm hours ago."

"Man, I have no idea how far I've walked, but I can tell you that I could pass out any time now."

"Okay just hang in there. Share your location with me on your phone, and I will come get you."

"Okay hang on, sharing now."

"Got it! Holy shit, you're all the way out on Bullytown Road, near Green Bank. I am on my way, buddy, hang in there."

I sure as hell hoped he got here soon. Well, at least Jill will be happy that I got my steps in today. Actually, I got my steps in for the next six months. I was too damn old for this, and I was going to be sore as hell tomorrow.

Chapter Thirty-Six

Stella

G and I weren't in our patrol car longer than five minutes when Margie radioed. "Hey, kids, trouble at our favorite campground. Six golf carts were stolen last night."

"On our way, Margie."

G shook his head. "How far can someone go on a golfcart?"

"Oh, you would be surprised. There are two scenarios that could play out here. Number one, the teenagers who are out roaming the campground all hours of the night were drunk, stoned, or bored, and we will find the golf carts submerged in the lake or left in the woods. Scenario number two, someone from inside the campground, with a truck, trailer, or van spent the night loading up and bringing them offsite. More than likely, they will repaint them and sell them." "Smart, beautiful, and all mine,"

G said, as he leaned over and kissed me on the cheek. "Any word from Brie? Is she okay?"

"Yes, she seems to be. She had a date recently with the bartender John from Piney's. He drove to Philly and took her to a really nice restaurant. She seems pretty smitten with him." "Smitten, huh, cute. I don't remember meeting him. I don't even remember her talking to anyone else but us, but it was so crowded in there. I couldn't take my eyes off of you. Brie could have spent time with the Jersey Devil, and I still wouldn't have known. Did you tell Brie about us?"

"I haven't had the chance. At first, I didn't want to tell her because she was going through so much drama and stress. I wanted to tell her on the phone, but she hung up quickly to head to a meeting. Oh, but before she hung up, she told me she saw my ex during her date. Apparently, he came over to the table and asked about me. She told him to go to hell."

"Hmmm, do I have anything to worry about, Stella?"

I took his hand and told him, "Thomas was my past, but you are my future. I am, however, a tad bit annoyed that Brie aired my dirty laundry to her date."

"No way, she really did? That is not cool!"

A line of travel trailers and recreational vehicles were parked near the entrance of Waving Pines Campground while the owners were inside the store registering for their campsites. It took a minute to maneuver around them before I could get through the gates. Beth was outside waiting for us. She looked terribly upset. She waved, and we pulled into a parking spot and met her under the awning of the store, sparing us the sting of the sun's incredibly brutal mid-day rays. She proceeded to tell us about the angry guests that she had been dealing with all morning. The campground was booked to capacity until the end of the month, so figuring out who did this may be damned near impossible. There were also no cameras installed anywhere except inside the store. The best we could hope for was recovery of the golf carts. I told Beth that G and I would drive through the campground and check the usual spots off road as well. I really felt bad for her. At her age, she didn't need this. Corporate life had to be looking better and better for her and her husband. Dealing with the public was never easy, especially the angry public.

G and I proceeded to drive up and down the paved streets. First up Cranbury Lane, then down Blueberry Drive, then driving over the bridge onto Jersey Devil Avenue toward the lake. No sign of the carts being driven into the lake, just people fishing, riding bikes, and headed toward the pool. After about forty-five minutes of slowly making our way around the campground, I decided to head back to the state park. It wouldn't be impossible to drive the golfcarts across a shallow part of the wading river and over to the park. No luck over there either though. I'd call Beth later and let her know. Hopefully, it was just kids that drove them into the woods as a joke.

I gave Margie a quick call to let her know we were mobile again. I pulled over to the side of road and put the cruiser in park.

"Did we stop to make out, I hope," G asked.

"Unfortunately, no, we did not. We pulled over, so you could drive today."

"Seriously? Awesome! To what do I owe this unexpected honor?" "Oh, I don't know. Let's just say you have earned my trust in more ways than one." I opened the door to trade places, but he held onto my arm and pulled me close to him. He kissed me slowly as his tongue tenderly caressed my bottom lip. I slid my hand down his chest but stopped myself from continuing further south. Neither of us would have the self-control to stop if I did that.

"You are killing me. I want to make love to you right now, Stella."

"Well, if you're a good boy and drive without incident, I can see that happening for hours later tonight."

He flashed me that sexy, naughty grin, the one that turned me on and melted my heart. I was head over heels in love with this man.

We patrolled the usual spots, the schools, the old, unnerving, psychiatric hospital, Lake Oswego, and of course, the bars. All seemed quiet today, and with just two hours left on shift, I prayed it stayed that way, too. I sent McIntyre a quick text and told him I would call him either tonight or tomorrow. Like a wrecking ball to my plans, Margie radioed to advise that once again we were needed at Waving Pines Camping Resort. This time it was a physical alteration involving several men. G hit the lights, and we were off. He was laughing now.

"What in the hell is so funny? This sucks, so close to end of shift."

"I just had this mental image of looking over at you in that seat thirty years from now, ready to break up campground fights in Pine Barrens. Think you'll still have all of your teeth?"

I just laughed and shook my head. "Keep laughing, G, ain't a dentist around these parts, not for miles and miles," I said in my best redneck voice. We were both still cracking up when we turned onto the road leading to Waving Pines. "Okay, we have to act professional now. No more laughing."

"Ten four, Officer Sexy."

Once again, Beth was standing outside the store looking completely defeated. "I am so sorry to keep bugging you. We had reports of a huge brawl back by the bath houses, but my security guards are now telling me those reports are false. Two teenagers were fooling around, wrestling and kicking at each other. I have to tell you both I am at my wits end with this place." She started to tear up.

I put my arms around her and hugged her. "Beth, it's not a problem. G and I understand the pressure you are under. Always call if you need our help. It is the end of the season, and people are wound up trying to soak up as much fun and sun as they can. It will get better."

"Oh, Stella, you are always so sweet. Oh, and wait, I wanted to tell you that after you left this morning, a man came to the store and asked me if the female officer that was on site this morning was named Stella. I told him yes, and he said he knew you from working together in Philadelphia."

Oh my God, I felt sick and suddenly weak, but I tried not to let it show. "Did you get his name?"

"No, he was a black fellow, particularly good looking, maybe forty-five or so. He was here with his wife and two kids. They checked out about an hour ago, though."

"Stella, are you alright?" G asked when we were headed back to our little precinct. "You haven't said a word since we left the campground, and you looked as if you had seen a ghost when Beth told you someone recognized you."

"I'm alright. Like I told you before, I just want to forget about my life in Philly. I'm not proud of it."

"Do you know the guy she was describing?"

"Yes, his name is Devon Walker. We weren't friends, but we were cordial. I didn't dislike him. I guess I just never made the effort to know him any better."

"Are you concerned about him telling people where you are?"

"No, they are detectives. If any of them wanted to find me, it wouldn't be hard." We pulled into our parking lot to find Captain Jesse and Joe sitting at the picnic table eating together. Joe immediately called us over.

"Hey, you two, what's new?"

"Nothing, why do you ask," I replied.

Joe grinned at Cap and said, "I told you so." I looked at Cap, and I knew right away that they knew about me, and G.

G cleared his throat. "Captain Jesse, I am in love with my partner. We are in love with each other. If you have a rule against relationships amongst colleagues, I completely understand. I will request a transfer, but I do not want Stella to have to do that. She loves it here." A period of uncomfortable silence lingered for just a few moments.

Finally, Cap stood and put his arms around both of us. "Don't be ridiculous, we are family, and Joe and I couldn't be happier for both of you. Now Margie, well, that may be a whole different situation altogether. You know how she loves to flirt with the younger men. She's such a cougar!"

"I will let her down gently," said G. With that we all had a really good laugh. I loved these people, my family!

We clocked out and headed to our cars. "Well, that is a load off my mind, Stella."

"Oh, I agree. I feel such a sense of relief knowing that we don't have to hide our relationship and the Cap has given us his blessing."

"So, how about I go home, take a shower, grab some clothes, grab some takeout, grab some alcohol, and then come by your place and grab you all over?"

I pressed my body to his and whispered in his ear, "You can grab me anywhere you want as long as I can slowly slide my tongue all over that beautiful, hard body of yours." I kissed his lips and walked to my car. He was still standing in the same spot, looking happily dumbfounded and, from what I could see, extremely aroused when I drove off.

I spent a few minutes daydreaming about making love to my love later tonight and then decided to give McIntyre a call back since I wasn't sure when I would be alone next. McIntyre picked up right away, he was good like that.

"Stella! Everything good with you?"

"Couldn't be better, McIntyre.:

"Do you have time to meet me at the Jacobs farm now? I want to walk you through what we have discovered so far."

"Yes, I have a few hours before I need to be anywhere. I am about twenty minutes out. See you soon."

I had to admit I was excited to see what McIntyre had uncovered. This experience was priceless for me. Working with McIntyre on a serial killer case was definitely a career booster for me, even if it had to be our secret. I would have never had an opportunity like this in Philly. Too many macho, self-entitled men in front of me. In a place like Philly, women in law enforcement weren't respected the way their male counterparts were, even if we were better at the job. I had to remember to tell McIntyre again how much I appreciated him involving me in the case. When all was said and done, and we had the unsub in custody, I imagined the FBI would pat themselves on the back and bring in the heavy hitter media outlets so that the world knew how brilliant they were. I had no doubt this case would end up with a book and movie deal for a quick-thinking writer. I was fine with that, really. I didn't need to be center stage, never did. I was just grateful to be involved and to hopefully catch this whack job.

I arrived at the Jacobs farm right on time. My car wasn't exactly off road capable, and this damn driveway was ridiculous. I crept at a stellar five miles per hour. Blueberries, despite the obvious lack of care, were visible on most of the bushes. I read that once they had rooted, they took care of themselves until late summer when they were supposed to be harvested. What a waste. There was money to be made here, people that needed food, which would soon be rotting. Hopefully, at least, the animals ate what they could.

I could see myself living on a farm like this, maybe refurbishing the beautiful old farmhouse that had been ignored for decades. I would love to have this much land. So many possibilities, maybe even a vineyard someday.

McIntyre was parked in front of the farmhouse, leaning against his car, talking on the phone, probably talking to his wife. God, I prayed that G was my soulmate, like Jill was his. G and I hadn't known each other long, but I loved him and could see myself spending the rest of my life with him someday. McIntyre was just getting off the phone when I reached him.

"Nice to see you, Stella. You look good, happy. New love in your life?"

How the hell did he know that? Was it that obvious? Was this what people in love, having amazing sex, looked like? "Wow, you are quite the profiler. Perhaps you should hold off on the retirement plan."

He laughed. "Not a chance in hell. My wife would go ballistic. Nope, I am sticking to the plan, which is why we need to catch the son of a bitch who murdered these people now."

"I totally agree. We need to catch him before there are any further victims. At some point, the media will get wind of this, race out here in droves, camp out, and report every hour on how little success law enforcement seems to be having."

"Exactly, I am too old for that shit. Been there, done that. So, from the beginning, this is what we know so far. The body of Kurt Jacobs was discovered in the state park. The coroner recorded the cause of death as blunt force trauma to the head and upper torso. Witnesses report that prior to his demise, Jacobs had engaged in a physical altercation at The Wander Inn Bar, in which he became violent with Sandy Brown. Post altercation, a stranger asked Sandy Brown for a location on Jacobs, which we assume that she provided. During our investigation, we further discovered that Kurt Jacobs and his brother, Roy Jacobs, inherited this farm from their deceased father. Inmate Roy Jacobs stated that he and his brother had not entered the other structures on the property, including the barn, since their father's death three years ago. They occupied the main house only. That changed when Kurt told Roy that he thought there were squatters living in one of the old barns on the property. Roy then instructed Kurt to confront the intruders and demand rent money if they wanted to stay. Question is, did that confrontation cause Kurt to lose his life? Crime scene techs recovered prints and trace evidence from inside the bar. The fingerprints were a dead end. The unsub is not in any of our usual data bases. Let's table the fact that numerous victims were discovered buried on the property for now. Sandy Brown, believe it or not, stopped by my office to let me know that she spotted the same handsome guy who was at the bar the night Kurt assaulted her. She reportedly saw him from the diner window, coming out of a liquor store across the street, Rosie's Packaged Goods. He was driving a dark small car. FBI is questioning the store clerk and printing the door. Maybe we get lucky.

"We believe we spotted the unsub approaching the property from that tree line ahead." McIntyre pointed to the tree line past the barn. "Unfortunately, the second time, after leaving the deceased body of Will Bayo, he eluded capture."

"Not one person will shed a tear for that scumbag, sexual harasser, Bayo," I hissed.

"True, true, but let's continue with what we know. With regard to Bayo, to the best of our knowledge, the only people who knew about him stalking and harassing Brie are you, your partner G, and your captain, right? Anyone else?"

"Actually yes, Margie and Captain Jesse's husband, Joe. Oh, and two women in Brie's office that were present when Bayo asked Brie if she was ever a bra model. Bayo covered his tracks by threatening the two women and then gifting them with nice salary bumps and promotions."

"Are you sure there isn't anyone that we're missing?"

"I don't think so."

"Perfect, now, something else you didn't know. I got really curious about what's beyond that tree line, so I took a walk. A very long walk that almost killed me, but nonetheless, it was worth it. I followed a path that, after about an hour, opened up to a clearing. Think of it as a bald spot in this thick forest. I am quite sure that the unsub spent time there, actually, I'm positive. I recovered empty beer cans, remnants of a campfire, and I discovered a larger path, capable of vehicle travel."

"The suspense is killing me, McIntyre. Where did the road lead?"

"I thought after hours in the blazing sun and no water, it was going to lead to my death, but at the end of this sort of dirt road, the opening narrowed just before it ended at an actual road. A small car could pass through, but not without sustaining paint scratches to the driver and passenger doors. That is a fact. A fact that could help us identify this bastard. I didn't know where I was, and I couldn't get phone service, and did I already say I am too old for this?"

"McIntyre! Where did you end up?"

"Bullytown Road."

"Not possible, that's got to be ten miles from here."

"Actually, it's twelve miles. So, with regard to the female victims, the coroner confirmed that time of death was about twenty years, give or take, some victims may be less. They weren't all killed at the same time. Stella, this guy has been at this for at least two decades. He also said that despite the condition of the bodies, he was sure they were sexually violated. Lastly, further tests revealed that all of the girls carried sexually transmitted diseases."

"How the hell can they tell that from a corpse?"

"Coroner said from extracting fragments of bone near the vaginal canal."

"So, based on the coroner's findings, you are assuming these girls were prostitutes, aren't you?"

"Yes, which would also explain why they were never reported missing."

Chapter Thirty-Seven

Augustus

"Pastor, are you okay?"

"Ah, Augustus, yes I am."

"Pastor, it's okay, you can tell me the truth. I heard what you said to the board members, and I can see that you are upset. Is there anything I can do to help you?"

"You are a very perceptive young man," Pastor replied with the grin of a proud parent on his face. "Augustus, do you know why I have dedicated my life to serving the Lord?"

"Well, I assume because you felt a calling to do so."

He smiled, "Yes, you are correct, that certainly is part of it, but I also wanted to help those most in need, the way Jesus did. Praising our God in a house of worship should not be only for the financially endowed. All should be welcomed without the expectation of an offering. Augustus, you have spent enough time getting to know this city to know that, above all, those lost souls roaming the streets that are homeless, or addicted to drugs, or selling their flesh, and those without money, they truly are the kind of people that I have always wanted to bring to Jesus. I want to tell them all about the miracle of Jesus. If they knew the love of Christ, really knew, their lives would be filled with meaning. No, no, I didn't choose this path so that I could bully people into giving money."

I sat down in the chair across from him. From his chair, he had leaned forward with his elbows on his desk and his face buried within. We didn't speak for quite a while, but it wasn't uncomfortable silence. I understood that he needed to wrap his head around what just transpired with the board members and decide what he was going to do next. Finally, he lifted his head from his hands with tears in his eyes.

"Augustus, I have made a decision. It is obvious to me that the board will forever be a brick wall, focused only on profit. A brick wall that makes it impossible for me to serve God and the people of this community as I intended. I am submitting my letter of resignation to the board tomorrow."

My heart sank, and I fought back the tears. "Where will you go?"

"Well, there is a vacancy at a wonderful Baptist

Church in New Orleans, in an impoverished and struggling, diverse community. A community that needs immediate help, needs to hear the word of God. I have already contacted the church and spoken to the board chairperson who offered me the position after just an hour-long conversation. I have a feeling that there wasn't many other pastors inquiring. I have to speak to my wife, but I know she will jump at the opportunity to go elsewhere. She has never been happy with the city life. She has never felt safe here in Philly, especially after dark. Within the next two weeks, I hope to be headed down to New Orleans."

I guessed Pastor could see the sadness in my eyes and sense my fear of losing the only person I could count on here in the United States because he smiled so kindly, with such compassion in his eyes. "Augustus, I would like you to come with us, but only if you want to, of course. I do get the sense that Philly isn't exactly an ideal place for you to put roots down, either."

"No, it certainly isn't. I guess I sort of feel like your wife does. It's just too busy here, too unfriendly, and the night scares me as well. I do not have a sense of security after dark, when all of the different people seem to pop up from nowhere. Can I think about it?"

"Of course, of course. This is a big decision, and you must be certain in your heart it is what you want. Pray, for God to give you the answer, and He will."

"I will, I promise. Oh, and I have good news for you. Today, I took the train from Philly to Burlington, which was a bit unsettling, and I bought a used car."

"Well, congratulations to you. That is just wonderful. Let's go outside and have a look."

After Pastor and I spent quite a while outside in the parking lot looking over my car and talking about his first car and how fast it was, we were both exhausted, said goodnight, and parted ways.

Of course, once I laid in bed, I couldn't fall asleep, too many thoughts swirling around in my head. I had less than two weeks to decide my next move, a move that, for all intents and purposes, would define my future. One thing was for certain, I did not want to go back to Germany, except to visit my family, but never for good. However, I also didn't want to live in Philly, especially without Pastor Dan. City life would never be a comfortable way of life for me. New Orleans could be an interesting opportunity, but despite my childhood nightmare, I also felt sort of drawn to Pine Barrens. Driving there with Pastor Dan that day, I felt good, not haunted like I assumed I would. I thought it would be the perfect place to face old demons, put my past behind me, and build on the foundation of the people in my life that

I was so incredibly grateful for.

Searching for the exact farm I grew up on could prove impossible. After all, I rarely saw my house and the farm from the outside looking in, my father was adamant that be the case. It could be completely demolished by now and turned into an amusement park for all I knew, but nevertheless, a part of me needed to at least try. I had money to rent a place to live, a decent car, and I could easily get a job. Maybe I could meet some new friends, too. I wouldn't even mind learning to bartend in a local pub that would be a great source of income and interesting people. Two weeks to make a major, life-altering decision at a pivotal moment in time made me feel very tired.

Chapter Thirty-Eight

McIntyre

Jill woke me up at 7:30 a.m. I instantly felt the headache I deserved after drinking too much Irish whiskey last night while Jill and I enjoyed a fire in our backyard. The cool air felt incredibly invigorating, and the smell of the salt air drifting from the bay was just enough to take my mind off the case for a while and clear my head. I sat up slowly, thankful that I didn't feel nauseous, too. Jill returned with a glass of water and Tylenol. She kissed me on my forehead and headed out the door to her yoga class. I grabbed my phone and saw that I missed two calls from Johnson, no messages though. I took the Tylenol and headed for the shower, but I didn't get too far when my cell rang again.

I answered with an annoyed, "Where's the fire, Kev?"

"How the hell did you know?"

"Know what? What are you talking about?"

"Brendan, the farmhouse at the Jacobs property burned to the ground last night. Completely gone. Fire Chief says an accelerant, most likely gasoline, was used to ignite the blaze. By the time the firehouse got the call and got on site, the house was completely engulfed in flames."

It's got to be our unsub, but why burn the house and why now?"

"Well, I've been thinking about that. It may be a message from our unsub, a warning perhaps, to leave him alone in *his* place. By the way, McIntyre, you were right. Prints on the beer can you found match the prints we lifted from the barn. Oh, and get this, the clerk at the liquor store said he is quite sure that he knows the guy we are talking about. He's going to call us if he sees the guy again. Thinks he is maybe thirty or older but doesn't think he's paid enough attention to his face to give a good, detailed description. He said that he has been coming into the store for a while now but couldn't be more specific than that. He did, however, say that the guy drives a dark colored car that looks like someone keyed the side of. You said it would be impossible for even a small car to make it through the opening to the woods you found without getting scratched up, right?"

"Right, in my opinion, it would be absolutely impossible. The opening is too narrow. So, we know this guy has some sort of connection with the Jacobs place, but think about it, Kev, some of those bodies have been there twenty years, right? Well, that would make our unsub what, ten years old when he started his killing spree? Could we be looking at more than one unsub? I know you are the profiler, but I think if we are going to figure this psycho out, we need to take a look further back. We need to find out everyone who owned the property prior to the Jacobs family. It's the only thing that makes sense. This guy either lived here at one time or something unbelievably bad happened to him here."

"I'm on it, Brendan. I'll reach out to the county for all records they have regarding the property. Hopefully, that will be the break we need."

"Wait, so we know this guy spends a lot of time at or near the Jacobs place, but also that he doesn't actually live there. He's got to be close by, though. Have the records bureau folks also give you the names of any males that have purchased property within a ten-mile radius of the Jacobs farm during the past five years. It's a long shot, but at this point, I will take it."

"I feel good about this, McIntyre. I'll call you as soon as I know something."

Just a few hours later, I was almost to my office, feeling much less hung over, when Johnson called again. "Dead end, buddy!"

"What do you mean, dead end?"

"Well, I called over to the records people, and as a result of an out of control, controlled fire, their records only go back ten years or so."

"Are you fucking kidding me? You're telling me that none of this information was computerized? How could that be?"

"Well, its Podunk, New Jersey, what do you expect? If it makes you feel any better, they had just hired a vendor to begin scanning data into an electronic filing system weeks before the fire destroyed the Hall of Records and all of their paper files."

"Nope, no, doesn't make me feel any better."

"On a positive note, Adelaide, the ninety-eight-year-old lady at the records bureau who I was speaking with, did say that she would try to locate the records for purchases within ten years. I wouldn't hold my breath, though."

"Actually Kev, I did have another idea. Perhaps we talk to some old timers that were here back in the day, like you know, the locals that may remember who owned the place prior to Jacobs. I'll call you later. I know where I am headed first."

I did know exactly where to head next thanks to Stella. Stella told me her landlord, Mr. Avery, was considered the unofficial mayor of the county. Everyone knew him, and he knew everyone who lived in his area of Pine Barrens. Perhaps he could remember who owned the old blueberry farm before the Jacobs family. I was praying this old guy could help me out. If not, I was at a dead end. I knew in my gut that our unsub spent time, perhaps even as a child, as a visitor to the farm. I had to get the names of the previous owners. The entire case hinged on this one piece of information. Didn't take me long at all to arrive at Mr. Avery's place. I pulled up just as he was locking up. Stella's car was parked at her place, and there was another car behind hers. Boyfriend maybe? She did look pretty happy when I saw her last.

Mr. Avery was struggling to get the door to lock when I approached him. "Hi, are you Mr. Avery?" Shit, he didn't hear me walk up. Poor old guy nearly jumped out of his skin, even grabbed his chest which really scared the hell out of me. I put my hand on his shoulder and apologized for sneaking up on him. He laughed it off. "No harm done, young man, what can I do for you?"

Stella was right, this guy was straight out of a Norman Rockwell painting. "Hello, Mr. Avery, my name is Brendan, and I am a sergeant with the state police. I am also a good friend of your tenant, Stella."

"Oh my, she is a wonderful girl, isn't she? I just love having her here. Actually, everyone around here has grown pretty fond of her."

"Mr. Avery, do you know whose car is parked behind hers?"

"Well, I believe that is her partner's car." He nudged

my arm the way old men do. "I do believe they are quite fond of each other, too." He giggled and blushed. "Do you want me to call over to her and let her know that you are here, son?"

"No thank you, actually, I came to speak with you if I may."

Mr. Avery and I sat at a table in his store with fresh cups of coffee he made us. The smell was intoxicating and was just what I needed after overindulging last night. I explained to him that I was working with the FBI on a case that involved the Jacobs property and that a fire had destroyed records of property ownership prior to the Jacobs's.

"Mr. Avery, Stella tells me that you have been here your entire life and that nothing happens around here that you don't know about, so I am really hoping that you can tell me who owned the property prior to the Jacobs family."

A strange look came across Mr. Avery's face, and he bowed his head, closed his eyes, and said nothing for several minutes. I was confused, maybe he didn't remember or maybe he didn't want to talk about it. It was as if I had opened the door to a memory that he had hoped he would never have to recall. With a sadness in his eyes, he finally spoke.

"Well, now that is a sad story, an incredibly sad story indeed. Many years ago, a family, I think they were originally from Europe or maybe Ireland, farmed blueberries out there. I don't know the last name, but the man's first name was Stefan. He had a wife and a young child, a son. I don't know their names. I only saw them from the window right there, and only twice." Mr. Avery pointed to the front window next to the door. "I remember looking out at them, waiting inside his truck while Stefan gathered supplies from my store. That poor woman had such pain and sorrow in her eyes that I just wanted to run right out that front door and hug her. The boy sat very still and close to his mother."

"Do you remember their names?"

"No, never did get their names. Stefan was not a friendly man. His eyes were cold, and there was a darkness about him that sent shivers up my spine every time he stepped inside the store. I did, once only, attempt to converse with him. I asked him what his boy's name was, and do you know what he said to me? Well, he looked me in the eyes and told me that it was none of my concern. Like I said, cold as ice. Then, just like that, one day, I heard they left town for good. Place sat abandoned for years, until the county finally claimed it and eventually put it up for sale. To tell you the truth, I was always curious as to why they left. He had to have been making a really good living selling his crops. I just pray that little boy and his momma ended up alright."

"Mr. Avery, did Stefan have people working for him

on the farm?" "Yes, I do remember that he always had a Spanish fella with him when he came into town for supplies or needed parts to fix his equipment. I did hear a rumor many, many years back that when the county took the land, they found undocumented immigrants, quite a number of them still living on the land and occupying the house, too. I believe the authorities deported them back to their own country, but again, it was a rumor. I certainly cannot swear it to be the truth."

I finished my coffee, as did he, and together we walked outside. I locked the door for him, handed him the keys, and thanked him for all of his help. He shook my hand with a firm grip and told me to come back for a cup of coffee and a slice of pie any time. I could not recall ever having a conversation with a nicer gentleman.

As I drove off, I glanced over toward Stella's place to see both cars still parked in her driveway. Interesting, Mr. Avery seemed pretty certain that Stella and her partner were romantically involved. If that was true, I hoped it didn't cloud her judgement. I needed her involvement in this case to remain confidential. Although Mr. Avery's information was helpful, it didn't get us any closer to discovering the identity of the unsub, especially without a last name of this Stefan. Then, like lightening it struck me. Could one of the males remains found out at the farm be that of this Stefan? Could one of the women be his wife? But if that was the case, where was the boy, and who was the other male victim we uncovered? Jesus, help me, I had more questions than answers now and a headache again.

Chapter Thirty-Nine

Stella

As I lay awake, mentally sifting through the information McIntyre shared with me, I could feel G's soft, warm breath in a steady rhythm on the back of my neck. He was sound asleep after yet another incredible late afternoon love making session. It was as if we truly became one being, the only being, in the height of the moment, unlike anything I could have ever imagined. That was the truest definition of the term "soulmate." I tried to fall asleep, but my brain was in overdrive. I managed to slip out of bed without waking G. He looked so peaceful, so beautifully perfect lying naked in my bed. I thought about softly, strategically waking him into an instant state of arousal, but my mouth was too dry for what I intended. I gently closed the bedroom door behind me. I wasn't used to walking around the house in the nude, but we began our sexual adventure at the front door, so I needed to collect my t shirt, pants, and g-string. As I bent over near the front door to retrieve them both, I heard a slight knock on my door, so faint that I assumed I had imagined it. I threw my clothes on quickly just in case it was Mr. Avery. I would die of embarrassment if he saw me like this, as would he.

As I slipped into my favorite yoga pants, I heard another knock, just a little bit louder this time. I opened the door with a big smile ready to greet the only person aside from G who stopped by: Mr. Avery. I was completely wrong and completely speechless. There on my porch, in my town, Thomas stood with a bouquet of sunflowers in one hand and a bottle of wine in the other. A flume of emotions sent my head into a chaotic, confused spin. It was at least a good minute or so before I could form a sentence, and that was when I unleashed the hurt and anger, I had carried for so long.

"What the fuck are you doing here, Thomas? How did you find my house? Who the hell do you think you are showing up at my front door, you coward!"

"Stella, please just hear me out, please! I tried to find you months ago, but your personnel file was sealed and no one at PD would tell me where you went. You stopped using the cell phone you had, and I didn't dare ask Brie. It wasn't until a friend told me that he saw you down here working that I had any indication where you had gone. Stella, I left the force when you left. I couldn't be there without you. I love you! I never stopped loving you!"

I did not respond, but I could feel tears forming in the corners of my eyes, as his every word stung my heart without mercy.

With that, G was standing behind me. He must have heard everything because he was fully dressed now. He and Thomas stood staring at each other until G broke the silence. "I am assuming you are Thomas. My name is G, I'm Stella's partner." They shook hands. Right then, right there, why didn't I say he was my boyfriend! Why the fuck didn't I add that? I saw the hurt in his eyes. Oh my God, I hurt him, how could I! He kissed me on the cheek and said he would call me later. I should have called out to him, should have made him stay and Thomas leave, but I just stood there frozen, watching it all play out, and before I could think, G was gone. My emotions got the best of me, and I cried hard. Thomas reached out to touch me.

"No, no, don't you dare touch me. I am finally over you, Thomas. G isn't just my partner. He is… he is the man I love, my soulmate."

Thomas now had tears in his eyes as well. "Stella, I am sorry, the last thing I want is to hurt you again. If you are in love with G, I will back off. I just want you to be happy. I want you to also know that I took the blame for it all. I told everyone at the precinct that I loved you and that I had planned on divorcing Jenna to be with you. No one blamed you, Stella. I did divorce Jenna, even though she wanted to go to marriage counseling and try to save the marriage. I loved you, that was the only relationship I wanted to save."

"Brie said she saw you out to dinner with a date."

"Oh, Stella, that wasn't a date, that was my lawyer. There has been no one in my life since you left."

"Well, I am sorry, but you are too late. After losing you, my job, and the city I loved, I ended up here. I thought my life was over. Some nights, the depression and the memories tortured me until the sun came up. I was in a very dark place. I had no one, not even my best friend, to hold me while I cried. I wanted to die. I did not want to live without the things and people I loved, but all that has changed. I love my job, my friends, this town, and most of all, G."

Thomas looked completely crushed, as he hung his head and said, "I understand. I love you, but I understand. I wish I could go back and change the past, but we both know I can't. Listen, I am staying in a cabin at Waving Pines Camping Resort. I am sure you know where it is." I nodded my head yes without making eye contact. "If you change your mind or just want to talk some more, please come."

I turned my back and went back inside. I stood with

my back against the door and held my breath until I heard his car drive away. Then, I sank to the floor, held my face in my hands, and cried for a long time.

I ran to the bedroom and picked up my cell to call G. No missed calls. His phone went straight to voicemail. I left him a message to please call me right away. I waited about a half hour before trying again, but same thing: voicemail. *God, please do not let him leave me, please.* The cell rang in my hand, and my heart jumped, but it was Captain Jesse. I took a deep breath and tried to sound cheerful.

"Hey, Cap, how are you?"

"Stella, I just wanted to see if everything is okay with you."

"I am okay, why?"

"Well, G called and said he needed a couple of days off to deal with some personal stuff that came up."

I was not sure what to say, but I figured vague was best. "Oh, I did not know that. I left him a message earlier to call me. I am sure he will when he gets a chance, no worries."

"Okay, you okay with riding solo tomorrow?"

"Absolutely!" A lie, of course, as the thought of not being on duty with G cut like a knife, but Cap did not need to know that.

I needed Brie. The minute she answered, I fell apart, babbling like an idiot, unable to catch my breath through the tears and nose blowing. Brie always had a way of calming me without saying. I was finally able to tell her what had happened today. Oh, she was furious at Thomas.

"How dare he, Stella! How fucking dare he! Oh, and I understand why you haven't told me about G yet, but I knew, I already knew by the way you two look at each other."

"Oh, Brie, what if that is all over now? What if G never comes back? Why did I let him leave?"

"Because you were in shock and not thinking straight. It's okay. It will all be okay. I can feel it. G loves you, and he will understand. Listen, John was supposed to come to Philly to my place for dinner tonight, but I am going to cancel. I'll be there tonight."

"I love you, Brie."
"I love you, too, Stel."

Chapter Forty

McIntyre

I thought it odd that I had not heard from Johnson in a few days, but I really had nothing new to add to the investigation, his investigation to be accurate, so I refrained from calling him. No news was not good news, though. Every day that passed without a new lead or viable information was one day closer to having this labeled unsolved. I wondered if Kevin considered involving the media in an effort to help solve this serial murder mess, but knowing him, even if he did consider it, he quickly dismissed the thought. These victims were killed decades ago with the exception of Jacobs and Bayo. We already knew that the killer, or at least one of them, was still in this area. The onslaught of media in the vicinity could force him to disappear forever. No, we needed to manage this quietly. It was our only hope of catching this guy.

I wanted to check in with Stella to see if she had been able to give any thought to the information I gave her, but I was not sure if she was home or working. If she was romantically involved with her partner, then he may be with her day and night. It was better to wait for her to have the opportunity to call me. I liked Stella a lot. She was a good kid, but I worried that sleeping with her partner could cause a lot of pain and heartache in the end. I really hoped that I was wrong, but I'd seen relationships between cops turn really ugly too many times during my career. Rarely did it end up in a fairy tale ending, ride off into the sunset situation, but for Stella's sake, I hoped it did.

Hours later, finally, the call I have been waiting for. I answered immediately, but he did not let me get a word in. Johnson sounded completely frantic, uncharacteristic of him.

"What the hell is wrong? Slow down, I have no idea what you're saying. Where are you?" "McIntyre, meet me at Jacobs, now. Hurry, man, please."

My heart was thumping fast, and I was driving even faster. Something was wrong, I could just feel it. The Kevin I had known for so many years was the definition of calm and cool, but the Kevin I just spoke to was rattled to the core and pissed off.

Chapter Forty-One

Stella

God, if I could only go back to this morning and fix this, scream at the top of my lungs that I love G, demand Thomas leave and never come back, I would. I would give anything for a redo of that moment. G still had not called, nor would he respond to the million, psycho ex-girlfriend type texts from me. I felt completely and utterly helpless right now. I didn't know what to do, where to go, or how to find him. I'd never even been to his place, not once, but I was certainly not going to ask Cap for the address. I couldn't, or he would know that something bad has happened between me and G. He didn't need this drama, it was not fair to him. I could go for a walk, but if G came back, I wanted to be here. I was so fucking pissed at myself. Stupid! Stupid! Stupid!

I showered, got dressed, grabbed a book that I had

been trying to finish for months, poured a glass of wine, and sat on my front porch. Despite the emotional mess I was, I felt peaceful sitting in the sunlight. The weather was beautiful this time of year in the barrens. I told myself that what happened next was beyond my control. It was up to G now to call me, forgive me, or tell me to go to hell. Thomas, the man that broke my heart, devastated me, and ruined everything about my past life that I loved, now sat just miles away at a cabin hoping I would show up and run straight into his arms. I wondered if what he had told me was true. Had he really desperately tried to find me? Was I still in love with him? Could you genuinely love two men at once?

Brie! Brie arrived just in time to keep my head from exploding from self-inflicted mental torture. She was early, much earlier than I expected, and I couldn't have been more grateful. I ran to her car as she stepped out, and that was it. Meltdown, act two. God, I needed my best friend right now more than ever. She hugged me tight and stroked my hair. "Stella, I'm here, it's going to be alright. We can figure this out together."

When I was finally capable of pulling myself together, Brie and I sat together on my front porch, each with glass of wine, and I told her the story from the beginning. She listened so intently, just like a best friend. I missed her so much. Her phone sounded a few times, and despite her super prominent position at work now and her new love interest, she never once picked her phone up to see who was reaching out to her. Nope, not Brie, she was right there in the moment with me. So very blessed.

I told her everything, from the first time I laid eyes on G to the events of this morning.

"Stel, I have to ask you, are you still in love with Thomas?"

"Oh, Brie, I don't think so, not the way I love G, but I care about him, and if what he says is true about trying to find me, well then, I feel awful."

"I'm sorry, but he's a cop and he couldn't find you? I find that a bit suspicious, and although, yes, he knows that I despise him, he also knows that if he had come to me and asked that I give you a message, or a letter, I would have. So, screw him and his bullshit about not being able to find you. I don't want to hurt you, you know that I love you, but that so-called meeting with his lawyer at the restaurant that night sure looked more like a cozy date to me. Forget about him, Stel. How could you ever trust him? He cheated on his wife with you. What makes you think he won't do the same to you?"

She was right, everything she said was true, and I needed to hear it.

Brie and I sat for hours on my front porch talking. She brought me up to speed on work as well. She said not one employee or board member attended the funeral service that Bayo's adult kids held for him. She heard that not even the wife showed up. That really told you a lot about the character of a person. She said things were wonderful at work now. Her first objective now that she was the decision maker was to re-evaluate the drastic and obvious difference in company salary ranges, men versus women, and rectify it. Brie said she had many previous conversations with Bayo about the unfair salary practices, but he would just laugh it off, commenting that she needed to accept it and get used to it. She was on a mission to empower her employees to be the best they could be and to know that they would always have a voice now. I was so proud of her. I knew that it was bad karma to feel as elated as I did about Bayo's demise, but he truly was a dark triad, deserving of what he succumbed to.

Chapter Forty-Two

McIntyre

I arrived at the farm quickly, even racing up the shitty driveway, though I was certain I would live to regret that car repair bill, to see a lot more FBI vehicles than I anticipated. What the hell was going on? I was stopped by an agent I didn't recognize. I held up my badge.

"You McIntyre?" the agent asked. I nodded, and he pointed toward the barn. "Johnson is waiting for you, sir."

I could see a group of crime scene techs in the field, working inside a yellow taped off section of the field next to the coroner's van. *Oh God, please tell me we don't have another body.* Johnson looked exhausted and angry as he approached my car.

"What's going on, Kevin?"

"Brendan, this is a fucking nightmare, not to mention

a career ender for some of these assholes."

"Is it another body? Did we miss one?"

"Oh no, that would be too fucking easy to explain. No, this is a brand-new grave with a brand-new victim!"

"How? I mean, that's impossible. You had agents sitting on this property and at the exit off of Bullytown Road, right?"

"Yes, of course, until last night when someone called in a possible terrorist act in progress on the Walt Whitman Bridge, which activated every available agency within a hundred miles. Caller said he saw middle eastern men strapping what looked like bombs to the bridge. So instead of calling me for further instructions, the idiots I had posted here just left, fucking cowboys. I suspended all of them. I am so pissed off right now, McIntyre."

"Johnson, this means that our guy must be law enforcement or at a minimum have access to a scanner."

"My thoughts exactly."

"Who is our victim?"

"No identification yet, no wallet, no keys, but buried headfirst, with no attempt to cover up the body completely. I think this fucking bastard wanted us to find this one."

"Maybe he got interrupted? Your guys see anything when they finally got their asses back here?"

"Nothing but a new grave. Let's go have a look, the coroner has the body now."

We walked toward the coroner's van together in complete silence. Doc saw us coming and unzipped the body bag containing our newest victim. He was covered in blood, but even so, he didn't look familiar to me. Maybe to be in his thirties, good physical condition, no wedding band, and no jewelry.

"Any tattoos?"

"Nothing so far, but I will know more when I get him back to my lab. I can tell you this, though, cause of death was once again blunt force trauma to the back of the head and upper torso."

Kevin stormed off toward the crime scene techs, yelling about the criticalness of being thorough, so I headed toward the barn to see if anything looked different.

From inside the barn, I had a perfect view of the new grave. Was that the killer's intent? To relish in the moment and admire his work, knowing he had sent the agents miles away on a wild goose chase? He certainly was confident, too confident. This guy no doubt had access to a radio or scanner, or worse, was a cop. Out of the corner of my eye, I caught a glimpse of something white peeking out from underneath an old metal shovel with a rotted wooden handle still attached. As I moved closer, I could see it was a waded-up piece of paper. I slipped on the crime scene gloves from inside my pocket and methodically moved the shovel, careful not to disturb anything. I picked up the paper, unfolded it, and just about fell to my knees.

What the hell was happening here? Oh God, Stella. Again, Stella's address. Did the victim bring this, or did the killer? Was Stella okay or had this guy harmed her? I knew that I had to get in touch with her immediately, and at this point, her captain, too. Time to come clean with Johnson about Stella's involvement, too. Jesus, this news was going to put this poor guy over the edge. I hoped he could forgive me.

Stella answered on the first ring. I didn't give her a chance to say no or ask questions. I just told her she needed immediately to report to the Jacobs farm and that I would have her captain meet us here as well, then I hung up. Next call was to her captain. I expected this guy to be pissed at me for not getting his blessing about working with Stella, but instead, he only expressed concern for her safety and said he would head out to meet me now. He was familiar with the place. Next, a conversation with Johnson, who was already headed my way.

I took my time, starting from the beginning about how I met Stella and who she was. I told him that she was helping at my request and that she had kept her involvement confidential, also at my request. He never interrupted me. I told him about Stella's address written on paper, now being discovered twice with respect to this investigation. He already knew about Brie and her involvement with Bayo, but I linked in the connection to Stella as well. I left out the part about Stella sleeping with her partner. When I was all done bringing him up to speed, I apologized. If the tables were turned, and he had involved someone I didn't know in my investigation, I would have been over the top pissed.

Instead, he looked me in the eye and said, "I'm not mad, Brendan. From what you have told me about Stella, I understand why you would want to involve her. She sounds more capable than some of these knuckleheads reporting to me. If she can help us catch this guy and close this, I am all for her continued involvement. At this point, my next step was to call in the local LEOs anyway."

We shook hands, and I was beyond relieved at his response. I brought him to the spot in the barn where I found the paper. He agreed that the unsub probably admired his work from right where we stood. We were both equally frustrated.

Chapter Forty-Three

Stella

"Thanks for driving me, Brie. McIntyre probably won't be happy that I brought you with me, but with two glasses of wine in me and the emotional day I've had thus far, I don't care."

"Stella, I know you said you can't tell me much, but how and why are you working with the state police?"

I sighed and said, "We were both on the same call, a murder in the state park a while back. He had jurisdiction but was willing to keep me involved. We think all of this, including Bayo, may be the work of one person, but that is all I can say. Please when we get there, don't ask any questions, just stay in the car. I don't know why he needs me, but his tone leads me to believe it's serious."

"Stella, will G be here?"

"No, he was never involved in this, so he would have

no reason to be here."

"You kept it from him?"

"I had no choice, and besides, this happened the very first day I met him. Cap will be here, though. Brendan said he had to call him in. I am praying he won't be mad at me. I can't handle any more men in my life shutting me out. Turn here, but slow down. This driveway will ruin your tires."

"My God, where the hell does this lead to?"

"Actually, hell is accurate. It leads to a true hell."

After we passed the charred remnants of the house, I could see the sea of law enforcement that had gathered. I looked at Brie and held her hand.

"This entire area is a crime scene, so please stay in the car until I get back."

"I will, I promise. I don't want to get you in any more trouble than you are already in."

We slowed down to talk with the agent posted, but he waved us by. Obviously, McIntyre let them know I was coming. I could see McIntyre and another guy standing in the barn. I asked Brie to stop near the barn and got out to walk toward them, chin up, trying not to look like a woman who'd been crying over a guy. McIntyre made the introductions.

"Stella, who's in your car? Your partner?"

"Damn, Brendan, always the investigator. No, it's Brie. We were out together when you called." He looked annoyed. Great, just what I needed today. I didn't give him a chance to say anything about bringing Brie along. "What is going on here, and why did you need me? I was really confused because I thought my involvement was a secret, but here I am being introduced to the FBI at a crime scene."

"The unsub dumped, well, actually, partially buried another body here last night. We don't know the identity yet, but it's a male, same cause of death. You up to taking a look at this guy? You may recognize him. He had your address written on a piece of paper on him."

I felt sick. Why the fuck was this happening to me? I took a deep breath. "Let's do it."

The coroner was just getting ready to pull out, but Johnson held his hand up to stop the van. An older gentleman rolled his window down and said, "Guys, the heat is our enemy. I've got to get this guy back to autopsy right away."

Johnson replied, "Sorry, Doc, we just need this officer to take a quick look. She's local and may be able to help us identify him."

With that, he jumped out and opened the back doors of his van. The body was inside an official FBI body bag on top of a gurney. He tugged at the zipper until it released.

Chapter Forty-Four

McIntyre

Doc unzipped the bag to reveal the victim's face, and like a scene from a movie, Stella let out an awful cry and fell to her knees. She was yelling for Brie who must have been watching this unfold from the car because she was already out of her car running full speed toward us.

"Stella! Stella, what's wrong!" Brie bent over and tried to pull her up to her feet, but Stella was motionless. She just sat on the ground sobbing uncontrollably. Brie looked up at me. "What happened? Why did she collapse? Who is in that body bag? Oh God, it's not her partner, is it?"

I looked at Johnson, and he gave me the nod. "Brie, would you be willing to look at our victim and tell us if you recognize him as well, please?"

Brie stood without reservation, walked to the van, and

looked at our victim. "Oh God, no, that's Stella's ex-boyfriend, Thomas. They used to work together in Philly. He is, I mean, was a cop. They had what you could call a bad, very public breakup a while back. He showed up, uninvited, at Stella's this morning. Her partner was there with her but left to give her space to talk to him. Stella eventually made him leave. Told him she was over him and in love with someone else. He did leave without incident but told her that he would wait a day or two to see if she changed her mind. He was staying at a campground here; in a cabin I think."

Brie immediately returned to Stella's side, who was still sobbing, but this time, Brie was at least able to get her to a standing position, hugging her tight. I motioned for Johnson to follow me, and we walked back to the barn.

"Okay, Kevin, this is not good, man. What Brie neglected to tell you is that Stella's new love is her partner. I saw his car at her house early today, which means that he was there when our victim showed up, and maybe became furious. Furious enough to follow this guy and take him out."

"Shit, McIntyre, where is her partner now?"

"Well, speak of the devil, I believe that is him walking toward Stella and Brie with their captain."

"Yup, from the way he is holding Stella and kissing her forehead right now, I can pretty much guarantee that he is her love interest. McIntyre, we need to know where he has been until now."

Chapter Forty-Five

Stella

"G, I'm sorry, I'm so sorry. I love you. I told Thomas I only loved you and that he had to leave and not come back. I was pretty mean to him, and now he is dead. Why is this happening? Who would do such a thing to him?"

"Stella, it's okay, I love you, too. I wasn't angry with you. I just wanted to give you space to figure out who and what you wanted. I was trying to do the right thing. I don't know who did this, but we will damn sure find out." He hugged me tighter. As awful as I felt about poor Thomas, I was so relieved that G hadn't left me.

Captain Jesse was standing by the barn now and looked to be deep in conversation. I had been so distraught that I had not noticed the coroner's van leaving, but at some point, it did. G, Brie, and I walked up to the barn. Johnson asked me if I was okay, and I nodded, yes. Then, he spoke to G.

"I understand that you and Stella are partners, under the command of your captain here, and that you are also romantically involved. Is that accurate?"

"Yes, those statements are accurate."

Johnson continued, "Is it also accurate that you were present when the victim, Thomas, visited Stella earlier today?"

This line of questioning was starting to make me nervous, and I knew exactly which direction it was headed so I jumped in. "Don't answer that, G. What is going on here? You suspect G murdered Thomas? If that's the case, you are wrong! Thomas and G shook hands and then G left my house so that I could finish my conversation with Thomas. G was not present when Thomas announced he was staying at a campground, and I never got the chance to tell him that, either."

McIntyre could see that I was getting irritated. "Okay, okay, no one is accusing anyone of anything. This is simple. G, where were you from the time you left Stella's house to the time you arrived here?"

G, without hesitation, said, "I was visiting with a friend that I haven't seen in a really long time, sort of a mentor of mine actually. His name is Dan. He is visiting from out of town and called me. We had lunch together. I can supply you with his contact information." G asked Johnson for his cell phone number, so he could text him what he needed. Easy.

Cap chimed in, "Okay, so from what you have told me so far, it seems that this unsub has connections to this property, has access to law enforcement or is a cop, but it doesn't explain why Bayo and now Thomas are dead. Two seemingly insignificant out of towners with nothing other than state of residence in common. Well, that and Stella and Brie."

"There must be another connection," I said. "No one else here knew about Thomas or about Bayo. I have told no one, not a soul. Brie? Oh my God, that's it. Brie, you told John, the guy you are dating about Thomas and Bayo, didn't you?"

Brie started to tear up, and I put my arm around her.

"It's okay. It's not your fault, just tell us everything."

Brie told everyone what I already knew. She met John, who was bartending at Piney's the night that we all went out. The same night Bayo followed her here, which she also told John. John traveled to Philly where he took Brie to dinner. During that dinner, Thomas approached Brie and John and tried to speak with Brie who told him off. At that point, Brie felt obligated to tell John the story of me and Thomas and how she suspected that if G and I weren't already romantically involved, we soon would be.

"Oh God, Stella, I am so sorry. All of this is my fault. Could John have done all of this, but why? I barely know him."

McIntyre asked, "Brie, do you have his cell number, and do you know where he lives?"

Brie shook her head, "No, I have no idea where he lives, but I do have his number."

Captain asked Brie if John knew she was coming to see me. Now Brie was inconsolable. This was all just too much for her to handle. I was really worried about her. I put my arm around her and then I answered, "Yes, she was supposed to have a date with him tonight, but she cancelled it for me. He knows she's here, and he knows why."

Johnson, while scanning the woods for any signs of this unsub, or John, or whoever he is, said, "Okay, I want everyone to leave now, in the cars you arrived in, with the people you arrived with. I want you all to go directly to Captain Jesse's office and wait for me there. We are going to put this to bed tonight." With that, we all disbursed as directed.

At 7:15 p.m., we were all present at the precinct, including Johnson. Margie had gone home, which was a good thing. Johnson had a plan, and he explained it slowly and in great detail so that there would be no mistakes made. He had completed his profile of our unsub and was certain that this was our one and only chance to catch him before he realized that we almost had this, him, figured out.

"Brie," Johnson directed, "will contact John and tell

him that G and Stella have made up and will be spending the night together, and therefore, she would like to meet him at Piney's for a drink to give Stella and G some privacy before she returned home."

Brie appeared nervous but agreed that she could flawlessly handle the task. Johnson advised that since the unsub has never seen him, he would be seated at the bar at Piney's. Once John arrived and was seated, Johnson would approach and detain him. Captain Jesse would be waiting outside in his personal vehicle ready to pick up Brie once Johnson was outside with our murderer.

Johnson further instructed McIntyre, G, and me to head to the Jacobs property and wait in the barn as soon as Brie had confirmation from John that he would in fact meet her at Piney's. Cap and Brie would follow Johnson back to the Jacobs place, where he was certain the truth would unfold. After about an hour of rehearsing Johnson's plan, we all agreed that we were ready to proceed. We watched in complete silence as Brie sent the text, worded just as Johnson requested, to John. She placed her cell phone on the table, and we waited. It didn't take long for John to accept the invite.

Hi Brie, that's awesome for them! I can be there in thirty minutes. Can't wait to see you again, followed by an emoji smiling face.

G, McIntyre, and I headed back out to the parking lot and jumped in McIntyre's car.

"You both have your service weapons, correct? We have no idea if this guy is working alone or with a partner, so we need to be prepared."

G and I both nodded. McIntyre had amazing patience, driving just under the speed limit and telling us about his wife's honey-do list that was now sixteen pages long. I thought he was trying to keep us calm and prevent us from over thinking the big moment. Johnson would only call us if John failed to arrive at Piney's. Otherwise, we were to wait in the barn after parking the car out of sight. I could see that the anticipation was becoming overwhelming for G. His brow was sheer with sweat, and he kept tapping his knee with his fist. I grabbed his hand and squeezed, but he didn't make eye contact with me. His eyes were focused on the road. I wondered if he even realized that I was holding his hand.

It took longer than usual to get there. It was already dark out. This close to fall, there were no longer 9:00 p.m. evenings to watch the sun set. McIntyre turned his headlights off, and by the light of the moon, we crawled our way to the barn. McIntyre drove past the barn and parked the car to the side of the building where it would not be seen by the light of Johnson's headlights, all part of the plan. The three of us stood inside the barn with just the light of the moon to see each other. We didn't talk much. G, most of all, looked the most stressed and nervous about what was about to happen here. I felt for him. I think my years as an officer in Philly better prepared me for this type of operation. I was nervous, but I was also excited and ready for whatever was going to go down.

I took a quick peek at my phone to do a time check, but I never did see what time it was. I shoved the phone back in my pocket and drew my weapon, as did the boys. A car was headed our way, two cars actually, just as we planned.

Johnson stopped his car just short of the barn and stepped out, and we heard him open the back door and say in a very stern tone, "Get out of the car, cuffs stay on, and walk toward the barn slowly. I know you are familiar with this barn, right? Isn't this where you enjoy the view of your work, John?"

We heard no response. The footsteps were just a few feet away, until finally, McIntyre pointed his flashlight in John's face causing him to tuck his head down quickly. I lit the lantern that had been left inside the barn, and McIntyre turned his flashlight off. Brie and Cap stepped into the barn. Brie had been crying, her makeup was a mess, and her nose was red. Poor thing, she was not built for this.

John slowly picked his head up. We all stared at him, trying to get a feel for this guy. Was he familiar? Had we seen him around before? He was a very good-looking guy. He would not make eye contact with anyone except G. They were both looking at each other as if they could see each other's souls.

John spoke, "Augustus, you are all grown up now. I have missed you, old friend"

G, looking as if he just saw a ghost, replied, "Javier? Is that you? You did all of this, but why? I don't understand, why?"

No one else spoke, but I was close to vomiting. Who was this man I fell in love with? I grabbed G by the arm and attempted to force him to look at me. "G, who is Augustus? What the hell is going on here? G, how do you know John, or Javier? I want answers now!" I found myself clutching my weapon that I had strapped at my hip. My head was spinning. I was angry, sad, confused, and way too emotional. G did not respond to my line of questioning. In fact, he still had not taken his eyes off of our suspected killer.

Javier took a few steps closer to G, and Johnson permitted it. Javier looked at G so fondly, as if they were in fact old friends or even family. "Augustus, you left me here a long time ago with a very bad man. I know you must recognize this place, old friend?"

G shook his head in disbelief. "Oh my God, no. This can't be it." G stared out into the darkness as if trying to understand or recognize something, anything that may

360

help him grasp what our strange suspect was saying.

"You still do not understand, do you, Augustus? You see, I saw what your momma did to your poppa when we were young boys. I saw it all from my usual hiding spot. It's okay, though, Augustus. I know what your papa was. He was the same thing he turned my poppa into, a monster." Tears rolled down Javier's face as he continued, "I watched what they did to all of the girls. I hid really good, but I saw it all. Pappa changed in a bad way, started hitting Momma and then raping her and the other wives right in front of me. After, he would laugh and call them useless whores. I killed him. I had to, for Momma. I killed him and buried him here amongst the frail and helpless souls of the girls our fathers raped and tortured together. I am not mad at you for leaving me, Augustus. My momma told me that you and your momma had no way of knowing the whole truth. She said you were both innocent like us. So you see, I come every night to visit the girls and to pray for them. I have no one else to care for. Some years later, Immigration took Momma and the others, but not me. I hid like I always did, in the woods, the woods saved me. Now, I protect you, too, Augustus, and your friends. I save you all from evil men that hurt people, who make girls cry and beg for mercy. That old man from the city was surely going to hurt beautiful Ms. Brie. I buried them all headfirst. Headfirst, Augustus, just like you and your momma buried your father. I believe you did that to make it easier for the devil to grab them and drag them through the burning gates of hell. You look well, Augustus, my old friend."

McIntyre did not give G a chance to answer Javier. He moved swiftly towards him and began to mirandize him in a clear and concise tone. Javier looked completely unaffected by this. Johnson held his hand out and instructed G to hand him his service weapon until we completely understood his involvement. G did as he was told without pushback. Although I tried my best not to, I was now sobbing. I turned my back to everyone and walked out into the night air to attempt to compose myself.

After a short time, Captain Jesse walked up beside me and put his arm around me. He cleared his throat and said, "Stella, I don't know what to say. The credentials G provided must have been doctored. Shit, to be perfectly honest, kid, I liked the guy right away, so I didn't do too much digging into his past."

"It's not your fault, Cap. Obviously, he had me fooled, too. Even worse, he stole my already fractured heart.

McIntyre appeared from the barn to let me know that G was begging to speak with me. "Stella, I'll tell him to go pound salt if you want me to. Just say the word," McIntyre offered.

"No, no, it's fine. Bring him out please." I took a few very deep breaths and watched as G made his way toward me, and Cap and McIntyre disappeared back into the barn. The pain and anguish on G's face seemed genuine to me, or maybe that was what I wanted to see. He reached for my hand, but I quickly stepped back and shook my head.

He pleaded, "Stella, I love you. I was not involved in any of this. I am shocked to see Javier. I haven't seen him since I was a kid, a lifetime ago. I admit, I have not been honest with you about my past, but only out of sheer embarrassment and shame. My father was an awful man, a serial killer. I followed him one night, out into these very fields apparently, although nothing seems familiar right now. Probably because I have spent too many years forcing myself to forget. I watched as he buried the body of a young girl, Stella. I was just a kid. No kid should ever have to see that. He proudly admitted to me that he was raping and killing prostitutes. He was seconds away from killing and burying me when my mother intervened and, with all of her strength, struck him in the head with a shovel, ending his miserable existence. Stella, I have never harmed a soul, I couldn't. Please forgive me. I will tell you everything you want to know, I promise, but please don't ever doubt how much I love you."

"Stella, we need to roll! I am taking you and Brie back to your house, now," McIntyre announced.

This time it was Brie who walked past G and grabbed my hand tightly. She had obviously heard what G said.

She leaned into me and whispered, "Stella, you need time to process this. Time to figure out how you feel and what you want. Please, let's go. Let me take care of you tonight."

I didn't look back as I walked hand and hand with Brie to McIntyre's car, but G's words nearly crippled me.

"Officer Stella, I love you!"

Wikipedia defines, in part, the Dark Triad as follows:

In psychology, the **dark triad** comprises the personality traits of narcissism, Machiavellianism, and psychopathy.[1][2][3][4] They are called "dark" because of their malevolent qualities.

Research on the dark triad is used in applied psychology, especially within the fields of law enforcement, clinical psychology, and business management. People scoring high on these traits are more likely to commit crimes, cause social distress and create severe problems for an organization, especially if they are in leadership.

Made in the USA
Middletown, DE
24 September 2022

10949173R00205